LOVE LANE

By Patrick Gale and available from Tinder Press

The Aerodynamics of Pork
Kansas in August
Ease
Facing the Tank
Little Bits of Baby
The Cat Sanctuary
Caesar's Wife
The Facts of Life
Dangerous Pleasures
Tree Surgery for Beginners
Rough Music
A Sweet Obscurity
Friendly Fire
Notes from an Exhibition
The Whole Day Through
Gentleman's Relish
A Perfectly Good Man
A Place Called Winter
Take Nothing With You
Mother's Boy
Love Lane

PATRICK GALE
LOVE LANE

TINDER PRESS

Copyright © Patrick Gale 2026

The right of Patrick Gale to be identified as the Author
of the Work has been asserted by him in accordance
with the Copyright, Designs and Patents Act 1988.

First published in 2026 by Tinder Press
An imprint of Headline Publishing Group Limited

1

Apart from any use permitted under UK copyright law,
this publication may only be reproduced, stored, or transmitted,
in any form, or by any means, with prior permission in writing of the
publishers or, in the case of reprographic production, in accordance with
the terms of licences issued by the Copyright Licensing Agency.

All characters in this publication are fictitious and any resemblance
to real persons, living or dead, is purely coincidental.

Cataloguing in Publication Data is available from the British Library

Hardback ISBN 978 1 4722 5746 8
Trade Paperback ISBN 978 1 4722 5748 2

Typeset in Sabon LT Pro 10.75/14.75pt
by Six Red Marbles UK, Thetford, Norfolk

Printed and bound in Great Britain by Clays Ltd, Elcograf S.p.A.

Headline's policy is to use papers that are natural, renewable and recyclable
products and made from wood grown in well-managed forests and other
controlled sources. The logging and manufacturing processes are expected
to conform to the environmental regulations of the country of origin.

Headline Publishing Group Limited
An Hachette UK Company
Carmelite House
50 Victoria Embankment
London EC4Y 0DZ

The authorised representative in the EEA is Hachette Ireland,
8 Castlecourt Centre, Dublin 15, D15 XTP3, Ireland (email: info@hbgi.ie)

www.headline.co.uk
www.hachette.co.uk

For Aidan Hicks

From the Imperial Training School, Wakefield:

Pip, I fell hopelessly, helplessly, completely and finally in love with you almost the first time I met you and I have gone on loving you, more and more every minute of every day since then, until now it has reached a point when I just cannot keep it to myself any longer.

From the Senior Cataloguer, Durham University Library:

Dear Sir,
Please find enclosed one white hair. Late owner: Miss Philippa Jean Ennion, aged 19 years, 9 months. Found by Miss Gill Piercy on Tuesday 10th of May 1949 at 11.13 a.m. Sent for interest and general information. Very rare. Please keep in cool, safe place.

From an exchange of letters
between the author's parents.

HARRY

ONE

For many years, Harry Cane and Paul Slaymaker were able to live the life they did, not only through scrupulous discretion, but because they never gave what they had a name or even put it into words. They owned adjoining farms a couple of miles outside the tiny settlement of Winter, Saskatchewan, and, because Harry had been married to Paul's sister and raised a child with her – until losing both wife and daughter to the Spanish flu in 1918 – it was generally accepted that the two men were effectively brothers as well as friends. It was known that, being sonless, each regularly helped the other out with tasks needing more than one pair of hardened hands, and not just during the wheat harvest, as many neighbours did, but throughout the farming year. This was accepted too, as it was known that Paul had lost a foot in the Great War, although he still rode as one born to it and managed his prosthesis so well his limp was barely discernible.

What nobody knew, not even the all-seeing postmistress, was that they were lovers and rarely spent a night apart, unless one of them was ill or more than usually exhausted. As with most long-married couples, youthful passion had burned itself down to a steady tenderness and the big bed Paul had built them from his own land's timber in their early months together was witness more often to conversation, yawning and quiet companionship than to any outlawed practice. Yet each remained the other's private lodestone, the one he would name in extremity, or in prayers, had they been praying men.

Their road to one another had been so beset with sorrow and obstruction that neither envisaged their future as holding anything but more of the peaceable same. Old age was a frightening prospect, as it was to any solitary person in such a remote and comfortless spot, but Paul chose not to think of it, just as he chose never to acknowledge in words the rare happiness they shared. Harry, if pressed, and being more of a worrier and planner, would have said they would surely find some solution in North Battleford, the nearest town: adjoining houses with a discreetly knocked-through attic, perhaps.

The decades after the Great War were no kinder to Canadian prairie farmers than to anyone else. It was a wonder that either Paul or Harry's farm survived. Wheat prices tumbled in the long recession that followed the war and a searing drought in 1924 drove several of their neighbours to abandon hard-won land to the savage rainlessness. All around them, families quit their homesteads, often driven out by crippling debts to banks, for whom emptied-out farms were surely of less worth than mortgages. It became common to meet whole households stacked up on ramshackle carts, mattresses and all. Most poignant were those who had acquired a car or tractor in better times and, no longer able to afford fuel, were now reduced to having the vehicle towed by a horse. Work camps and soup kitchens were set up by way of poor relief. Teams of desperate men were set to building bridges, repairing roads and, further north, felling trees.

Then rose a false dawn – a succession of record harvests that saw the rail network expanded further and brought fresh settlers in, many moving onto farmsteads not long reclaimed by the banks. The price of wheat rose and fell alarmingly, so that farmers formed cooperatives, the better to negotiate a stable price for their grain and plan ahead.

Harry fell into the habit of cooking double quantities of food so there might be something to offer the skeletal women and children who regularly walked wearily up his track. Paul and he were lucky in having an orchard, chickens and a cow between them, but, such were the wants of the hungry and desperate, the henhouse had to be kept padlocked by night, the cow led into a shed and locked in, even on the hottest nights. Regardless, they were reduced to cooking the gophers they would once have paid village children to catch and drown as vermin. These tasted not unlike rabbit, especially if the gravy was sweetened with fresh chunks of ripe apple.

It was at the bleakest point of the early 1930s, when the dust storms off the blasted land were leaving little drifts of earth under every door and heaped on every windowsill, turning the windowpanes brown, that the woman and her boy showed up. Paul and Harry had just finished a punishing day of harvesting. Paul and the labourers hired for the day headed off to bathe and sleep. They were entirely caked in dust and dirt, resembling so many pitted, kerchief-masked statues, the reddish grime emphasising their lines and sweat runnels.

They were sitting in the shade of an apple tree, she and the boy, both thin as wire and so deeply tanned that their blond hair looked almost white. She stood as they approached, and Harry saw she had been sitting on a stuffed old carpet bag he guessed contained all her worldly possessions.

'Are you hungry?' he asked, as he always did. Paul thought he was soft. 'I'll be eating soon and could spare some.'

'I don't want charity,' she said. 'I want to work.'

Harry began to demur. 'Harvest is finished,' he said. 'Such as it was.'

'I trained as a dairymaid,' she said, 'back east. I can milk and make cream and cheese. The boy can look after hens, knows how to spot the rooster chicks: it's a gift he has.'

Harry gave his usual, honest answer, that he couldn't afford to hire anyone permanently but that they were welcome to eat something with him and bed down in the barn, provided they didn't smoke out there.

He had made a pie, more vegetable than meat, and there were stewed apples and cream. They ate together on Harry's veranda, talking little as the autumn sun dropped below the horizon and a chill stole out with the shadows. She fed the child before she ate herself and he soon fell asleep with his head in her lap.

'He's seen more in his short life than I hoped to in my long one,' she said. 'I hope it hasn't marked him.'

'Your husband . . .?' Harry began.

'Dead,' she said. 'He was helping us into a goods train

and fell. It was quick but horrible and the boy saw it all. He'd thrown the boy aboard before jumping himself and falling. The worst of it was not being able to stop the train – box car riders are lower than vermin – so we were just carried away into the night, leaving him where he lay.'

It occurred to Harry later that her terrible tale didn't quite hold together, that there was nothing to have stopped her and her boy climbing down when the train next stopped and riding back the way they had come, to reclaim the body.

She and the boy duly bedded down in the barn. Harry woke to the smell of baking and found she had not only taken the padlock key off its hook in the kitchen to fetch the eggs and let the hens out, but had swept and mopped the house's ground floor and made soda bread for breakfast. The boy had been set to curry-combing the two horses, then to gathering up windfalls in a log basket.

'You didn't need to do this,' he said, ashamed of his momentary fear that his exhaustion the night before had made him forget to lock the house.

'We always sing for our supper,' she said.

The soda bread was better than anything Harry ever made himself. She said the trick was to use soured milk, of which thundery weather gave them no lack. She introduced herself as Dimpy O'Connor. Her child, older than his hungry frame, was Davy. He raced over to accept a slice of warm, buttered bread and a glass of milk then hurried back to the horses, having asked their names.

'He loves the countryside,' she said. 'Never happier than

with a horse to care for or a lamb to nurse. It's been tough for him, living on the road like this. And without a father, of course, he protects me, so he's growing up too fast.'

She was pretty, Harry saw then, for all her hardened manner. When people spoke of women with heart-shaped faces, he had always dismissed it as a sentimental figure of speech, but her face, he saw, truly was heart-shaped, with broad, smooth cheeks, a delicately stubborn chin and even a widow's peak where she had tugged back her pale hair under a cotton scarf. She gazed admiringly over at the boy, Davy, and her eyes caught the morning sun so that their grey looked almost blue.

Just then Paul came riding across from his place, unrecognisably clean after the grimy figure she might have glimpsed the night before and no longer masked against the harvesting dust. Even after all this time, with his hair shot through with silver and his habitual frown making his expression sombre, Harry's blood sang a little on seeing him, especially in the saddle, where his limp wasn't evident. Harry raised a mug of coffee in greeting and saw Dimpy's careworn face similarly lit from within.

'This is my brother-in-law, Paul Slaymaker,' he said. 'Now I'm sure he could use a dairymaid.'

Paul's utter lack of small talk, accompanied by a tendency to gruffness around women, was undoubtedly what had kept the mothers of the parish from pushing unmarried daughters his way over the years. Far from being off-putting, the knowledge that he slaved on heroically, despite having lost a foot to the war, would otherwise have made him all the more appealing to cosset and cherish.

True to form, he fairly interrogated Dimpy O'Connor, but she made her answers calmly, using a low tone, as if with a skittery horse. Then the boy, Davy, emerged from the barn, wanting to know every detail of Paul's mare. Since the all-too-brief joyful years before the war, when he had doted on the little niece, Grace, who now lay with her mother, Petra, in a grave at the edge of Harry's orchard, Paul had been even shyer of children than he was of women, guarding his heart from further hurt. Now, he not only answered the boy's questions but, with a nod of assent from the mother, lifted him onto the saddle, climbed up behind him then trotted up the track to the boundary line before cantering back to the house. At a stroke, the boy was his to command, the mother, grateful.

Paul was appalled by her story, as Harry knew he would be, but it was the boy and the thought of what he had witnessed and been put through that made him offer them a cabin behind his home. It had been designed by his late sister as a summer kitchen, so was equipped with a stove and a sink, but had long fallen into being used as a store for everything from apples to rat traps.

Harry had not been a party to the conversation so assumed money had been discussed, that she and the boy were getting a roof over their heads, but were also to be paid a wage for helping out around the place as a dairywoman, cook and housekeeper. But there had been no such conversation – she was invited, not hired – and that ambiguity paved the way for what followed.

All that autumn they lived in the cabin and Paul continued his routine of visiting Harry after dark several times a week. Then winter descended with unusual ferocity, confining each man to his house, and, when the weather relented a little, Paul's visits did not resume. Concerned he might be ill, or have had an accident, Harry rode over and discovered that Dimpy and the boy had taken refuge in the house as the water supply to the cabin had frozen. So of course, with witnesses living in, the nightly visits had to cease.

Just as he had never discussed or even acknowledged in speech the fact of his visits, now Paul made no direct reference to their having so abruptly come to an end. The mother's and son's change of address was announced as part of their usual agricultural small talk – between grain prices and weather. Lunch was pressed on Harry, lunch during which Dimpy and the boy sat at the table like family, not hired help, and she corrected the boy's table manners with the quiet confidence of a woman entirely at home. Harry did not know if she was sleeping in the spare room, where Paul and his sister Petra had long ago nursed him back to health from pneumonia; in Petra's room, which had long assumed the unhappy character of an undusted shrine; or in Paul's own bed. The mere fact of her arrival in the house signalled a drastic alteration. With the spring thaw, Paul rode over – with a gift of one of her delicious apple cakes and some tasty soft cheeses – to announce that he was marrying her, and to invite Harry to be his best man. Harry had guessed enough to appear to accept the news with equanimity. Paul had evidently been worried Harry would raise objections, as his relief at his friend's calm made him positively talkative.

For years, Paul now admitted, he had been under constant pressure from the women of the parish to take a wife, having none of Harry's immunity as a widower whose tragedy still caused them to drop their voices and men to sigh.

They walked, as they tended to, talking intermittently of drainage and fences, pests and the wheat cooperative of which Harry was chairman, while Harry thought of the weight and musk of Paul's body and of how he liked to be kissed on the neck, while Paul, he suspected, was thinking only of drainage and fences, pests and the wheat cooperative. When Paul rode home again, with Harry's warm congratulations, Harry stepped quietly back inside his house before being assailed by a storm of grief that made his knees buckle and left him rolling on the floor before the stove like a dog in pain.

He knew the change was irrevocable, as Paul's decisions tended to be, that he must get up off the floor eventually, get the hens in, feed the horses and accept that life would continue, but differently. Yet the change felled him as news of a death would, and he lay there, crying at intervals, with the licence of a man bereaved.

And, of course, he did all a best man should: stood at Paul's side, handed him the ring from a little pocket in his waistcoat, kept silent when asked if there was any cause or impediment et cetera, and raised a toast to the bride over the awkward little lunch afterwards. Duty done, he retreated into living the life he had gone to great lengths to appear to be leading for years, that of a respected widower. He steered meetings of the wheat growers, he attended those of the school governors, and he acquired and trained a handsome pointer like the one he and Paul had briefly adopted back in 1914, as so many English settlers abandoned dogs when they sailed off to enlist.

His house had always been isolated. The plots on two sides of it had never been taken on, thanks to rumours that the Cree – who had been displaced from them – had cursed their earth on being forced to leave it. The isolation had never affected him except, sometimes, in the winter months, because Paul was only a short ride away. With Paul no longer slipping over at night, Harry's house felt as remote as his rain-sodden tent had done when he was first breaking and fencing his acres and regretting his madness in thinking he could survive in such a spot. Now, as then, he talked to his horses a lot as he worked. He talked to his dog incessantly.

He was no longer a letter writer, since he had fewer and fewer people to write to as his years in Canada progressed. One or two friends and acquaintances who had lived in Winter or North Battleford before moving away might write occasionally and he always wrote back, politely, within a day. Posting or receiving letters involved a trip into town to the post office and he found he didn't often have the time to go expressly, so post-office trips tended to be combined with his weekly trip into Winter with a horse and cart for provisions. There were rarely letters for him, but there were sometimes things he had sent off for through catalogues – seed, spare parts, the warmer socks and underwear he liked. Everybody shopped from catalogues so these deliveries the postmistress would leave, ready to be called for, but personal letters aroused her interest and, if she saw Harry tying up his horse on the street, she might leave her position to call out to him from her door, waving an envelope for all to see.

On this occasion, there was even colour in her sallow cheeks.

'Mr Cane!' she called. 'A letter from England. A woman's hand, I think.'

She clearly hoped he would open it on the spot, but it was so long since he had heard from anyone back home, as he still thought of it, that he was frightened of what it might contain. He thanked her, tucked it into his breast pocket without even glancing at the handwriting, and went swiftly about his other business, freshly aware of it whenever he reached for his wallet.

Back home, he set the horse in its paddock with the others, untied the dog, put the kettle on the stove then sat at the kitchen table to take the thing out at last.

The navy-blue handwriting was unfamiliar and extraordinary. It was florid, with deep loops and emphatic dots and crosses, a decorative, emphatic hand so far removed from the dutiful copperplate taught in schools that it spoke equally of flair and independence. He flipped the envelope and saw the return address was from a mansion block in Battersea – not a place anyone he knew would have ventured – but perhaps the war had altered London drastically. He had read an article somewhere about the crisis it had caused in finding servants and how unmarried women so greatly outnumbered the surviving eligible men that they no longer felt obliged to stay at home but were striking out on their own, taking jobs, renting flats and living with a freedom that was almost masculine.

He knew his first wife, Winnie, had long since moved on. He had barely arrived in Winter than her lawyer sent through divorce papers for him to sign, and he hoped she had found lasting happiness with the department-store owner her bullying brothers had forbidden her from marrying initially. But, once settled, he had persisted in sending their daughter, Phyllis, a birthday card every year so she would not think he had forgotten her. He sent them to the only address he had for her: her formidable grandmother's Thames-side villa in Strawberry Hill. He heard nothing back. Assuming Mrs Wells had not died or moved away, he hoped that little Phyllis got to see the cards even if she was forbidden from writing back or had no wish to. He always wrote her new age in brackets beside her birthday in the year's seed merchant calendar, so as to keep tabs and not persist in sending her anything too childish as she grew up. The general stores and post office did not offer a sophisticated range and, once he had calculated that she had progressed beyond the age when he could satisfy her with a donkey in a bonnet or kittens in a basket, he took to buying the smallest possible watercolours in the arts and crafts tent at the annual North Battleford show. These he would fix by their corners to a piece of folding card in which he would write her a birthday greeting.

Once Grace was born, and he had a wife and daughter in the house again, he kept the practice up from a kind of guilt and, after Grace and Petra were dead, he persisted from a kind of fear. But still he heard nothing back.

He heard nothing from his brother, Jack, either. Jack's wife, George, had obliged them to break off contact, but Jack had promised to look after Phyllis and Harry knew he'd have been in touch had anything happened. As a horse vet, Jack would have gone to the front to care for the countless horses wounded on the battlefields. Harry had religiously scoured the published lists of the dead, looking for Paul's name in them, and he always looked for Jack's, as well. Neither man was ever listed, so he assumed Jack had returned home safely, as Paul had. Since then, he dreaded a letter from Cheshire in George's brusque hand telling him Jack had died.

This was not from George, however. The first words he read on opening it were *Dear Father*, and at those his eyes swam with tears so that he had to set the letter down for a moment to blow his nose.

BETTY

TWO

Betty and Terry had met when she was out of mourning for her mother and had at last won the battle to have her long hair shingled in the latest style, but was nevertheless regarded by the Aunts as too young to be *out*. Living as Granny did on the river at Strawberry Hill, they were all fond of pottering in boats and were stern critics of men who thought they could row. The Henley Regatta had been a fixture in the household's calendar ever since Aunt George had found Uncle Jack there (which was also how Betty's mother had come to marry his older brother, Harry). Even the Aunts who had married persisted in making an occasion of it, and admired the physiques of the competing men and boys quite as openly as people at the races assessed horseflesh. Aunt Julie, who insisted on a French pronunciation of her name, especially when her sisters shortened it to Ju, had developed an exhausting, shelf-like bosom since bearing her first child, and would tell anyone who would listen that the pains of giving birth to such a huge baby had left her in agony and sipping gin for a fortnight. One might have thought these twin experiences would have put Ju off all men and marriage, but she continued to take a keen interest in both, watching the races through her mother-of-pearl opera glasses and nudging Betty hard when she spied a rower she found especially toothsome.

'Marry money, by all means, Betty,' she had said, 'but at least make sure he's an *oarsman*; then at least you'll be happy in one department.'

Betty had said, 'Yes, Aunt Ju,' although the pronouncement left her baffled and picturing shops.

Terry won a cup – he was an extremely fast oarsman and very competitive – but had caught Aunt Ju's opera glasses even before that, and she steered herself into position to congratulate him, towing Betty with her.

'Very well done,' she said. 'You're a big man to be handed such a dainty cup.'

He laughed at the tiny piece of silverware clasped in his bear-like paw. 'I thought I might eat my breakfast egg from it,' he said. And he introduced himself politely, pretending only to be interested in Aunt Julie, who in turn introduced him to Betty, whom she labelled, 'My poor, motherless niece.'

'I'm motherless as well,' he said, briefly taking Betty's hand, and winking at her. 'I assure you; it does get easier.'

Aunt Ju couldn't leave them alone together, naturally, as Betty was far too young, but she steered him back to their noisy party on a nearby terrace, pretending she wanted him all to herself, then slyly waving him and Betty to a little sofa in a corner that had just been left empty.

Betty's upbringing and household was overwhelmingly feminine, and she was used only to her distant, rather frightening uncles, who tended to treat her – or talk about her in her presence – as though she were less a person than a family pet. And they were somehow all wrapped up in externals – beards, suits, watch chains, cigars – none of them remotely appealing, whereas Terry was beardless, an overgrown boy and, in his tight rowing shirt and long shorts, seemed almost as naked beside her as the young men she had let herself glimpse at the beach in their sagging, knitted swimming costumes.

'I'm sorry,' he said. 'Bit hot. I never seem to get hot when I'm on the water, but then, a little after a race is done, I boil over.'

'That's quite all right,' she said. 'Let me fetch you a lemonade.'

She needed to step away from him for a minute, as the tang of him was filling her nose and making her blush. When she returned with his drink, he politely stood up again, looming over her briefly and making her colour again so that all small talk left her. But he chattered, so much so that she sensed he was nervous too, which made her relax sufficiently to prompt him with questions to keep him talking.

'Always ask men about themselves,' Aunt Kitty had told her. 'You might learn something, and they'll be flattered into thinking you're intelligent and a good listener.'

He was in the army, with the Highlanders, though he wasn't remotely Scottish but from Newmarket, where his father was a solicitor, and an uncle was a racehorse vet. His mother was a great beauty who had died when he was a small boy. His father had remarried and had three more children with a second wife. Betty admitted her father had left for Canada when she was small and that her mother had died when she was only twelve, so that she had been raised by aunts and her grandmother.

'How is that?' he asked. His directness was disarmed by his eyes wrinkling up in silent laughter.

'Not always easy,' she admitted, 'although that feels disloyal. I love them very much and they're good to me.'

'No child should have to feel grateful for being treated well,' he said, almost indignantly.

'Do you like your stepfamily?' she asked.

'Very much,' he said. 'But it's not the same; it can't be. And I was sent away to school – nowhere special, place called Framlingham – so I've always felt myself a bit, well, apart, you know?'

'I know,' she said. And she did, of course, and, for what felt like an astonishingly long time, neither of them spoke while they simply looked at each other. She felt his eyes run all over her, quite as though he were touching her, so she was glad she was wearing her newest white summer dress with the lapis beads everyone said brought out the blue of her eyes and the scent Pattie had sent from Paris. (Granny disapproved of the scent because it smelled of the boudoir, she said, and young girls should smell only of roses or lavender.)

Betty found she was looking him all over as well, from his twinkling eyes and good head of brown hair down to his large, capable hands and rather smart French watch and long, hairy legs and then, swiftly, because the legs were so very unexpected, back to his kind face and engagingly gappy smile.

'I like your teeth,' she said. 'They're friendly, somehow.'

'Good for whistling through,' he said, and gave a little whistle.

'I can do that,' she said. 'It's the only good thing about having teeth like a rabbit.' And she let out a whistle that was far louder than she had intended, like a hockey mistress calling foul, at which he threw back his head to laugh and she wondered how it would feel to touch his long, strong neck and run her fingers over his Adam's apple. Game aunts notwithstanding, she had led a scrupulously sheltered life, largely taught at home by governesses, and knew no boys her own age, so had only very recently begun to notice men's Adam's apples and be fascinated by them.

'Do you like dancing?' he asked.

'I love it,' she said, though she had only ever danced at home.

'I could take you for a spin in my car and we could go dancing,' he said. 'How would that be?'

'I would have to ask the Aunts,' she said. 'I'm not going to be a deb or anything like that, but I'm not really out yet. Not at all, in fact.'

He grinned. 'I don't mind that,' he said.

So she asked Aunt Ju, who kissed her and said the apple hadn't fallen far from the tree because her father had been so handsome too, and agreed that Terry could take her for a drive and a dance, but only if she came as well. 'To chaperone and to give a stout old trout some fun.'

So Ju had taken her home in high excitement and dressed Betty up in one of the younger aunts' evening gowns and Ju had become quite as pink-cheeked and had dressed up too, in a rather racy beaded one. When Terry had arrived to collect them in his little sports car, Ju had gamely insisted on being helped up into its dicky seat so that Betty could ride in front. And they had gone into town for supper and dancing at Searcy's, where Ju met old friends, and paid little attention to quite how closely they were dancing.

Terry was so much taller than Betty that she could comfortably rest her head on his chest, and he could plant kisses on the top of her head to make her laugh.

'Our timing is bloody terrible,' he told her, and admitted that he had never got over his disappointment at having been too young to enlist in time to fight in the war so had fixed to go out to Sarawak as a policeman instead, 'because some chap I met said it was a great adventure and I thought I'd like to see the world a bit before I settle down and do something my father would approve of.'

She thought her heart would break, meeting this delightful boy only to have him ship out to the Tropics where, from what she had heard, anything might happen, but then he said, 'I know it's a tall order and you're frightfully young, but would you wait for me?'

'Of course,' she said, as nobody had asked her something so romantic before. 'Will you write to me, so I know where to write to you?'

'Of course,' he said. 'So long as you don't correct my spelling. And my handwriting's like a drunk doctor's.'

Betty laughed and he kissed her on the lips this time, rocking her close against him so that she blushed furiously, and he apologised, and she said that was quite all right, before Aunt Ju came to tap him on the shoulder with her fan.

The Aunts and Granny took her interest in Terry, and his in her, as a sign that she was *ready*. Her mother, George and the older sisters had all been sent to be finished by nuns in Belgium, but that had been in another era, when the family had money and realistic expectations of acquiring more of it by marriage. Instead, Betty's favourite of the Aunts, a luscious ex-actress called Pattie, invited Betty on a train tour to Paris, Venice and Rome by way of finishing her and to save her from the – not always benign – influence of her younger sisters.

Betty had always thought the Aunts glamorous and naughty, with their exquisite clothes and worldly humour and murmurs of *pas devant l'enfant*, but Pattie, she knew from sitting very quietly in window seats or deckchairs so that people forgot she was there, was not only an actress-turned-Parisienne but had once been the mistress of an aristocrat, and the family had briefly held its collective breath in case he *elevated her*, as Ju put it. Whatever his intentions had been, the war had come, he had died almost at once, along with one of the Uncles, and Pattie had reformed to the extent of training as a nurse and going to the theatre of war. There, in a twist of fate worthy of the sort of novels the Aunts passed amongst themselves, she changed the dressings on Jean, the wounded French officer who would sweep her to a new life, and contracted the TB that would soon cut it short.

Betty adored Pattie, from her glorious hair to her deep contralto voice, and naturally confided in her about Terry, whose letters she had paid a maid at home to intercept, and she listened gravely as Pattie gently explained that some boys were just for practice and that, however strapping and handsome he might be, it was rarely wise to accept the first man who came along. It was, she said, the single greatest advantage upper-class women had over middle-class ones: the season, with its exhausting round of balls and parties, gave young women a period of licence in which to try different boys on for size. They still made poor choices, of course they did, but Pattie believed fewer of them ended up trapped in the wrong marriage by impulse.

'You're not a beauty, darling,' Pattie told her. 'You've always known that. But you have your dear mother's natural flair and big, china-blue eyes and those will last long after beauty has gone.'

For a few weeks, Pattie enjoyed lending Betty her finery, dressing her up and parading her as the other Aunts had never done, teaching her a few things the nuns might have taught her – which sauces went with what, how to eat plaice and oysters, what to do with her legs on sitting and how to address people correctly, to cope with them and thank them for their hospitality. And she taught her useful things the nuns' curriculum would never have covered, most of which came under the general heading of Keeping Men Happy. She taught her how to enjoy drink without getting drunk, and how to ignore Italian men who cried out *Guarda la Bionda!* while also storing up their admiration. Pattie also taught her the facts of life, not only slipping her an invaluable little illustrated booklet, which did wonders for her schoolgirl French vocabulary, and encouraging her to read *Colette*, but also explaining the various ways a wife could avoid becoming pregnant while not denying, and even enjoying, her husband. All this wisdom gave a timid girl courage.

Pattie repeatedly said that she advised her because she no longer had a mother to do it for her, but Betty could not imagine her mother having ever been so frank and practical and, as the glorious, giddying trip drew to an end, she found the grief for the mother she had lost was entwined with a new, unspeakable one for the mother figure she gathered she would shortly lose as well. For Pattie, the trip around Europe with her motherless niece was by way of a bittersweet last hurrah.

Betty, returned to Strawberry Hill feeling far from a girl if not quite yet an adult, and amused the Aunts hugely by her new taste for Dubonnet. After everyone had quizzed her about Paris fashions and Italian hairstyles and insisted that she parade for them in the dresses Pattie and Jean had so kindly bought her, it was made plain that, for all her subterfuge, the Aunts knew about her already faltering correspondence with Terry and disapproved, for discreet enquiries had been made and he was found to have no prospects. As a motherless girl with an effectively unmentionable father and nothing to her name beyond the modest contents of a post-office savings account, she could only afford to marry for love if the man she loved was rich.

They proceeded to give her what Ju called *a poor girl's season*, pulling strings to have her invited to garden parties and riverside picnics, to concerts and tennis tournaments, whist drives and charity fundraisers. Terry's letters, so funny and keen at first, had rapidly become perfunctory and infrequent as he was drawn into the demands of his policework in Sarawak and what sounded like a hectic social whirl out there, so she let herself be distracted in turn, even though she found she was using him as the yardstick against which to measure the boys and men paraded before her, finding most too short or too skinny and others too obviously judging her for her lack of education or fortune or, worse, seeming to like her precisely because they weren't especially educated or fortunate themselves.

Betty was raised in the awareness of being a poor relation, even a burden, and keenly aware that her education imparted first from a happy village school, then from a succession of vindictive governesses, was full of glaring gaps. She had seen neither as problematic until now. Perhaps because she had never had to endure the cruel exposure and teasing of boarding school, it was only now that she felt herself prodded back and forth around the cattle ring of a marriage market that she became acutely conscious of the slightest of her physical failings, her wayward hair, her slightly protuberant front teeth, her unfashionably generous bosom that had to be bound flat.

She did not love the man who finally stepped forward from the pack, but she liked him well enough. He was conventionally handsome, and was a barrister, which the family liked as two of the uncles were in law. He was popular because he made people laugh, he drove a sports car, which was fun, and, when he singled her out whether to dance with her, talk to her, lead her to a dinner table or draw her away from some other man's clumsy attentions, she felt herself protected, rescued even, for which she was grateful. He was, the Aunts all said, *a catch* and she couldn't understand why he picked her and had not been snapped up already by one of the girls with an inheritance, a trust fund and a more fashionably boyish figure.

Betty played for time when he proposed. Aunt Ju had said it did not do to appear easy by saying yes straight away. She wrote to Terry saying she wanted to wait still, but needed encouragement to do so, as she was now coming under pressure. No reply came, even after the usual two weeks, though she had enclosed her most recent photograph. She had read some of Granny's Somerset Maugham, so was beginning to understand that a Far East posting was beset by temptation, that all those hard-drinking, bored married women in their bungalows might have been as much Terry's reason for travelling to Sarawak as any wish to prove himself a man through the work there.

She looked about her as she waited to hear back. By now, all the Aunts were married – 'Not a maiden among us, dear,' Kitty liked to joke – and marriage seemed to have liberated them into having more fun rather than less. They were forever visiting Granny's house at Strawberry Hill, as it was large enough to cope with them all and, in an odd way, their husbands seemed to matter slightly less to them than their sisters did. The Uncles were another matter; though they liked to dominate conversations and bully both Granny, the Aunts and Betty, their visits were rare, and Betty suspected this was because their wives felt outshone and out-talked by their sisters-in-law, who were formidable en masse.

The greatest warning against marriage was Granny, who had endured twenty years of it to a man she cheerfully admitted was a brute, and bore him an eye-watering fourteen children despite their lack of compatibility. 'It's to avoid your Granny's fate that you need to read and absorb this,' Pattie had said of the little pink booklet she lent her.

So Betty said yes, and a brief period of triumph ensued, beginning with the huge South African diamond in her engagement ring. She continued the round of parties, but now always at his side and he called at the house several times a week. He became a firm favourite of the Aunts, as he teased them and made them laugh, and they often commented on how beautifully he danced and how lucky Betty had been to land him. The only one to voice any doubt was Granny. On two occasions, when they were all chatting in the garden, she had said something to the effect of *we should let you young people enjoy some privacy*, but nobody had moved and Kitty had joked, 'Oh, they'd be lost for words without us.'

Shortly after, Betty had called in on Granny as she often did in the mornings, to sit on the ottoman at the foot of her big bed while Granny drank her tea and ate arrowroot biscuits, whose tumbling crumbs she blew into the lacy mystery of her cleavage.

'Are you happy, Betty?'

'Perfectly,' Betty said, instinctively turning on her finger the large ring whose size was worrying her.

'This should be the happiest time in any young woman's life, but you seem . . .' Granny broke off, blew more crumbs and sipped tea from the large breakfast cup she favoured. 'You're not marrying to be good?'

'Good?'

'Your dear mother married to be good, because your uncles wouldn't let her marry for happiness and I worry it cast a cloud over you. Disappointment sort of soaks into a person's fabric like a stain.' She broke off again to look at Betty sharply. The morning sunlight glancing off the river flashed on her little spectacles. 'Are you ever alone with him?'

'Of course,' Betty said. 'When he takes me somewhere in his car. He's very sociable. Very popular.'

'Is he not . . . I don't want to give offence, dear, but is he not a little light on his feet?'

'He's a very good dancer,' Betty assured her. 'Far better than I am.'

'Dear girl,' Granny sighed. 'Now I really must get dressed and see how many we are to be for lunch.'

Her gentle queries awoke a slight uneasiness which Betty tested for herself, finding more occasions to be alone with him. A certain nervousness, an extra hilarity came over him, she realised, when they had no audience – quite the reverse of the usual response to privacy. She also began to judge his kisses and his touch against the very few she had received from Terry before he left for Sarawak, and realised that these he kept for when they were seen, as though her private self held less value for him.

Shortly after that, they went to a tennis party and Terry was there, unexpectedly back from Sarawak. He looked Betty up and down and said my how she had grown up, in a way that made her suddenly recall the more continental suggestions in Pattie's pamphlet. There was no time to hide her engagement ring, so she decided to brazen it out.

'Pretty, isn't it?' she said.

'You said you'd wait,' he reminded her.

'Spoken like a man who doesn't live with his grandmother and several aunts. Besides, you'd stopped writing.'

'I hate writing.'

'It shows. And what you do write's illegible.'

'Is he rich?'

'Yes. But . . . he's not you.'

She had forgotten how tall he was, and how athletic his build. He could have broken the fiancé like a twig.

Terry fetched them both a long glass of what she thought was just lemonade but turned out to be a Tom Collins, and it went straight to her head as she was thirsty and hot with self-consciousness.

'Where shall you live?' he asked.

'London, I expect, as he's a barrister.'

'Very good.'

'Are you home for good?'

'I'm not sure. I thought I was but the girl who said she'd wait, didn't . . .'

'That's not fair,' she said.

'Sorry. But bloody hell, Bets.'

'If I had waited. If you had written more letters and I had waited—'

'I'd have asked you to marry me,' he said, and she gulped the last of her delicious drink to stop herself exclaiming and its iciness burned her throat. 'But the dreaded Aunts would have made you say no, of course, as I've not much money and couldn't stump up for a whopper of a ring like that carbuncle on your finger, or drape you in silks and mink, as I'm sure the lucky bounder will do.'

'He's not a bounder.'

'No. Of course not.'

'He was just here. And he asked when I thought nobody else would and . . .'

'What?'

'It's been bloody awful.'

'You are ripping when you swear, Bets.'

'Don't be silly. What does it mean when people say someone's a bit light on his feet?'

He frowned, finished his drink and looked around them.

'A bit pansy,' he said. 'You know. A bit concert party.'

She wasn't entirely sure she understood. 'What Aunt Pattie calls musical?' she asked.

'That's the idea,' Terry said. 'Often the life and soul, enormous fun at a party, but no use in a tight corner and often treacherous to boot. Why on earth do you ask?'

'Nothing really,' she told him. 'Just something Granny said. You do know I've no money, either. Not really. Father had lots, but Uncle Frank invested it badly, I think, which was why Father left us to go to Canada, and poor Mother said she wasn't cut out to be a pioneer and then she died and . . .'

'I say, old girl. Never mind. Here.'

Without warning, she was shaken by emotion. Not a great storm of it, just the sort of wind to bring down blossom in an orchard. Terry shielded her from view of the tennis players and spectators, and passed her a spotlessly clean and well-ironed handkerchief. She used it, and he waved it away when she tried to hand it back.

'Yours to cherish,' he joked. 'Will it be a big wedding?'

'He has three sisters who want to be bridesmaids,' she said. 'Haven't met them yet but he says they're a hoot.'

'How ghastly.'

'Quite. And Granny will insist on hosting as the bride's family is expected to. As you know, she has a big garden by the river where we can fit a marquee – we did that for Kitty's wedding, and Ju's – but I know she can't afford it and, with so many sisters already married off, my uncles are already pulling faces.'

'You should elope.'

'*What?*'

'If he loves you, you should elope. You've nothing to prove and it saves everyone the fuss and cost and nonsense.'

'How would that work?'

'Perfectly respectable. Pick a day. Make an appointment at Chelsea Registry Office, or whichever suits, and Bob's your uncle. You send everyone a nice telegram when it's done.'

She tried, and failed, to picture her fiancé agreeing to such a thing. 'I . . . I think he's rather looking forward to all the fuss and cost and nonsense.'

Terry pulled a mock lugubrious face. 'Oh dear,' he said, at which she laughed. 'Hooting bridesmaids it is. I promise I wouldn't have put you through all that.'

She stopped laughing then, and saw he was telling the truth.

To be fair, she ran the idea past the fiancé as he was driving her home later that afternoon. 'Why don't we just elope?' she asked.

Sometimes she worried his car was the thing she liked best about him. It was low-slung, white and sporty with room only for two – a piece of selfishness so brazen that she wasn't sure how it made her feel.

He was in sunglasses, which robbed his face of all its usual animation. She liked him in them as he was otherwise a little too animated for comfort. Was animation in a man unmanly, she wondered. Was it, to use Terry's phrase, a bit *concert party*? She was in sunglasses as well, and her Italian silk headscarf, which she hoped rendered her face as impassive and unreadable as his.

'You funny thing,' he said. He often called her that. 'What on earth makes you ask?'

'It's such a huge expense for Granny.'

'Did the Aunts not teach you it's vulgar to talk about the cost of things?'

'Of course they did, but in private it's allowed. And a wedding's such a performance with all the dresses nobody wears again and the food and champagne and wine nobody needs, and the marquee and chairs and tables and flowers.'

'Well, a table's not much use without chairs, my pet.'

'The date's not set yet, or invitations printed. If we just elope, we save all that waste and bother.'

'Whatever would people think?'

'They'd think us romantic.'

'They'd say my family didn't approve of you. Or that I'd got you into trouble.'

'Small chance of that.'

'Phyllis!'

'Nobody calls me that. You know they don't.'

'I think it suits you, my funny little Virgilian shepherdess.'

They had to stop for a long queue of cars on the Embankment. He hated having to wait for anything.

'Oh, get a move on, will you, you stupid cow!' he shouted, and a matronly woman crossing the road stopped to glare at him. 'Oh, not you,' he said. 'I was shouting at . . . Oh never mind.'

Suddenly, Betty realised it was the perfect opportunity. While he was huffing and puffing and failing to charm the increasingly cross pedestrian, she slipped off the engagement ring, which she saw now was embarrassingly large, an impossible thing for an ordinary girl like her to wear, and she dropped it smartly into the car's little ashtray, let herself out and boarded the first bus to pass in the opposite direction.

It was the boldest thing she had ever done. It took two buses, a train ride and a short walk for her to make her way back to Strawberry Hill, plenty of time for thought, plenty of time for her to ask herself if she had any regrets. She decided she would only take him back if he was man enough to follow her home and be waiting for her, with flowers and a heartfelt apology when she arrived.

He didn't, of course, because she had wounded his pride.

She hurried up to her room and fired off a letter to him before anyone could have time to find out and try to dissuade her. She apologised for leaving without explanation, she wrote, but it was the only way as he was such an expert persuader. He had done nothing wrong, she said. She had simply realised that they came from drastically different worlds and had different expectations of marriage.

The Aunts were shocked, but also excited by the drama of it and made her repeat the story over and over. They only asked once why she had called the engagement off. Her saying that he was light on his feet worked like a charm and Aunt Ju slowly closed her eyes in the way she had when she needed to land emphasis and murmured, 'Only a *real* man will do for Betty.'

Betty had briefly worried that the only address she had for Terry was care of the police force in Sarawak, but he was there at the very next dance she went to, looking so tall and handsome in black tie, that she almost regretted she wasn't going to be seeing him in morning dress as she walked up an aisle in an antique veil. They eloped within the month, married in Chelsea Registry Office with the laughing next couple as their witnesses, and moved into a top-floor flat in a mansion block overlooking Battersea Park.

Granny cried, the Aunts all said *how romantic* and the generosity of the presents rained upon them was a mark of everyone's gratitude at having been spared the fuss and expense of a wedding.

It was a piece of the purest luck that they had been reunited. For all his bluster about her not waiting for him, he now admitted he'd assumed she'd given up on him as a hopeless correspondent. Judging from a Sarawak album of his, he had no lack of women happy to help him enjoy a high old time out there, ride on the back of his motorbike, go swimming with him or get up in fancy dress. Not presuming to contact her once silence had fallen, he had made use of his policing experience to sign up for a traineeship with the Prison Office, had just spent a few months training at Dartmoor prison and, when he ran into her again, was shortly to become deputy governor at Wormwood Scrubs. When she thought how easily she might have cried off the tennis party with a headache, how easily she might have married the wrong man, it left her quite dizzy.

THREE

Betty wrote to her father. They had no contact of any kind while she was growing up. This had never struck her as odd in childhood. At first, he was just one of a list of things the pained expressions of the adults around her taught her not to mention and then the Great War, which claimed one of her uncles, killed so many fathers or brothers that it became bad form to ask after the absent, and new acquaintances simply assumed her father had died at the Somme.

It was Terry's questioning and suggestions that made her write. They enjoyed a short trip to his family by way of a honeymoon and it left her feeling painfully her own lack of parents. She had pestered Granny and retrieved the precious photographs her mother had never displayed of Harry Cane as a debonair bachelor with a lavish cravat pin, and as a handsome young husband with Betty as a solemn baby on his knee and a comically serious terrier on the occasional table at his elbow. With some pride, she told Terry the few scraps she knew, that her father had inherited a fortune from one of South London's first horse-drawn bus services, and that he and his younger brother, Jack, a dashing vet, had married two sisters, her mother and her sporty Aunt George. Jack and George had also eloped, amusingly, and settled many hours away in Cheshire, but then a certain frost had descended between them and the rest of the family after Harry decamped to Canada.

In telling the story, she felt afresh the deep, quiet sorrow of her mother's life – that she had loved another man the uncles hadn't let her marry – which in turn surely explained Harry's emigration and his never having sent for her once he settled.

'We should visit him,' Terry said, who had devoured the books of Grey Owl and loved the thought of the great Canadian outdoors and a wild life of bears, guns, riding and impossible weather.

Dear Father, she wrote. *I realise, writing that, that those are two words I have never written before. I am sure I should have written to you but the Aunts (I always think of them with a capital letter) were so very controlling, especially after Mother died, and it's only now that I have left home to start a life of my own that I feel able to put pen to paper. I do hope this reaches you. I copied this address from Mother's little address book in the hope that farmers stay put! There is no house name or number, but Terry says you probably don't have postmen if Winter is as remote as it looks on the map.*

Terry is the reason I'm writing, really. His name is Terry Ennion, and we were married in Chelsea Registry Office. We're poor as church mice, so we eloped to spare our families any expense, but the Aunts are being generous with bits and pieces now that we've told them, and I've been forgiven. I've known him for ages. We met when he was a bit of a hero at the Henley Regatta. Isn't that how you met Mother? Or was it how Jack met George? I get in such a muddle with all their lovely stories. Anyway, I was very taken with him but too young and he was hopping mad at having been too young to enlist in the War, so signed up to be a policeman in Sarawak for a year or two, and I promised I'd wait. So here we are, and I wanted you to know.

I doubt you ever come back to visit England – I'm sure you'd have told me if you did – but, if ever you do, Terry and I would love to have you to stay in our little flat. There's a spare room and views over Battersea Park to the bridges and even a balcony where we have squeezed two rattan chairs on which to drink sundowners.

I'm so happy, Father, and hope you are as well.

Terry's time as an officer in the Imperial Police has set him up well to train as a Governor in the Prison Service. He has to take a course, then we hope he will land a deputy governorship somewhere. We've been told the trick is to agree to go wherever he gets offered a post, so we may not be in Battersea for long, but I'll be sure to let you know if we move. It sounds grim, I know, but the job comes with Civil Service pay and pension and they provide a house!

Meanwhile I am learning (slowly) to be a wife. To shop and cook and even clean, though I hope we'll soon be able to hire a girl to do the rough, at least, or even a maid.

Ah well. I expect you are full of questions. I know I am. No rush to respond but Terry and I wanted you to know of our happiness.

I have no idea how to sign this off!
Your long-lost daughter,
Betty

HARRY

FOUR

Betty. So she had switched to her middle name. He supposed times had changed and Phyllis was now thought antique and stuffy. She had enclosed a cutting from *The Times*'s marriage announcements column, which revealed that Terry also went by a second name, having been christened Sidney. She also enclosed a frustratingly tiny photograph of the two of them on the steps of Chelsea Town Hall, he, an athletic giant, she, a buxom blonde in a smart silk frock and jacket, a chic hat, whose brim half hid her face, and a bold slash of lipstick.

He didn't know if he was more surprised that she had suddenly got in touch or that her mother had died, and nobody had thought to tell him. Touchingly, the marriage announcement made it sound as though Winnie and he were still married, so evidently, she had not, after all, married the rich admirer she had initially been kept from accepting.

Harry wrote Betty a considered response then made a fair copy, as his penmanship had suffered from underuse. He congratulated the happy couple, wishing he were still rich enough to write them a useful cheque rather than add to what was by now probably a collection of toast racks. He had no camera and knew nobody who did. Prairie people tended to rely on itinerant photographers who sometimes set up shop at fairs or shows, but the hard times had made their visits rare. He found a photograph of himself, however, looking rather severe in a group shot of staff and governors with assembled children taken a few years before. He also took up a sharpened pencil to draw her a sketch of his house.

Letters took a long time to cross the country and then the Atlantic, of course, but she had evidently been raised to reply to them within a day of receipt. He remembered her mother, Winnie, long years ago in the impossible idyll of their early marriage, dutifully seeing to her correspondence at a little desk after breakfast, the waves and gull cries of Herne Bay coming through an open window.

Betty replied by return. His letter took ten days to reach her, and hers a further ten to reach him.

Though he was sensing already that she was enough the niece of her aunts to put a bright and witty slant on every story, she told him the sad, unvarnished tale of Winnie, who had succumbed to breast cancer after a botched operation performed, astonishingly, at home. Winnie's wealthy first suitor had indeed returned to her orbit after Harry left, but she had proved scrupulously honourable, accepting no financial support from him directly, so that money he gave was always *for the family*. And then her less scrupulous younger sister, Kitty, who their mother, Mrs Wells, had married off to a man she never loved, announced she was divorcing to marry a millionaire. It transpired Winnie's admirer's patience was finite, and one Wells sister was as good as another.

Betty had only learned the truth long after from her Aunt Pattie. Pattie had become her protector and adviser after Winnie's death and, having escaped into respectability herself, felt able to enlighten her niece about family secrets from which Betty had been shielded. When Harry had last seen Pattie, she was a statuesque member of the Gaiety chorus line, being kept by a minor aristocrat, but the war had changed all that too. He found he was glad to hear of her attaining respectability, and that she had proved a friend to Betty, and sad that she had died so young.

It was so strange hearing about the family he had long fought to put out of his mind. They and their messy concerns had become as remote to Harry as characters in a novel, but, like any keen reader, he found their stories drew him helplessly in again and each of Betty's chatty but surely wilfully obtuse accounts left him full of questions and hungry for more.

When she wrote about Pattie, it reawakened his old pain at the speed with which she, her mother and her siblings had practised on him then cast him out, and his old guilt at his infidelity to Winnie. Of course, he wondered how much Betty had been told. She had been so small when he left that perhaps she had never cared enough to ask, or she had swallowed the official story that he had made poor investments or been dangerously profligate and lost a fortune as easily as one might mislay a handkerchief.

They had exchanged several letters before he dared ask after her uncle Jack. She made no mention of him, so Harry guessed he had reneged on his promise to look after her. There was a distinct coolness in Betty's tone when she finally wrote about Jack and her aunt George, but perhaps it was simply geography – that their house in Cheshire had been unfeasibly far from Strawberry Hill and so connections withered. She enclosed a small photograph of Jack, thick of waist in his country tweeds, a horse-faced George and matching daughters around him.

Harry wrote of her cousins from duty rather than with much affection, but, even so, he did not let her realise that all communication with his brother had been severed long ago. He found he felt gratitude that Jack had returned from the trenches unscathed, but found the unsmiling image of him so remote from his memories that it awakened nothing warmer in him, neither dislike nor regret.

Betty announced, quite abruptly, that she and Terry had moved to Barnes, that he had a granddaughter, Pip, and that Terry was now deputy governor at Wormwood Scrubs. He sent warm congratulations on both counts, enclosing some little Cree beadwork slippers for the baby.

There was a further update to announce a second daughter, Adèle, nicknamed Whistle, and a change of address to Governor's House, HMP Chelmsford. But thereafter the cares of motherhood and Terry's job evidently consumed her and made her letters a little dutiful and dull. In fairness, he was surely boring her in turn as life on a small prairie farmstead was profoundly uneventful and the gossip and chat had been largely on Betty's side.

She posted him photographs of the granddaughters as they grew, with occasional glimpses of her and Terry: she, stylish with a touch of Pattie's voluptuous vampishness; he, moustached, tall and increasingly bald. He imagined Terry enjoyed perhaps being the only man in the household and was becoming what Dimpy, in a rare show of wit, called *a harrumph.*

Harry had kept his family news from Dimpy. Excluded by Paul from the process that had led to his marrying her, he initially kept the correspondence to himself from a petulant impulse to enjoy a secret of his own. He kept secrets from Betty as well; as her letters became only occasional and part of the texture of an unexciting life.

It gradually became clear that between him and Paul there would be no stealthy resumption of their old arrangement. What lay between them had been deeds alone, never acknowledged in words, so its abrupt cessation left only their daylight conversation. That talk of yields and seed quality, of animals, trees and weather went from being shot through with the encoded promise of the night to come, to being merely what it seemed. At first, Harry dropped a few clumsy hints, but Paul answered these with only the briefly frozen expression of someone politely ignoring a companion breaking wind, and the implied rebuff chilled Harry in turn. They did not argue; they simply ceased to see one another alone, unless some farm task demanded it.

His first reaction was that he could not bear a future as the happy couple's well-intentioned neighbour. He could sell up, he thought, while he was still young enough to start a new life elsewhere. North Battleford was a pleasant enough spot, he decided, after a morning of walking around the place. He could buy a cottage there, somewhere he could have a garden and continue to grow his own fruit and vegetables, but enjoy that small measure of anonymity a town might afford.

He spotted two or three such places, picket fenced, cedar shingled, whose prices were surely within his means. He even wrote to Betty about the idea and was encouraged that she seemed to support the proposal, writing back that he might also settle somewhere in England where she and Terry could *keep an eye on him.* But then he had his farm valued, thinking he could tell anyone who asked it was for insurance purposes. The forces that had made the cottages seem so affordable had also grossly devalued agricultural land, and the price that would be raised, if it could be raised, would leave him nothing much off which to live. Perhaps, he confided in Betty, he could buy somewhere with a large enough plot for him to become a market gardener and make a small living that way? But her reply was less encouraging, suggesting he was too old for the labour involved and would be better off staying put but farming less or even, Terry's suggestion, renting his land out to an eager neighbour, someone keen to farm but not yet established enough to buy land of their own. He sensed she thought him a feckless timewaster – the spoiled wastrel of her Aunts' genteel calumnies.

It was Dimpy who changed his feelings. Happy and secure as she had never dared hope to be, her primary gratitude flowed not to the man who had married her but to the man who had first taken her and her boy in, then put his bachelor neighbour her way. She brought him pies and cheeses, butter tarts and chokecherry jelly – not so differently from any good neighbour of an ageing, childless widower – but then she lingered to talk, and Harry had, all his life, been easier in the company of women than men. By degrees, they cautiously opened up to one another and, quite without noticing, became friends.

The feeling that time could not change, however, was Harry's towards her boy. On that first sunlit morning when Davy made himself at home in the barns and then gravitated to Paul, instinctively seeking out the stronger man, Harry had seen the unpleasantly triumphant way he stared down from the saddle of Paul's horse and had found it impossible to warm to him since. There was a watchful, calculating quality to him, at odds with the usual spontaneity of boyhood. Knowing it was surely born of a hardscrabble life made Harry feel guilty, but did not alter the way he felt.

That discomfort intensified over the years as Paul so evidently relished having a boy he could treat as his son. He taught him to shoot, taught him farming skills much as he had once taught Harry and, as the boy, who had little time for school but proved naturally industrious, grew into a young man, soon had him mending fences, digging ditches unsupervised, tasks Harry would once have helped him carry out.

Davy regularly asked for details of how the neighbours were related, how Harry had enjoyed a tragically brief marriage to Paul's sister, how she and their little daughter were buried among apple trees on the boundary between the farms. He raised the subject almost every time they were all together and glanced from man to man quite as though he hoped to catch one of them out in some inconsistency.

When Harry once found an opportunity to raise the matter on a rare occasion when he was alone with Paul, Paul dismissed his concerns.

'All children want to pin down how their families fit together – it's only natural – and we're all the family he has or knows. You're family too. He just wants to be sure we won't disappear the way his father did.'

Thus, he shamed Harry to silence, but as the months, then years, passed, Harry found he could never relax around the boy and the boy sensed it. Harry believed Dimpy came to be unsettled by the boy as well. She sometimes murmured how very like his father he was becoming, in a way that suggested there had been things about his father she did not wish to see again.

Paul's withdrawal was a sadness, but not a tragedy. They were both ageing. Harry was still lean and fit – farmwork saw to that – but the dangerous fire that had landed him in such terrible trouble all those years ago and led to him putting all he loved in jeopardy, now flickered and flared where once it had given off a constant heat. Had they lived together – impossible thought – they might by now have reached the stage of sleeping in separate beds or separate rooms even, prizing sleep over intimacy. He found he was relishing the solitude that previously might have frightened him. He knew Paul for a deeply private man and wondered how he coped with marriage's steady erosion of privacy; between wife and stepson, it seemed he was never alone now.

FIVE

Not long after the O'Connors moved in with Paul came almost a decade of agricultural disaster, not only more droughts and blinding dust storms, but plagues of pests that had only arrived because of all the alien wheat being grown: western bean cutworm, wheat stem sawfly and even clouds of locusts that had the Bible-beaters out in force, preaching on street corners and the radio alike. Farmers were instructed to fight back with a mixture of sawdust, bran and sodium arsenate, to little avail. In the middle of it all, there were harvests excellent enough to feed hope, but which sold for a fraction of their old value, as there was now so much competition from other parts of an empire recovered from the war they were now calling Great.

Like many farmers, Harry had never thought of himself as political and was used to feeling that government understood little about agriculture and its needs. He instinctively shied away from crowds and any kind of mob behaviour, and was repelled by the steady rise in popularity of the Ku Klux Klan in the prairies, where the perceived enemy and engineers of national poverty were not the blacks but the Catholics, or cat-lickers as the O'Connor boy called them, usually before spitting. But even Harry felt a small swell of engagement when the newly formed Farmers Left Party was elected towards the end of the thirties.

The Great War had devastated the prairies' newest settlers, first by taking away so many men who never returned, then by the Spanish flu, which Armistice celebrations had spread with fatal efficiency to any community large enough to host a patriotic parade or hoist a flag. Still, it had been a conflict that felt European, *over there*. The new war made its presence more directly felt, not just in the familiar pressure to grow more wheat to compensate for interrupted trade routes, but in the establishment of huge air corps training camps. One of these was only a few miles away near North Battleford and housed fifteen hundred mechanics, many of them British.

Not only were the quiet prairie skies suddenly noisy with yellow Harvards, exciting local youngsters into enlisting as soon as they were old enough, but suddenly there were platoons of trainee pilots eager to help get the harvests in. They enjoyed stripping off to swim in Harry's slough at the end of each day's work, camped in the orchard and on Harry's terrace, and cast a temporary sylvan spell across the place. Harry enjoyed their company immensely, even as it marked him out as officially an oldster.

Davy O'Connor enlisted, though not for the air force as, to his fury, his eyesight was too poor, but for the navy. At least, as an airman, he might have been trained in the prairies. As a sailor, he was put on a train for Vancouver, with the likelihood that his leaves would be spent far, far away. Dimpy was beside herself with anxiety. He was not a letter writer, unsurprisingly, and neither was she, but she made herself one, even asking Harry's advice in the matter.

(He was deemed more English than Paul and therefore thought to have better manners.) All she received for her every two or three offerings were maddeningly uninformative, barely literate postcards. Harry knew, because she rode over to show him each one. And, quite the wicked uncle, he caught himself hoping Davy would not return. Not that he would die – Harry wasn't a monster – but that, like countless sailors before him, he would be seduced by the brighter, more varied culture of the coast, far more alluring than travelling back to the dull predictability of the farm.

It was Paul, however, who went out and did not return. On a bitterly cold night, snow thick on the ground and more due from a gunmetal sky, Harry had finished supper and was about to turn in early to save fuel when he heard a horse whinny close by. Cursing, assuming it was someone lost, he pulled on coat and hat, stamped into his boots and lit a flashlight. He recognised Paul's new horse at once – a chestnut stallion with a distinctive black eye mask and feathering.

He'd have assumed Paul had hurried out of sight on some errand even, as was common with them both at their age after a long, cold ride, to head for the nearest tree for an urgent piss. The reins were dangling onto the ground, however, rather than tied round the veranda's hitching rail and there were no footprints in the snow leading away from it. The poor animal was half frozen and Harry led it to the stable where it could eat at least and be slowly thawed by a blanket and by proximity to one of his own horses. Then he took the other, saddled her up and rode slowly out into the dark, following the tracks clearly left by Paul's horse in the snow. Both he and his horse knew the terrain, but the mare picked her way gingerly and fresh snow began to make visibility so poor he was on the point of giving up when he found him.

Paul lay in such an unnatural, humped-up position that Harry's first glance took him for a rock or an untidy pile of lumber. The illusion was completed by his thick winter coat having tumbled forward to cover his head and hands. He was already stone cold. The one comfort was that, from his undignified position, it seemed clear death had taken him as swiftly as a bullet, and he had not been lying there in the snow for hours, fearing death's approach as he prayed for help.

Harry had always been slighter than Paul. The other's bearish weight – even the simple comforting weight of one of his arms across his chest – was one of the things Harry had missed about him, particularly on cold nights. In death he was doubly unwieldy. Happily, the mare Harry had brought out was as biddable and patient as a gundog, and remained rooted just where Harry needed her, as he first dragged Paul into a sitting position against the nearest tree then, in a slow, staggerly dance, worked him up onto his feet to lean against it. He had to throw Paul's arms over his shoulders and inevitably ended up with his face panting against his cheek and bull-like neck in an embrace that might have been designed to reflect their last decade: one still yearning, the other withdrawn and unresponsive. Then, in lumbering parody of a two-step, he brought him round from leaning against the tree to leaning against the horse, who he spoke to soothingly to keep her from stepping away too soon. He rolled Paul round against her, lifting his arms from over his shoulders to flop them across her saddle. Then he had to put his head between Paul's legs and heave with all his strength, and – almost breaking his neck in the process – drive him upwards with his shoulders.

Only the pain and effort of it made the violent intimacy bearable and, once Paul was up there, his meaty rump to the falling snow, Harry wept as much from relief as sorrow.

Like any farmer, he always had rope in his saddlebag and a knife in his pocket, and he worked with them swiftly, cutting lengths to lash Paul's thick belt to the saddle's pommel and, for the extra stability it might give, his wrists to the girth strap. Finally, his sweat chilling rapidly in the freezing air, he led the mare slowly to the nearest fence, which he used as a mounting block to let him clamber up behind the saddle, his legs stretched wide across her bony rump, his boots only just reaching the stirrups he had not thought to adjust first for the greater distance. Then he took the reins, thanked the horse and set her picking her painfully slow way over to Paul and Dimpy's farmhouse.

Harry cried again as he rode, cried freely under cover of snow and darkness, one hand on the reins, one laced, for steadying and comfort, under Paul's belt. Paul's shirt and vest rode up as they went. He ungloved the hand that was under the belt and spread it for precious minutes on the small of Paul's back, feeling the familiar fur there and the heft of the man before cold drove him to tucking vest and shirt chastely back into place, tugging his glove back on and sliding his fingers under the belt again.

Dimpy had been looking out, of course, frantic with worry when Paul failed to come in for supper as snow began to fall. He was so obviously dead that it spared Harry having to tell her, though of course she wanted all the details he had to offer, and it comforted him to comfort her.

He built the coffin himself – Dimpy agreed that Paul's Scottish tastes were for the austere and simple – and the obsessive measuring, planing and sanding of his lover's last bed gave Harry a focus for grief he could not voice.

He suggested Paul would have liked to be buried beside his sister and niece, on land the two of them had cleared from virgin prairie, but, surprisingly for someone whose church attendance was sporadic, Dimpy said she could not bear the thought of him in unconsecrated ground like a suicide, so, once there had been enough of a thaw for the ground to be diggable, Paul was laid to rest in the orderly, desolate churchyard where Harry, who had long been a regular attender and twice a church warden, visited him each week after communion.

SIX

Davy didn't come home for the funeral – in all probability the aircraft carrier he was now on was somewhere in the far Pacific. If only he had come home and laid claim to the acres he was now free to farm on his mother's behalf, Harry might have extricated himself.

With the rapid improvements in farm machinery being adopted all around, farms were getting bigger, swallowing up their neighbours, and the land continued to empty out of people. In some spots, little settler towns like Winter had become almost derelict, become places youngsters drove through at night for thrills. Farms selling up was the most obvious sign of change, or railway stations falling into disuse when there was less call for trains to stop at them. A subtler symptom was the shrinking of schools to the point where they were no longer viable. Once a school went, the church and post office would shortly follow. Harry was still on the board of governors at Winter's school, there being nobody to replace him, and the board's numbers would soon overtake those of the children being taught there.

Despite this depressing dwindling, the price of land was said to be creeping up a little, boosted by high wartime demand for wheat and the yields improved by mechanisation and weed control. Harry could have sold up and escaped to North Battleford, but he didn't because of Dimpy. With no Davy to help her, the land she had inherited would have overwhelmed her, so, though his ageing body and grief for Paul made him ready to stop, he felt honour-bound to stay on and do his best to run two farms concurrently, just as he had back in his youth when Paul had stormed off to fight in France and left Petra and him shorthanded.

It was utterly draining and, night after night, he fell into a sleep like death, often before he could find the final energy to undress. But there was a kind of consolation in labour, in driving through, and he grew as fond of Dimpy as her hedgehog nature would allow. They never discussed their grief, but he knew she could see he suffered. Just once, after a rare occasion when she had come to church and joined him in setting flowers on Paul's grave, she said, 'I think you feel it harder than I do because you knew him longer. You knew him young.'

He could think of nothing to say in response, and she did not seem to expect anything, but he was glad that she had noticed – grateful, even.

Davy survived the war, but did not come home immediately, choosing to loiter in Vancouver.

'It's exciting compared to here,' Dimpy said. 'The last thing he wants is to run a farm. He'll find a way of getting rich there. Davy was always sharp.'

Unlike other mothers nearby, stricken by the loss of sons or tremulous at the prospect of their safe return, she seemed clear-eyed and unsentimental in her appraisal. Davy was no better a communicator than he had ever been and when Dimpy declared she was sure he wasn't coming home to her, Harry dared to believe her. He briefly fantasised that he and she would live out their lives side by side in increasing isolation as the rest of Winter emptied out, living off her cheeses and his apples and the bread she baked from their own flour.

Dimpy was wrong, however; Davy had delayed in order to marry. At some point in the war, he had been converted to a hand-on-heart brand of Christianity by an evangelical fellow gunner, who had even seen to it that he was baptised during a shore leave when their messmates were getting drunk and queuing for whores. When his gunner friend was blown to pieces and he was spared, Davy took it for a miracle and gave up alcohol and women on the spot. The dead evangelist became his private saint, and God efficiently filled the father-shaped hole in his life, as Paul had tried to do.

He had indeed been seduced by the briny glamour of Vancouver and drawn in by a very new evangelical church there, where he had fallen for a former navy radio operator.

Dimpy made excuses for him as ever. She hadn't been invited to the wedding because it was a quiet, private ceremony and Davy knew it was almost impossible for her to leave the farm at that time of year. She proudly displayed a studio photograph of Davy and his wife, a victorious-looking blonde whose name, Maxine, Harry found he kept forgetting. He had never known a Maxine before and wasn't sure that he wanted to now.

Gradually, it dawned on him that, having worked

through her fairly brief mourning for Paul, Dimpy was starting to like having the place to herself. She had let herself run a little wild, like an untended orchard, and had finally put on some weight, which suited her. Now that she had Harry on hand to help, she could live her life as she wanted. After the terrible years she had spent with her first husband and on the road, she had stumbled, as Paul's sister had before her, on the peculiar, rough-handed liberty the prairies gave a woman, away from all the nonsense forced upon her in town. Alone on her own acres, she could wear practical dungarees and a man's hat, if she had a mind to, and since Paul's death she increasingly had done. If she remarried or if Davy had returned to the farm after the war, she might have felt obliged to revert to feminine type.

During a summer lull, when her wheat was sown and the farm could briefly spare her, Dimpy asked Harry to mind the place for her while she paid a visit to the happy pair in Vancouver. He drove her to the train and noted the effort she had taken to look presentable, even stylish. He saw her nervousness at the novelty of travelling with a ticket she had paid for.

It was only to be a short visit – three nights – and he imagined she'd have felt awkward staying longer as Davy and Maxine lived in a one-bedroom flat, and she would be sleeping on their sofa. Her report on return was guarded. Vancouver had some stunning views, but was very crowded after Winter, and with people of all colours. Davy and Maxine were very Christian, she said.

'I mean, they talk about it without it being just a Sunday

thing. They say grace at breakfast. Maxine even asked me if I was saved. I said I certainly hoped so!'

Beyond that, she did not pass comment. She was not an enthusiastic person, so it was hard to tell if she had liked her daughter-in-law or not, but she said they were very settled there, very involved in their church and its social life.

Having hinted to Betty that he might be selling up, Harry felt able to write that he was probably staying put for now and even repeated his suggestion that she, Terry and the two girls might come on a Canadian adventure. He sensed money was short with her, however. Any holidays she mentioned were of the cheapest kind – a converted train carriage on the Kent coast, a caravan rented from the back pages of *The Lady*. It was unlikely they would come. Besides, Terry's work was as demanding as that of a parish priest. After cutting his teeth as a deputy governor at Wormwood Scrubs then Parkhurst, he had been promoted to governor at Chelmsford. He had spent the war as governor of the prison at Norwich, where he ran the local Home Guard. From there he had been transferred to Durham, which the family had loved, and where Pip had become engaged *at a <u>very</u> young eighteen* to Terry's deputy, of whom both parents were immensely fond, though they insisted on a long engagement. And now there was talk that they were to be moved yet again, this time to Liverpool, which Betty dreaded.

Betty had told Harry that, like vicars, prison governors were housed on the job, and handsomely so, but it seemed it was also a little like army life in that their families were regularly uprooted. There was also a weight of discretion whereby it was bad form for wives to know, or seek to know, the day-to-day details of their husbands' work, beyond things like carol services (interminable handbell performances) or breakouts, which could not be ignored. There must have been loneliness as well. Used to the crowded social life of the large family in which she grew up, it was a strain to find it was not on to befriend anyone locally apart from the deputy governor, chaplain and doctor and their wives – if they had them. It often struck Harry, reading her letters, that, although she lived in cities, her social life was as limited by form as his was by isolation.

Betty was sufficiently a Wells to have a bottomless appetite for the harmless stories he told her of Dimpy, the postmistress, Davy or Maxine. In return, most of her stories were not of people she met on the street, discouraged as she was from fraternising with officers' wives, but from what she gleaned from family letters: updates on the numerous Aunts and their confusingly plentiful offspring.

For a full year, a year in fact of young Pip's long engagement, all seemed settled, and Harry embraced the arrival of such excitements as a bigger radio and a tractor, content that no greater upheavals were in store. He stopped thinking of retirement to a cottage in North Battleford and, on his weekly visits to Paul's grave, dared imagine he would end his life as he had, quietly and on his own acres.

But families rarely stand still. After a surprisingly long time, Maxine announced that she was expecting. Davy's work as a carpet salesman was not bringing in enough for them to afford to rent a much larger flat and it turned out she was a daughter of the prairies, having been born and raised in the settlement of Unity, just two stops east along the Saskatchewan line from Winter. Despite never having visited Dimpy there, she decided she wished to give her babies the wholesome prairie upbringing she had known.

Poor Dimpy could hardly refuse her own kin and could not pretend that the help of a fit son about the place would not be preferable to relying on an elderly neighbour. So Harry watched as she cleaned and repainted so that she might give her room to the young couple and the second room – Petra's old one – to her grandchild, while she moved out to the annexe where she and Davy had first begun their life when Paul took them in.

Harry continued to support her as friend and neighbour, but he was conscious of mentally pulling in his neck, turtle fashion, as Davy and Maxine, who was exactly as he had imagined her, made their presences felt, and not merely as Christians for whom, apparently, Winter Church was insufficiently muscular in its Christianity. Maxine had money set by, as an only child of long-dead parents, and Davy used this and bank loans to modernise, buying the latest machinery, including one of the new combine harvesters, which required the immediate building of an ugly new shed.

He had been sly as a boy. Manhood, war, Jesus and marriage had made him more confident yet no more likeable or adept at disguising what he wanted. He drove Maxine over to Harry to introduce her and show off her pregnancy. The poor woman was so big with child it was a wonder she could climb out of his car.

'It's gonna be twins, for sure,' she said. 'They run in our family.'

'We're hoping for one of each,' Davy put in.

They called him Uncle Harry, as if by prior agreement. It was not a thing Davy had ever called him as a boy.

'So sad I never got to meet Davy's stepfather,' she said, sipping the barley water Harry had poured her. 'I gather he was like a brother to you.'

'Oh, they were close as close,' Davy said.

'Paul was my brother-in-law,' Harry stated. 'And the best neighbour a farmer could have.'

'I love your veranda,' she said. 'We should add one of these, Davy.'

'Full of schemes is Maxine,' Davy said, and winked. 'Thank you for looking after Mother while I was gone,' he added.

'She could run the place single handed,' Harry told him.

'Well, she can take it easy now we're here.'

'She likes to be busy,' Harry said.

'She's teaching me to knit,' Maxine told him. 'For the layette for these two. Sad to be all on your own here,' she added.

'I'm used to it,' Harry said.

'But you'll be wanting to put your feet up before long,' Davy told him.

'Since you've no boy to take the burden off your shoulders,' she added. 'I heard about your little girl. Sad.'

'I've another daughter,' he told her, 'by my first marriage. Back in England. She has a family of her own, so I'm not exactly all alone in the world.'

'Oh,' Maxine said flatly, and something in her face closed down. 'How nice. Davy never said.'

'Davy never asked,' he told her, with a teasing smile at Davy, who scowled, looking uncomfortable in his smart visiting clothes.

'I heard you were looking to sell up,' Davy said.

'In a tiny place like Winter,' Harry said, 'you hear a lot of things, not all of them true. I've had the place valued a couple of times, out of curiosity and for insurance purposes.'

'Ah well,' Davy said then, standing to indicate the visit was at an end. 'If you do ever decide to sell, I hope you'd consider selling to us.'

'It would make sense,' Maxine added, heaving herself upright. 'Combining the two farms. Those new machines need bigger fields and wider gates. Farms are expanding now to hold their own. And this house would be just perfect for Mother.'

It took him a moment to see that she meant Dimpy.

Harry held the car door open for her. She was wearing a scent that made Harry want to sneeze. He did his best to sound considerate.

'If ever I decide to sell,' he told them, 'I'll be sure to give you due warning. But I'm not the rich man I was as a boy; I'm afraid I'd need the best price the market could offer.'

'Oh, you stay here just as long as you like,' she said, patting his arm. 'Davy's just restless. Wants to sort the whole place out, to modernise. The boxes of junk he's throwing out to make space! My eager beaver . . .'

Dimpy was far too loyal to breathe a negative word

about the happy pair, but Harry saw the tightness around her mouth when she spoke of them now, saw how, when they insistently brought her to church with them each week, she was as guarded in her good behaviour as a hostage.

After that initial visit, and its crude statement of intent, Davy and Maxine stayed away. Her twins arrived safely, and Harry gave them a pair of pear trees in celebration. It had been as much for Dimpy's pleasure as theirs and, sure enough, it was she who eventually thanked him for them. Her hands were full now, helping with the babies, and he only saw her when the family was on parade at church.

Then, either from some windfall or Maxine's savings, Davy acquired the long-neglected plot the far side of Harry's farm. Fences and hedges were tugged up, gigantic wheat fields duly created – from which Harry was quite sure the next bad wind would sweep half the soil – and he was glad to learn the young family had effectively built a brand-new house in the wreckage of the old, leaving Dimpy to the place Paul had built and which was, after all, hers.

SEVEN

When Davy returned for another visit, it was unannounced and alone. Harry had spent a long day ploughing. He had mechanised to the extent of acquiring a little Ford tractor and plough and, although it was infinitely quicker and easier than walking behind an ox or Clydesdale mile upon mile, the long hours sitting in the open on a juddering steel seat left him chilled and numb and, he confessed to himself, feeling his age. All he wanted was to feed the dog then soak in a hot bath with the radio murmuring close at hand.

A problem with living somewhere so remote was that unwelcome visitors were doubly so. There was no hiding from them when they lurked on the veranda, only looming from the shadows on your approach. The dog barked at him, of course.

Davy still looked more like a travelling salesman than a farmer; it was as though the man, or his wife, had a pathological fear of dirt. He was paying other men to get dirty for him, Harry had heard. He would like that. Like being the boss of them. The only good thing he had picked up from Paul was how to stand straight and unashamed, but he still had trouble meeting a man's eye.

'Davy,' Harry said. 'What a nice surprise.'

'You always did have fine manners,' Davy said. 'Uncle

Harry.' He added the title with an unmistakable air of mockery.

'What can I do for you? Come on in to the warm so I can see your face.'

Harry took the key down from its hiding place, let them into the house and turned on a light. Electric light was better to read by, but it still came as a shock and its unflattering harshness made Harry miss the old softness of the oil lamps he still occasionally lit by choice. He riddled and woke up the stove, and threw some logs in it, then slid the kettle to the hottest part and set down a can of meat for the dog.

Neither Dimpy nor Davy kept a dog. He wondered if it was because of their time living on the road and occasionally having dogs set on them when they called at a hostile farmstead. Maxine, Harry felt sure, thought them unhygienic and ungodly. Dimpy kept a large and expressionless cat to keep vermin away, though he had never seen her pet it or even heard her call it anything other than the cat.

'Sit, Davy.'

'No, no. I won't keep you. I can see you're cold.'

'Well, I'm sitting, because I'm tired. Please, Davy. Sit.'

Reluctantly, Davy sat across the table from him.

'So,' Harry said, 'things seem to be going well for you. You're thriving, I hear, over at the old Schmidt place.'

'Yes, God be praised. Now that Maxine has rearranged and remodelled it the way she wanted.'

'Good. You'll have a good tonnage of wheat to sell at the year's end.'

'Should do.'

'Sad they wanted to leave such good land. I suppose after losing their son in the war, they were disheartened.'

'Have you thought more about selling, Uncle Harry?'

'I have, especially at the hardest point of last winter, but then I realised there's nowhere I'd rather be.'

'Maxine and I were thinking you might want to reconsider.'

'Oh?'

'When we moved out, Maxine took away boxes of old farm papers and such to make more room for Mother to spread herself. I don't think Paul had a bonfire in his life, there was so much of it. I was all for burning it, but Maxine insisted on keeping them. She's careful that way, said there could be legal or financial papers in there we might need some day.'

'And were there?'

Harry knew well Paul's impatient way with letters or bank statements or instruction manuals, how he would read them once, scowling a little, as he was in denial about needing reading glasses, before stuffing them into the nearest cupboard or drawer. *Adding to the wood*, he called it. By the time Dimpy met him, the place must have become quite the fire hazard, but she was an orderly woman, and Harry had assumed she would long since have tidied and swept every drawer and cupboard in the place. But then he remembered that she was not a woman who read. From the few times he had seen her handwriting, he knew that she was barely literate, so perhaps she had retained the respect of the unlettered for the potential of documents to instruct and control.

'Most of it was just junk,' Davy said, 'but Maxine insisted she go over it all. She's like a terrier with a rat. She'd sit by the fire with another pile of papers some evenings, or out on the veranda.'

'She got her veranda, then?'

'Yes . . . She got a veranda.'

Davy sighed and Harry almost felt for him. Maxine was not a woman who would ever be satisfied. She would drive a man, and a brittle quality to her smile made Harry suspect she was a woman with a private temper.

'But then she found a letter. A sort of love letter, you might call it. It was old. Folded and folded and tucked away, of all places, inside my stepfather's driving licence. Of course, Maxine was touched by it at first. Given the date on it, she thought it must be from some pretty girl he left behind when he went off to war. She doesn't know your handwriting the way I do. That very fancy, queer way you write your E's.'

Harry felt slightly dizzy. No warmth was yet reaching him from the stove, and he had been out on the tractor after dewfall so was damp as well as chilled.

'I expect you'd like to see it again, after all this time,' Davy said.

'I don't know what letter you can mean,' Harry said. 'I'm very cold, actually. I should run a bath.'

'Of course. I kept the original, as it's precious, really, a thing like that. But I had Maxine write it out, to refresh your memory.' Davy stood and took a crisp envelope from his jacket pocket. He gazed at it. 'If a thing like this were known, you couldn't possibly stay on here,' he said quietly.

'You, a school governor, a former church warden, a pillar of our little community. You might not be arrested at your age, but nobody would want you where there were children. Nobody would want to do business with you. I always sensed Paul was twice the man you were. Mother sensed it, too. You showed us kindness and took us in. I've never forgotten that, but it was him she was drawn to. The real man, not the abomination.

'Let me know what you decide. You'd best put it in a letter rather than call at the house. It doesn't bother me so much. I was in the navy, after all; I know men without women become animals. But Maxine would prefer not to have you step across the porch . . .'

He said nothing further, not even goodnight, but simply placed the envelope down near where he had been sitting, then put his spotless hat back on and let himself out.

Harry did not move until he heard the car fire up and drive off, then he went out to set the bath running. The gas-fired cylinder produced very hot water, but slowly, from a narrow-mouthed tap. Leaving the bath to fill, he turned on the radio to the sort of serious talk he preferred to dance music, a discussion of peace or the United Nations or some such, something that would wash over him as the talk of adults might pass over the head of a sleepy child. Then he topped up the dog's water bowl, locked the front door and carried the envelope to the light to open it.

Maxine's handwriting was cursive and tidy, quite without character. She used blue ink, the washable sort, of course. He had quite forgotten the words he had used, but remembered every word of the letter they were answering, as it was the only love letter Paul had ever sent him, posted on his way to the trenches where he would lose a foot and mercifully be taken prisoner. It had always been precious, not because it was the only letter Paul had ever sent him, but because it was the only time he had acknowledged in words what neither of them ever said out loud. Harry had carried it in his wallet ever since, until time, rain and frequent handling had caused the paper to fall apart. The letter was purely talismanic by then for he soon had the words by heart, there were so few of them.

Your face, like your voice and your touch, is tucked away in my heart, from where I can summon it night or day. Your photograph, like this cheap writing paper, would soon grow stained and crumpled from damp and much folding but the thought of you is indestructible and remains as fresh as on the day I left you.

Poor little Grace was almost more upset about the dog than she was about you! Harry had written back. *Or perhaps the two of you are muddled up in her head and it's easier for her to say she misses the dog than the uncle? Your sister is her usual stoical self, angry with you on the outside and buttoning up whatever pain she feels. She has been working like a Trojan. Insists I teach her to plough come the spring, if you're not back by then.*

If you're not back . . . I know I should be patriotic and write only morale-boosting sentiments but I'm afraid I can't, and it would insult your intelligence. I miss you more than words can say, Paul. It's like a growth inside me, heavy, malign, eating my strength, there the moment I wake, there when the cat wakes me, or I roll over in the night.

Oh yes. We got a cat. Or it got us. Just showed up in the snow, mewling to come in. No one can settle on a name. It doesn't laugh like you, or smell as good, and it bites, but it's a weight in the night and that helps a bit. Harry's reply had gone on to be cruder, far less measured, and dared to spell out just how Harry ached in Paul's absence and just what he missed him doing to him. He remembered, reading the words again, that, by not signing the letter, he believed he would enable anyone who read it to assume it was from a lovelorn girl.

It was a measure of the discretion of their relationship that he had no idea his letter had ever reached Paul, still less that he had kept it in his breast pocket to his dying day.

EIGHT

Betty almost certainly had no inkling how much power she was given over Harry's future. As soon as the farm sale was agreed, he wrote to her, suggesting that he could finally visit her, if she would like that, but the delay in waiting for her response was such that he felt he must have an alternative plan in mind in case she said no. He took a trip back to North Battleford and found a couple of places he could rent, if need be, with the sale money carefully invested. They were modest places, but one he especially liked was a sort of studio apartment with a shared garden. It lay on the ground floor, so was suitable for an old man whose knees would probably give out the moment he no longer had a horse. The town had a library, a good market, even a cinema. He could imagine being very happy there, in a quiet sort of way.

But then Betty's response arrived, full of apparent enthusiasm, suggesting he telegram his arrival details and saying how very much she and Terry and Whistle and Mollie the dog were looking forward to meeting him at last. Her letter was opening a window, but it was also closing a door, and he quickly set about booking his train and boat tickets rather than pay much heed to a tingle of regret.

Dimpy had no idea how little her son had paid him for the farm. The sum was so insultingly low that Harry's solicitor was clearly alarmed that Harry was not in his right mind accepting it. He was a church warden and had one of those faces that could shame a boy into good behaviour with no more than a sigh. Without saying anything to Harry, he said something to Davy that improved the offer, although he protested that it was still well below the market rate.

Harry silenced him in the end by saying that there was no one else he wanted to sell to. And this was partially true. He would much rather not have sold to a nasty piece of work like Davy O'Connor, but he liked the thought that it would soon be Dimpy who moved into his little house. However ambiguously, she represented a precious link with Paul and would, she had assured him, take care of Petra and Grace's grave. She had also astonished him by saying she'd take on his dog, that it would stop her feeling nervous on her own again if she had a dog about the place. Harry could tell she was finding it a strain to live on top of Maxine and the clamorous twins and was looking forward to the relative silence of his house.

He asked her over to see which of his possessions she might have a use for. He had travelled nowhere, discounting day trips, since he'd arrived to clear, plough and fence off his quarter section in the early years of the century, two world wars ago. Most people, he had seen, came to acquire more and more things the longer they stayed in one place. His long-ago mother-in-law, Mrs Wells, had lived so long in one house, through the bearing and marrying-off of fourteen children, that she joked it would take an archaeologist to find her when she died, as her house had accrued so many layers of pictures and furniture, of drapes and bibelots. And he had known men and women there in Winter line their houses with books and rugs like a protective layer against the wilderness, or death, perhaps.

He had been like them once. When he first married, as a rich young Londoner, he had enjoyed making house with Winnie beside the sea in Herne Bay, showering her with the tasteful best of everything. Then the process of losing first a large chunk of his investments, having to give up his house to move in with Mrs Wells and then giving up still more when he set out to be a homesteader, had been a brutal education in the vanity of laying up possessions. Even so, he had travelled out to the prairies with a preposterous quantity of clothes, including evening wear, and a canteen of family silver. The smart clothes had long since succumbed to time, mud and moth. The silver had survived, and it pleased him to leave it in its velvet-lined box for Dimpy to eat with.

Perhaps because he and Paul had built the house and much of the furniture in it by hand, he had never seen the need to gussy it up. He liked to see the joints and the pegs of the place. When he lay in bed, there was a distinct indentation he could see where Paul's hammer had missed its aim and dented the wood to the side of a nail. To see it was to remember the man who had helped him build the place from a huge, impossibly daunting kit brought over from the station on a cart. And although, like many a Canadian, Harry kept sane through the endless, isolating winters by reading, he had never seen the need to keep books about him like so many trophies, but would cheerfully give them away to the library or the school when he had finished them.

Dimpy was disturbed by how little he was taking with him to England.

'Being reunited with a father you've never known is daunting enough,' he told her. 'But to have him show up with trunkloads of stuff?'

Still, he humoured her by boxing up things she did not need but which he, in some vague future, might need again, and stacking them on the rafters of a weatherproof shed. She seemed relieved when he did that, so he could tell his lack of paraphernalia unsettled her, quite as though she'd caught him preparing to walk into the slough to drown, rather than making the trip back to England.

Dimpy drove him to the train and insisted on waiting to see him off. She hugged him on the platform, hugged him hard, which amused him as she was not the hugging type, but perhaps she had decided she would never see him again, so that dignity didn't greatly matter.

'I'm a lousy letter writer,' she said.

'That's all right,' he told her. 'Just think of me sometimes. And don't let Maxine bully you. She has no imagination, and controlling people is a sort of panic reflex in her. You'll be doing her a favour if you gently put her in her place occasionally.'

The train journey – a day and a night to Winnipeg, where he had a few hours to stretch his legs and eat some lunch – then twice as long again to Toronto and then out to Halifax, was an adventure in itself, and wildly sociable. He had not seen so many people in a long while, everybody wanted to talk and, as at least two second honeymooners told him, he had a listening face.

It was far more comfortable than the settler train on which Harry had first travelled out. That had an uncushioned wooden interior and men had been obliged to bed down on its floor, as that was more comfortable than trying to sleep on the punitive benches. This train was abundantly upholstered. It slowed down obligingly whenever there was a bear or a moose visible from the windows and it boasted an observation car, where he spent mesmerised hours at a stretch watching forest and river and more forest slip by. The socialising or, rather, the talking at his listening face, tended to happen at mealtimes, as lone travellers like Harry were placed at random for their meals by the maître d', never with the same people twice. After years of living in near silence, he found it exhausting. He soon learned to pretend he was asleep if he needed peace, only it was hard to resist for long the lure of the scenery flashing by.

If the train had come to seem claustrophobic, the *Empress of France* proved more so. Harry could only afford the cheapest ticket that Canadian Pacific offered to Liverpool, which gave him a shared berth with an extraordinarily tedious pig farmer from Moose Jaw, and access to a boomingly cavernous tourist-class dining room and mock-Tudor bar and lounge. The pig farmer, who seemed to think it a wonderful coincidence that two farmers from Saskatchewan should have ended up in the same cabin, had never sailed before, ate hugely on their first night, then spent the rest of the crossing being loudly sick from the bottom bunk, each copious outpouring accompanied by a groan of outrage that such misery was even possible. Harry, who had excellent sea legs, sat out long hours in the dining room or bar, oppressed by the hearty cavortings of the couples all around him and doing his best to fend off the approaches of the handful of brave lone women his sort of age. There was a dance contest, communal sing-alongs and then, on the third night, an uproarious attempt to improvise a sort of ice hockey by sliding around on the dance floor in stockinged feet in pursuit of an ice cube. Harry was no more a drinker than he was a smoker, but he ended by huddling on a cushioned stool at the bar, nursing a whisky and wishing the sea would get even rougher to drive everyone to their beds.

The barman was a silver-haired man with a marvellously Scandinavian look of contempt. He was wearily polishing glasses for something to do, while keeping half an eye out for damage or injuries. He caught Harry's eye and winked.

'You could always escape them by turning in,' he said.

'More than I can do.'

'I'm sharing with a man who wants the world to know nobody has ever been as sick as he is,' Harry told him. 'It's almost quieter in here.'

Together they watched a woman triumphantly thwack the ice cube with an umbrella handle into what passed for goal, and met each other's eyes again during the whoops that followed.

'But it is a bit . . .' Harry began.

'What is it a bit?' asked the barman.

'A bit . . . Noah's ark.'

The barman seemed to take a moment to understand then slowly grinned in agreement. 'There is another world,' he said.

'When we finally reach Liverpool, you mean?'

'No. On the next deck down.'

'There's a level below this?'

'Sure there is. For the staff. Something tells me you'd be right at home down there. Here, Marco?' He clicked his fingers for a younger colleague, who was valiantly swabbing down tabletops and clearing up the mess being left by merry passengers on every side. 'Take my friend, here, to the staff bar.'

'Yes, Mr Petersen,' the youth said. 'This way, sir.'

And he led Harry through a service door marked *Private* and into a mysterious, undecorated part of the ship, a part that actually looked like a ship rather than pretending to be a picturesque building on land.

'You won't be alone,' he told Harry. 'There are always one or two passengers on each crossing who prefer to come down here, as they feel more at home. Even from first class where, you know, you'd think they have everything. Here you go, sir.'

He opened a door into a low-ceilinged room that was a sort of maritime equivalent of how Harry dimly remembered a London pub. There was subdued lighting, and dance music playing on a gramophone. Members of staff and a smattering of passengers – revealed by their lack of uniform – were drinking and chatting at two convivial tables. The young guide, with the impeccable manners of a bright, young hostess, introduced Harry at the nearest table, where there was an empty chair.

'Hello, everyone. This is . . .'

'Harry,' supplied Harry.

'This is Harry. He's on his own. Be nice.'

'All got a bit much for you, ducky?' asked a portly man whose pocket bore a badge that read *Purser*. 'There's a lot of it about. What are you having?'

Harry found himself welcomed warmly into a world he had not imagined could exist. They were all men, though some, like the purser, were fairly feminine in their solicitude. Some were in pairs, recognised and apparently honoured as such, others adventurously single. They were keen to hear his story and, for the first and possibly only time in his life, he found himself telling some of it, which was giddying.

On the remaining nights of the crossing, he repeatedly explained that he was about to be reunited with the daughter he hadn't seen since she was a toddler, and the reaction was always a shocked disbelief that made him start to wonder if he was a blind fool to be making the journey. Only the portly purser responded calmly, laying a hand briefly on his arm to say, 'Well, you'll never know unless you go, ducky. And I expect there are things you want to say to her.'

Harry had never gone so long without fresh air, walking the turbulent corridors, from the acid stink of his little, wood-veneered cabin to the bottomless, empty talk of the dining room to the echoing whoops of the bar and – now that he knew the way – down the service staircase to the cosy snug on the deck below. He was having, or listening in on, conversations that left him as dizzy as an inexperienced climber on a mountainside. It gave him the curious sense that – in transit from a young world to an older one – he had stumbled onto yet another, that was altogether older and wiser than either. By the time they had passed Ireland and were nosing into the mouth of the Mersey on a dazzling April morning, he was left with the slightly panicky feeling of someone worrying they'd bought a ticket to quite the wrong place.

BETTY

NINE

It was extraordinary to feel she had a father finally, a man who would respond if she wrote to him, and that all it had taken to reintroduce him to her life had been to write a letter to the bewitchingly simple address that had been there all these years, written in her mother's tidy hand in her almost empty address book. Just as the move to contact Harry had been prompted by Terry, so the sudden flush of daughterly affection in Betty was fed by the happy transformation that love, Terry and marriage had wrought on her life. With his gruff affection, tweed suits, height and pipe smoking, his faux-grump way of exclaiming *Good God, Bets* and fiercely protective instincts, Terry was, she came to see, the daddy for whom she had never dared admit she yearned. Obviously, he didn't pick her up and whirl her around when he came home from work, the way she had enviously watched friends' and cousins' fathers do, but it was how she felt inside when he kissed her as he came through the door and exchanged his coat and hat for a stiff Scotch.

Betty had adored her mother and her granny and, for all her dread of the Uncles, always thought the Aunts funny and stylish and full of womanly wisdom she feared she would never acquire. It was only once she married Terry, however, and began to keep house for him, first in their tiny flat with the balcony, then in a little cottage in Barnes with cows grazing across the road, that she realised the extent to which she had always felt oppressed by their pity, by being *Poor Betty*, fatherless daughter of a woman without prospects, obliged to earn her keep by being always helpful, witty and attentive.

Nothing in Aunt Pattie's pamphlet had prepared her for the wildly undignified, sweaty reality of sex. Once she was experiencing it on a nightly basis – it was a point of pride in Terry never to miss a night, even when he was shattered or when Betty herself was – she began to examine other married women in wonder, and to ask herself if the respectability they pulled about them in butcher's queues and doctor's waiting rooms, at haberdashery counters and when giving instructions to housemaids older than they were, was a reaction to their bedroom lives. Or were they all in a state of yearning, and was Terry what the charlady's paper called *a sex maniac*?

Apparently, the family way of regarding her father as unreliable, somehow hopeless, was so inculcated in her that, once Betty admitted that they were in touch, nobody expected anything of it, neither a handsome (or any) marriage settlement nor a congratulatory visit. It was enough for Granny and the Aunts to know he was alive and unchanged. He might have been living on Pluto for all the interest they took.

Privately, Betty was a little hurt. Even allowing for the way men of his generation expressed so little emotion, she had expected some warmth once they established contact, but his letters, amusing and ironic, remained as calm as if she had simply walked in from the room next door or returned from an afternoon stroll, not been missing from his life for nearly three decades. When she explained that she and Terry would love to visit but could not possibly afford it, he did not offer to pay their fares or offer to visit himself instead. She told herself that, of course, it was impossible for him to leave the farm, but it was a wheat farm, not a dairy one, and even a town girl like her knew that, once planted, wheat could surely be left to grow for a few months unassisted. But then she looked about her, at the businesses going broke, the men laid off, the signs of desperation, and realised things would be no easier in Canada, and were possibly worse. So she simply, if sporadically now, kept up their correspondence. She sent him pictures of the children, first Pip, then bewitching, needy Whistle, of dogs, and simple seaside holidays. And, whenever someone new asked, she rather enjoyed their polite bafflement when she said that her mother was dead and her father, a wheat farmer in Saskatchewan.

In the narrow display of life's possibilities her mother and the Aunts had laid out before Betty, like the cards in a fortune-telling, women were entirely defined by what their husbands did unless they failed or chose not to marry and became governesses, schoolmistresses, nuns or actresses. Marrying money, as her mother had done, in theory guaranteed happiness since the husband would be content and therefore so would his wife, but her father's fortune had dwindled to the point where he was reduced to farming and she to dressmaking. A terrible lesson there, therefore. Marrying into the Church was generally held to be a terrible burden, fit only for the very high-minded. Marrying into the army was a not much better prospect, however exciting the dress uniforms, because the risk of widowhood was high, as was that of a life of hobnobbing only with other army wives. Marrying into the Prison Service had never been mentioned, but Betty soon learned it combined elements of Church and army in the way the wife's days and dealings were circumscribed.

While Terry was deputy governor at the Scrubs, Betty had lived a nearly normal life in their sweet little house in Barnes from which he drove to work and where she had little sense of his job impinging on her days at home with dog and baby. When she was expecting Whistle and he was moved on to be deputy at Parkhurst on the Isle of Wight, they had to move to the island, of course, as it would have been an impossible commute, and they were given a house on the edge of the prison's estate. Suddenly, their socialising was curtailed to a level as narrow as that in an old novel: the governor and his wife, the chaplain and his wife, the doctor and his wife and anyone suitable Betty happened to befriend in church, but she was so very busy with a toddler and then with a toddler and a new baby to care for, as well as having to make a proper lunch and supper every day, as Terry enjoyed popping home for those and to *see his girls*, that she barely had the time or energy to notice, much less complain. By the time he was promoted to become governor of Chelmsford, she had spent enough time chatting to the Parkhurst governor's wife to know what to expect and how to behave. The job always came with a large house attached to the prison, if not quite inside its walls, larger than they could possibly fill or fully furnish and usually impossible to heat. The better salary at least meant they could employ a cook and a maid. Contact with prisoners – *the men*, she was to call them – was an almost daily occurrence as the trusties, usually men on long sentences who had earned points for good behaviour, helped out around both house and garden, often using skills they had learned when free, from carpentry and plumbing to repainting a child's bedroom or hanging wallpaper.

She had a kitchen table made in one prison workshop and several pairs of curtains run up in another, so well-crafted that they travelled with her from posting to posting. The uprooting was the chief similarity to army life – it was rare to stay at any prison beyond five or six years for fear of friendships and favouritism destabilising a governor's authority.

Hardest, for a woman raised on the delights of gossip, was the need to hold one's tongue. Betty understood the most basic rule, which was that you never asked, either directly or indirectly, what crime had landed a man inside.

'You're dying to know, of course,' Terry said. 'So, often enough, are they. But it just isn't done. Just assume they're all murderers and rapists and be your sweet, polite self with all of them.'

'Always better they think you a bit hoity-toity than that they know you, or think they've got something on you,' the governor's wife told her.

This particularly became the case with the declaration of war and the imposition of rationing and shortages, ache though Betty might to accept someone's offering of their cousin's under-the-counter bacon or a couple of crab caught by their boy at the weekend. She had to be utterly impartial and law-abiding, suffering the same deprivations as everyone, sometimes more so.

These behaviours soon became second nature to her. The part she found hard was holding back with Terry.

'It's not like a normal job in an office or a hospital or on a street,' the Parkhurst governor's wife told her, 'where he comes home, puts up his feet with a drink and you can soothe his brow and have him tell you all about it. It's much better never to ask and never to encourage him to tell. He has trusted colleagues for that. With you, he'll need to relax, and he can only do that by leaving the job behind when the guards wave him through the gates. Tell him about your day, about the children, talk about the news or what you're reading. Anything but the trouble on C wing or the suicide or the awful noises you heard over the wall while you were working in the rose bed.' The governor's wife could see Betty thought she was exaggerating and laid a hand on hers for emphasis. 'I'm deadly serious,' she told her. 'Think about the reality of the job: he's spending all day dealing with and talking to and punishing truly desperate men, often the dregs of society, people you wouldn't want your child to sit beside on a bus. He absorbs their stories, their worries, their fears. That's a terrible burden. When he comes home, he needs a total break from it all, not wifey asking him to tell her all about it.'

Betty came to see that Terry's bluff, all-chaps-together, firing-on-all-six exterior masked a deep sensitivity and that, however much he might joke about the men sometimes, or delight in mimicking this one's accent or that one's wayward syntax when asking for a favour, they affected him deeply. He told her stories about his time in Sarawak sometimes, where his policing days were now a distant adventure, and she sensed the stories of rugby-tackling a drunk native who had scalped someone with a machete, or trapping a murderer who had fed his victims piecemeal to the huge local crabs, were his way of offloading in coded form the stresses of his days in prison.

They had the luxury of space, so that the children's noise and toys could be confined to a big nursery while the adults enjoyed a measure of elegance elsewhere. In at least two houses, they had enjoyed a breakfast room as well as a dining room and, as both their girls grew noisily adept at the piano and, in Whistle's case, the flute as well, they even had a music room. Betty worried that by growing up in such large houses, with prisoners standing in for servants for all the mundane jobs, the girls would acquire taste beyond their means.

Terry's second prison as governor had been Norwich, where they spent the dark years of the war, desperately missing the girls, whose little school was evacuated to a grand old house in a quiet corner of Norfolk, while Terry's experience as a lance corporal in the Royal Highlanders came in useful as he commanded and trained the local platoon of the Home Guard. Much their happiest posting had been Durham, where the girls, as young women, benefited from the overspill of culture that came from living beside a cathedral and a university.

Betty's own education had been so tattered and incomplete a thing that she was daunted by how much her daughters both seemed to know about art and music, at least. Having often suffered from the caprices and thoughtless cruelties of adults when she was growing up, she had been determined not to favour one child over the other, but nature intervened to ensure the girls were never equal. Long of leg and face – *coltish* was often used of her – Pip had always been her father's daughter, almost like the son he never had in her eagerness to run fast and be fearless. Whistle was everything Pip was not, arrestingly beautiful – a blue-eyed blonde with the sad, thoughtful look of Terry's late mother – but almost frighteningly sensitive, as though she lacked Pip's protective layers. As a child, she would give way to tears, rage or terror at the slightest prompting and the sensitivity had stayed with her to the point where Betty had consulted a doctor or two for reassurance, worried the girl had inherited some darkness or instability from a previous generation or should, perhaps, be taking medication to steady her febrile nature.

Terry lacked Betty's patience. He couldn't bear the noise of babies crying or the unreachable rage of toddlers and continued to walk out of the room when, in her teens, Whistle was occasionally overcome with anxiety. He took it personally, as though it was a failure in him that he couldn't calm her simply by his presence. It was Betty who often spent hours at night lying beside Whistle to soothe her until she fell asleep. Pip, who adored her sister, and had been protective of her from childhood, blamed it on the war and Whistle's terror of air raids. Sometimes, she even chided herself for having naughtily drawn her sister, in dressing gown and slippers, out from their airraid shelter, in the fragile weeks before their school was evacuated, for the dangerous thrill of watching a dogfight in the night sky.

Both girls remained artistic. Pip, who never stopped drawing, had an eye for fashion and meticulous recall of what anyone she met had been wearing, and pined for art school. Whistle, who had won a competition for her poetry and played her flute beautifully, could have thrived in music college or even read English at university. To her abiding shame, Betty had pretended to believe them when they said they were happy to take jobs at sixteen, because money was short and because neither she nor Terry had been educated beyond school. They had both inherited a suspicion that highly educated women scared men away.

For a while, Pip worked as a typist for an estate agent, where she rather got into trouble for amusing herself writing overly flattering descriptions – *charming outdoor facilities, great scope for an energetic gardener with vision*, etc. – until she charmed her way into the perfect job as an assistant librarian at the Durham University library. Young for her age, she was soon agog at the things she learned about love and marriage while chatting with the older librarians on their lunch breaks. She developed crushes, inevitably, on stammering students or handsome widowed professors who called in to borrow or return books.

But then, quite suddenly, she announced that Terry's new deputy, Mike, had proposed to her. Being a diffident, old-fashioned boy of nearly thirty, he formally asked Terry for his blessing and acquiesced when Terry and Betty insisted on at least a year's engagement as Pip was only eighteen and knew nothing of the world. Mike was a dear man, dryly funny, kind, more suited to the priesthood, Terry said, than the Prison Service and, perhaps because he had lost both parents, Mike had rather adopted them, writing to Betty more often than Pip may have realised.

Soon after the wedding, the prison commissioners had upended their lives, moving Terry to take on the prison in Liverpool – Walton Jail as the locals called it – and putting Mike in charge of a new officers' training course in Wakefield. The newlyweds had a nice enough little house just across the way from Wakefield Prison on Love Lane. Betty, though, felt the wrench of the new distance between them painfully, especially with petrol still rationed, and found Liverpool overwhelming and grim after Durham.

Always the strong one, her daddy's girl, Pip had horrified her and Terry by almost dying in childbirth a little over a year after her marriage. Her twins arrived a month early, at home, rather than in hospital where, Betty was convinced but dared not say, the boy might have lived. As it was, he died within an hour of his birth, while the equally tiny girl held on to life, tenacious as her mother. She was now in round-cheeked health, though a poor feeder.

Whistle undoubtedly benefited from not having a bossy older sister around to compete with her for attention at last, but in Liverpool, without Pip there to cover for her, her night terrors, the snobbery she used to mask her fear of new people and loathing of crowds, were cruelly exposed. She claimed to find all the talk of babies boring and mocked Mike behind his back as White Fang, for his neglected teeth, but she was turning into an almost alarmingly beautiful young woman, her blonde hair, white skin and full lips bright as a flag in the city's downtrodden crowds. Betty had taken to dropping hints and photographs to well-connected cousins in the south, who might be in a position to invite Whistle to what she considered more superior parties and dances than would come her way in Liverpool. She and Terry had few friends there, and no close ones. Betty had, at least, found a good flute teacher, a Jewish refugee from Austria who played with the Royal Liverpool Philharmonic and had encouraged Whistle to talk about music colleges and London and scholarships. Instinct told Betty that Whistle would never cope with studying on her own in the city, let alone with the pressure of auditions for a scholarship.

Yet again, she felt, everything depended on the generosity of the Aunts and their families.

TEN

It was a crisp day with a blue sky and a vigorous breeze, a day for pegging sheets on an orchard washing line. Terry said she was imagining it, but in Durham her wash had usually come in clean whereas here in Liverpool they had a railway nearby and there were invariably greasy smuts that drifted down and left a mark behind if rubbed. Mrs Stapleton, the daily of whom Betty remained nervous, claimed she kept a bone-dry nailbrush handy for removing them, but, when Betty had tried this on one of Terry's best white shirts, she had only smeared it and been obliged to scrub at the stain with Omo before washing the thing all over again.

She disliked housework with a passion and resented living in a city so dark and dirty that dusting and hoovering and mopping and polishing were no sooner done than they needed doing again. Her girlhood had not been grand, but there had always been maids and cooks, and Granny and the Aunts had never so much as held a duster. Ladies should always be ladylike, Granny told them, and there was nothing so unappealing in a woman as being red in the face from bending and rubbing.

When Betty and Terry were first married, they were sufficiently in love to be poor merrily, which, along with the romance of it, had been why they eloped. Letting him see her tame her flyaway hair and magnificent bosom in a spotty scarf and apron while she earnestly taught herself to do her housework from a manual had been a kind of flirtation. And Betty still dusted every room in a clockwise direction, so as to miss nothing, just as the manual had advised.

Though a year old now, she still thought of the car as their new one, bought to cheer her up on moving. Terry had always had a weakness for cars. It was an extravagance like the others, though a practical one: a smoke grey Morris Minor with maroon upholstery and a mole-coloured soft top. With her dark glasses, very red lipstick, her best French headscarf on and driving gloves she had purchased as they matched the seats, she knew she cut a dash. Driving it with the roof down in the sad streets around the prison might be seen as a provocation, but it lifted her spirits to be noticed a little, and Terry liked her to be noticed. The trick was not to smile or give any sign of knowing eyes were upon you: that would have been what the Aunts called 'fast'.

The long chain of Merseyside docks excited and alarmed her in equal measure. She had sometimes joined the Aunts on *safaris* to the docks in London to meet or wave off friends or relations, and loved the bustle, the huge ships, the suggestion of dreamy refinement, evening dress at sea, dancing the nights away to an on-board band, the classes reassuringly divided off from one another with doors and silk ropes. And yet ships sank and she knew all the palm-court finery, all the dressing for dinner, was a distraction from fear.

Betty saw people in the docks she'd never noticed elsewhere: black stevedores, their arms and thighs like the statues Pattie had approvingly shown her in Florence; Chinese, their beautiful clothes bright flashes beneath drab western overcoats or mackintoshes. These people fascinated her and she longed to stare, but she could never shake off the stories the Aunts used to repeat of nice girls snatched by Chinese thugs and sold into the white slave trade, or more recent tales Terry had repeated of how black men, Louis Armstrong a notable exception, because he worshipped him, all dreamed of possessing a white woman and bringing her low.

Father's telegram had said he was on the *Empress of France* and gave his approximate disembarkation time, so she had done her research. Unlike the Cunard line ships, which docked in the heart of the city, near the Liver Building, Canadian Pacific ones arrived far closer to the prison, at Gladstone Dock in Bootle. True to her telegram back to Harry, she had worn the red leather driving gloves and red headscarf so he would see her wave from the crowd. It occurred to her that he would recognise her before she saw him. She had sent him several recent pictures of her with Terry or with the girls, but the most recent she'd been sent was one of Father in a group of Winter School governors, in which his face was deeply shaded by a hat brim. Otherwise, all she had were the pictures of him in debonair youth.

It was a handsome ship, white with two buff funnels. Father had said nothing about which class he'd be travelling in, and two gangways were attached to the sides to ensure that first and tourist classes kept scrupulously apart at sea remained apart at least until obliged to mingle on dry land.

Watching the smart men and women on the first-class gangway, Betty thought of Terry's silver matchbox holder. It was a beautiful, heavy thing, designed by Omar Ramsden in the perfect likeness of a suitcase, tiny buckles and straps and all, with Terry's initials on one side and, on the other, the surely flirtatious message from *the grateful passengers whose burdens you shared.* He had always maintained it was given to him because he carried the bags for a couple of wealthy families on his long voyage out to Sarawak, but, jealous to a fault, and knowing there were perfectly good staff on board for such things, Betty had always pictured some wearily chic wife having it inscribed for him in recognition of a shipboard liaison. It stood on the table by his chair beside the fireplace, polished by her, filled with matches by him, ready for lighting the fire or his pipe, a suggestive object that had to be explained afresh to each new admirer who picked it up.

She had tried to keep a level head about Father, ever since her bitter disappointment when he had said he was coming home to celebrate her wedding to Terry over twenty years before and never made the trip. Right up until the moment she checked her lipstick in the hall and pulled on her gloves and scarf, she had braced herself for a last-minute second telegram saying Father had been unavoidably detained on the prairies, that the farm sale had fallen through or that he had changed his mind and thought it best he stayed put.

She had lavished real care on preparing the biggest spare room for him, the one with its own sink and with a little bathroom directly across the landing. She had one of the trusties paint it duck-egg blue to offset the dark-blue velvet curtains the previous governor's wife had left behind. She had framed a set of antique maps Pip had found in a junk shop, which Terry assured her were suitably manly. She risked perching a sweet yet sad photograph of her mother as a shy young woman on the chest of drawers she had aired with fresh lavender bags for his clothes. Worried she was working too hard, Terry had pointed out that her father had been living in a log cabin, or something little better, for the last forty or more years and would be used to roughing it, but she was mindful that Father had left England when he and everyone he mixed with had servants.

'He will have standards,' she said, remaking the hospital corners on his bed and wondering, yet again, whether two pillows were sufficient or whether she should find two more.

She knew few old men. All her uncles – *the Wicked Uncles*, Terry called them – had either died in the Great War or in the decade after, as though the women in the family had taken all the strength and left the men strutting but vulnerable. Terry's father was still alive, at an astonishing eighty-two in far distant Newmarket, but he was cossetted by Terry's stepmother like some precious antique, and whenever Betty said how well he was keeping for his age Terry would snort that it was all down to his tailor. Her father would have enjoyed no cosseting, she reminded herself. He had lived a tough life, much of it out of doors, so he would be toughened, a time-silvered garden bench rather than a silk-upholstered armchair. For weeks, she had been examining any old man she saw in the street, or in the regular queue of prison visitors, looking for his imagined likeness, but, she realised, the face she kept picturing was little changed from the plush one in the old photographs, greying at the temples perhaps and possibly bearded.

Betty couldn't help but focus on the first-class passengers, all in hats, the men mostly in lightweight summer suits, many of the women in pretty summer dresses, full-skirted in defiance of rationing, coming down the gangway quite as though they were entering a garden party, rather than descending to the noise and grime of a dockyard. She imagined that her father, her long-lost daddy – though she could not possibly use that word at fifty-two, she found herself thinking it – would be chatting affably to friends he had made on the ship, a distinguished English couple who had been visiting cousins in Toronto or taking a walking holiday in the Rockies – then he would spot her, step away from his interested companions, raise his hat to her and walk over, unable to stop smiling, his teeth as white and perfect as a GI's.

'Phyllis,' he would say. 'Or do I call you Betty now?' and he would ignore her gloved hand to sweep her up in a hug. Because he would be taller, of course, as tall as Terry, and strong from years of farming and eating healthily. He would sweep her feet off the floor, maybe even swing her around him. 'Let me look at you!' he'd exclaim. And he'd apologise for the lost years and promise to make it up to her in the time they had left. She'd straighten his tie, he'd touch her cheek in fatherly wonder and they'd walk arm in arm behind the porter wheeling his smart leather trunks through customs.

'Mrs Terry Ennion?'

He had come from the tourist-class gangplank, out of her line of view. He would once have been her height, or a little taller, but age had stooped and shrunk him. He wore a dark suit so old that the fabric was shining in patches and there was an obvious hole from moth damage on one shoulder. He looked far older than he was – like a man who had been through a series of shattering ordeals or a war. When he smiled broadly, she saw the resemblance to his brother, her handsome uncle Jack, but the effect was marred by lack of teeth.

'Father,' she said, stupefied.

'Little Phyll,' he said, and sounded so kind that she hugged him rather than kissing him. He smelled quite strong, and she wondered what washing facilities, if any, he had enjoyed on board.

'How was your crossing?' she asked.

'A little cramped compared to the high style I enjoyed last time I made it, when you were a child.'

'Oh dear.'

'I don't get sick, but the man in the bunk below me had no sea legs whatsoever. I spent most of the journey walking around to give him space.'

His eyes, she saw, were exactly the colour of hers, though, stupidly, she had not expected him to sound so un-English.

'Your voice,' she stammered.

'Have I become Canadian?' he asked. 'How depressing. In my head, I still sound the way I did when I first met your dear mother.'

'You sound like someone in a Western,' she said. 'Terry will be delighted. I think he's read every Zane Grey the library has in stock.'

'Oh dear.'

'The car isn't parked far away, but do we need a porter for your trunk?'

'My trunk?'

'Your luggage?'

'Oh. This is it.' He cheerfully lifted a battered cardboard suitcase. She hoped her shock wasn't obvious.

'How practical,' she said. 'I always pack far too much. I hope you'll be warm enough. It may be April, but I'm afraid the house is a bit of a barn and Terry calls the upstairs the Arctic Wastes.'

'Oh, I'm well used to cold.'

As he walked beside her, she noticed his feet. He wasn't wearing shoes, or certainly not what she recognised as shoes. Terry wore sturdy black lace-ups on weekdays and equally sturdy brown brogues at weekends. Trained at boarding school, he brushed them every night before he brushed his teeth. She had noticed he judged men on their shoes as fiercely as women judged one another's hats. Shoes that were anything unlike his, especially correspondent shoes or, his particular loathing, suede ones would see the wearer condemned as a *sewer*, a *poodle faker* or a *spiv*. He regarded the prisoners' obligatory black lace-ups as part of their rehabilitation. Betty was certain he would look askance at the leather boots Father had on. With decorative tooling and a significant heel, they were like something cowboys wore in films and looked distinctly odd, not to say orange, under his shabby dark suit. And his tie was a sort of bootlace.

She knew it was silly of her, but she felt self-conscious leading him across the busy street to her car, which in turn made her deeply ashamed as this was her father.

She opened the boot to place his tiny case inside then let him into the car.

She chatted nervously as she drove, about the car, which was still quite new so her pride and joy, about the extravagant sports cars Terry had driven early in their marriage, like his Lagonda, about rationing, about Liverpool and what a shock it was to be living there after the relative civilisation of Durham.

'It's not that I'm a snob, at least I hope I'm not,' she said, 'but I miss having kindred spirits and I've not found any here yet.'

She realised she was talking while Father said nothing at all. When they had to stop in a queue of traffic, she glanced across and saw that his pale eyes were flickering here and there at the people passing on the pavement. She couldn't begin to imagine where he had come from – men emerging from long sentences in prison looked less broken than he did – but she sensed it was very different to this.

'Did you spend time here on your way out to Canada all those years ago?' she asked.

'Not really,' he said. 'It was all a bit of a rush. I spent an evening with Jack and George somewhere then they drove me to the docks to embark. I don't remember any details.'

'I expect it feels very crowded after... Winter,' she said.

'The ship was pretty crowded,' he told her, 'but this is rather terrifying.'

'Sorry.'

'Oh, I dare say I'll adjust. When I left England, people had better manners.'

'Oh, I'm sure their manners haven't changed, but people are short of money here, and they're often in a hurry. Bloody man!'

She swore at a driver who had swerved to the kerb in front of her so that she had to indicate and wait to pull out past him. Father laughed and she laughed with him.

'Sorry,' she said, driving on. 'I get rather hot-tempered behind the wheel. Whistle, our younger girl, who's still at home, says it makes my veins stand out like Popeye's.'

He glanced across at her. 'You look entirely civilised,' he said.

Betty made an effort not to prattle as she drove him the short distance to Walton, but felt she must defend the city against dour first appearances, so told him about its wealth of Georgian houses and unfinished rival cathedrals. She answered as best she could any questions he put to her. As they drew nearer, she felt she needed to explain a little, to prepare him.

'In most prisons, the governor's house is actually inside the prison complex, behind walls and gates and guards. Nice in a way, as you never worry about being burgled, but it does add to the sense of isolation, almost of being imprisoned too. Our house here is actually on the street, just outside the prison walls, which is nice in that friends and relations can simply knock on the door and don't have to be waved through by a guard. I'll give you a spare key and you can come and go as you please once you're settled in. Not that there's much you'll want to see on our doorstep – pretty grim, I'm afraid – but there's a parade of shops nearby where you can get a newspaper and a haircut or razor blades, things like that. And a tobacconist where Terry gets his Three Nuns. Do you smoke?'

'No,' he said.

'I used to. Terry got me into it when we first met. I think he rather liked me smoking as he thought it made me look fast, but I had to stop because – it was too silly – I'd got into the habit of smoking out of the corner of my mouth, like Marlene Dietrich, I suppose, and it gave me a great nicotine stain in my hair! Thank God neither Pip nor Whistle smokes, though Pip's husband Mike is as glued to his pipe as Terry. The two of them together are quite like father and son. Terry works long hours in the prison, so you'll probably only see him at breakfast, but he pops home for lunch most days, unless he has an official visitor, and for supper, of course.'

She felt she ought to tell him what was almost certainly going to happen in the prison soon, to prepare him, but she had developed such an ingrained habit, had been so trained, in fact, not to talk about Terry's work unless it directly affected her – as in a house move – that she found it hard to speak to Father about it. Maybe she would later on. Once he was settled. The poor man had more than enough adjustments to make as it was.

However tough the neighbourhood, they lived in a handsome Georgian house – huge compared to the house he had built in the prairies, she imagined. The garage was in a fanciful tower that formed one half of the prison gates. An officer happened to spot her car as she pulled up and he hurried to open the garage doors for her. She liked to think that impressed Father a little.

He insisted on carrying his case and, hoping to deflect from his wounded pride, she told him an indiscreet story of how Terry hoarded petrol in jerry cans hidden on the garage rafters in case rationing got any more severe or continued much longer.

'You must be exhausted from your trip,' she said as she let him into the hall. 'I'll show you to your room and run you a nice hot bath.'

He was yawning uncontrollably suddenly, so she knew her instincts were right. 'Up to the Arctic Wastes,' she said, leading him upstairs. 'There's already a hotty in your bed to air it, but I'll fetch you a fresh one to warm your feet and maybe a sandwich on a tray for your lunch?'

'You're very kind,' he said. 'I confess I hardly slept on the crossing with my cabin mate being so loud about feeling sick.'

'Oh dear.'

He liked his bedroom and immediately sat on the bed and started taking off his curious boots. His socks were in a terrible state, she saw.

'It's a washday,' she lied. 'Give me anything you'd like

adding to the tub and, once it's dry, I can tackle any mending or darning that needs doing. Terry sees to it that I've always a mending pile on the go. Your little bathroom's over here. I put Pear's soap in there, as Mother always loved it, so I expect you did too. There's a towel and a flannel for you.'

Hating herself for wittering so inanely, she pulled the little crank that sealed the bath – which was antique but very comfortable and not one of those mean hip-huggers – and set the Ascot running.

'This runs very hot,' she warned him, 'but it's slow.'

'Just like my one at home,' he said.

She pointed out an old dressing gown of Terry's on the back of the door and left Father standing in his ruined socks, suddenly nervous he might start to undress further in front of her.

He was humming quietly in his bath when she came back upstairs to bring him lunch on a tray – a ham sandwich with a dab of mustard, two pickled onions, an apple and a bottle of pale ale. She put a fresh hot water bottle in his bed. It was early summer but there was not an ounce of fat on him, and she felt sure the sea crossing would have left him chilled.

She hesitated before opening the wretched cardboard suitcase then told herself he was her father, not just another guest. She had sensed a deep restraint and privacy in him, as well, which was easier to broach when he was out of the room. She unfastened the case and made a swift bundle of his dirty shirts, socks and underwear, which, as she had feared, left the case all but empty, and hurried downstairs to wash them. She made mental notes. From years of laundry, she knew what Terry owned and wore. He was far too tall for any of his old suits or jackets to be any use, but his shirts and vests, pants and socks would fit, and she could discreetly take some to Father's room to tide him over until she could take him shopping. But they would surely need a visit to Terry's tailor – he had used a Liverpool one recently when he admitted that his old suit trousers needed letting out. At least the impossibly old dark suit Father had travelled in was not his only one. There was a tweed one in the bottom of the case, which she examined while hanging it up to let it unwrinkle. It was an attractive tweed – green with a subtle pale-blue fleck – a hint of the young dandy in the old photographs.

She had no idea what a new dark suit would cost, only that money was never wasted on better fabric and a good tailor. Terry's good shirts had lasted for years, even before she effected repairs like turning their collars.

As she hoped he would, Father climbed into bed and fell fast asleep. When she came up, after putting his underwear to soak in one bucket and his socks in another, to take away his lunch tray, she found him tucked up and softly snoring. She drew his curtains as quietly as she could, feeling how absolutely strange the situation was. The sensation intensified downstairs as she scrubbed and washed his shirts then got to grips with the more intimate challenge of socks, vests and pants. She had always loathed housework for its tedious futility, but laundry, like cookery, at least felt personal. When dusting – because Mrs Stapleton only did fires and floors – she could work herself into a futile rage against an unwanted crowd of fault-finding mythical visitors, whereas turning a collar on one of Terry's shirts or replacing a button on one of Whistle's blouses was to think of them, which was easier.

ELEVEN

The first post had brought a letter from Pip. She was an assiduous, funny letter writer, peppering the pages with her clever little drawings of this woman's awful hairstyle or a Horrockses housecoat she had seen in *Vogue* and longed for, but couldn't possibly find in Wakefield. Behind the jollity, it was clear the hard realities of being a wife and mother were hitting home, and she was bitterly lonely in Yorkshire. Her days had become a treadmill of cleaning, cooking, serving meals and wheeling the baby on long walks with the dog so as not to feel so trapped. She was having great difficulty coaxing Henrietta, the baby, on to solids and felt sure stewed apple was surely not sustaining enough. And how was her long-lost grandpa, she asked. Did he look like a greying Gary Cooper? Was he going to go galloping at Formby with Whistle?

Betty had repeatedly explained to both girls that their grandfather was not a cowboy but a thoroughly respectable wheat farmer; their vigorous mythmaking was impossible to stem, however, and they'd long since christened him Cowboy Grandpa.

Before tackling his laundry further, she sat at her desk, Mollie the dog resting a head on her feet, to write back that he had arrived safely and was sound asleep, but she'd be showing him the best of Liverpool tomorrow and taking him clothes shopping. *Urgently needed after several decades on a remote farmstead, poor love.* She recommended Pip try the baby out with brains, which Pip had loved at that age.

Soak them for an hour in salted water, rinse them off them gently tease off any skin or bits, then cook gently in some milk for about fifteen minutes. No more. Thicken the hot milk by pouring it into a roux then add plenty of chopped parsley. It has just the consistency of scrambled eggs, so most babies love it, and of course they're too young to be silly about what it is!

She thanked God Pip was so level-headed and capable – *bossy*, Whistle called it – and so much her father's daughter. She never harboured grudges and, if something upset her, she said so at once then moved on. She had always been the noisy, more confident child, and her sister had needed the lion's share of everyone's emotional energy. Any child Pip raised she would regard as a potential playmate and friend, whereas she worried that Whistle might be one of those mothers who regarded children as competition. Pip had been broody from the moment she knew there were babies in the world to be scooped up and cuddled. Betty had never forgotten her amazed and happy declaration, on dandling some baby cousin when aged about eleven, that babies' heads smelled of shortbread. Whistle, on the other hand, had been declaring since much the same age that babies and talk of babies made people idiots.

Whistle had finally found herself a clerical job, as she couldn't type, in a large law firm in the city centre. She made heavy weather of having to wake up and breakfast and leave on time and had already claimed at least two days off for sickness, but she was evidently enjoying working among other women a little older than she was and having money to spend. Betty hoped she would be learning a little of the world and its ways as Pip had done at the university library. One of the better-settled cousins had kindly invited Whistle to a regimental ball in a few weeks, miles away in Wiltshire, and Whistle was already fretting about what to wear and how to dance and Betty in turn was fretting that so much seemed to be riding on a single party.

Before the war, a girl of Whistle's beauty would have had a mantelpiece crowded with invitations, but rationing and bereavements and shortages had made everyone so cautious and life rather colourless.

Once she had all Father's things washed and pegged out to dry in the back yard, Betty took him up a cup of tea and a slice of gingerbread lest he sleep too long and spoil his night. She showed him the small pile of things she had borrowed for him from Terry's dressing room while his own clothes were drying.

'I expect you've packing cases and so on coming over more slowly,' she said, and he laughed and told her that this was all his worldly wealth now.

'Well,' she added, to cover her confusion, 'perhaps we can take you shopping at some point? I'll be getting on with supper when you come down. Just follow the sound of swearing and crashing lids and you'll find me.'

'Do we dress for supper?' he asked.

'Heavens, no!' she exclaimed before understanding that he was teasing her.

'Only I hadn't realised Liverpool would be so smart,' he added as she was leaving the room.

She left worried she had hurt his feelings, but when he came down shortly afterwards, he seemed perfectly cheerful. He made a nice fuss of Mollie, who was getting on in years, and took a short turn around the district with her on her lead while Betty lifted potatoes and spring onions and cut a lettuce for their supper, for which she had already poached a piece of salmon. Then she settled him in the sitting room to pore over albums of old pictures of Mother, and of her in her youth with Granny and the Aunts, while she whipped up four glasses of gooseberry fool.

Terry and Whistle arrived home almost simultaneously so there was a nice hubbub to welcome Father afresh. She knew they were both a bit aghast at the state of him, but too polite to show it. Terry interrogated him about all things Canadian, and Whistle wanted to know all about his Clydesdales and how often he saw bears or cougars. She had repeatedly devoured the works of Jack London and admitted she had nicknamed her brother-in-law White Fang. Seeing Father instinctively cover his mouth when he laughed at this, Betty told him about the National Health Service and said how readily Mike had been equipped with smart dentures.

'I'm sure we could get you seen, Father, while you're here,' she added, in what she hoped was a kind voice. 'Mr Eade is so nice. I'm due for a check-up so I can put in a word. There's so much we need to sort out for you,' she went on. 'You probably need to meet Terry's bank manager and we should see about your pension payments; when I asked at the post office, they were most uncertain. You do have a pension?'

'Do I?' he asked, with a hint of a smile. 'I'm not sure I do.'

'I'll have a word with Bob,' Terry said.

'Bob is Terry's solicitor and a bit of a wizard.'

'His hair's too shiny,' said Whistle.

'Whistle!'

'Well, would you want to touch it?'

'He is a bit of a Brylcreem boy,' Terry admitted, 'but he knows his onions. Now, sorry, my dears, but I must head back in to work for a while. No, no. Stay put.' He waved Harry back into his chair and was swiftly gone.

'Oh, God, it's tomorrow, isn't it?' Whistle began.

'Yes,' Betty told her, 'but you know we don't talk about it. Take your grandfather back to the sitting room and play him something while I make coffee.'

Both girls had a handful of pieces they played reliably well. Whistle played her Chopin preludes and her French pieces about cuckoos and chickens while Father looked again at the old albums and amused her and Betty with stories about how his brother eloped with formidable Aunt George. He wanted to know all about Pattie's life after she ceased to be a Gaiety Girl and a kept woman. Although the loss of Pattie still felt sad and raw to Betty after thirty years, she could see how, for Whistle and now Father, it had become a piece of sad romance: a childless love match cruelly cut short.

'I still have some of her gowns in a trunk with old ones of Mother's and mine,' she admitted. 'They've been in there wrapped in quantities of tissue paper and lavender since before I met your father, darling.'

'Perhaps she could try them on?' Father suggested. 'One might do for her debut.'

And the way he pronounced *debut* made Whistle laugh and Betty saw, with relief, that, for all the awkwardness of his being there, they might yet find common ground.

'Oh, could I, Mummy?'

'Of course. Just not tonight, as the trunk is vast, and we'd need your father and one of the men to heave it down from the attic.'

Betty laid plans to visit Mr Eade the dentist and perhaps the emerging cathedrals the following day with Father, or at least make a trip to the Walker Gallery, but Whistle made them promise to keep a ride on the elevated railway for when she wasn't working and could come too. Mention of the trunk of dresses had Whistle taking out the albums again to marvel that her grandmother, who she had never known, and the great-aunts, had once been both young and glamorous and then, by common consent as Father was yawning again, they elected not to wait up for Terry's return from the prison but to go to bed. Whistle was now quite giddy and sang Father a comic song as they climbed the stairs.

Betty saw Father to his room, kissing him on his weather-beaten cheek as she said goodnight, then slipped into Whistle's room to warn her about the morning.

'Don't forget you need to be off for work bright and early tomorrow, darling, as there's bound to be a big crowd outside, larger than usual, I expect, because of all those ghastly articles that have been appearing.'

Whistle rarely looked at newspapers as they were full of things that worried her, and she worried enough. The reference to what was due to happen in the morning threw her into a panic.

'Maybe I can stay home and tell them I'm sick?'

'Well, that would be silly. You want to keep that job, and last time you stayed home you said it made you feel trapped. Just set your alarm a bit earlier and you can slip out well before anything happens. You barely eat breakfast anyway and you can always call in for a coffee and toast at Lyons. Just leave here before seven and you'll be fine.'

'Those poor boys!'

'Don't talk about them. You'll only upset yourself. Would you like me to brush your hair?'

Brushing Whistle's hair had always soothed her, so Betty sat on the side of her bed while Whistle turned away slightly, and spent a few minutes slowly drawing the heavy brush through her hair until the gold shone and Whistle's breathing had slowed. Betty had dreaded another long night of stilling her panic. The poor girl was fearless of taking a high hedge on a horse, but had a terror of dying in her sleep or catching polio and ending her life in an iron lung or a wheelchair or even getting lockjaw from a bramble scratch when out walking. Still, her fears, when they took hold of her, could leave Betty worn out and full of sleep-chasing worries of her own that only a mug of Benger's would soothe.

TWELVE

Early on in her marriage, once they had met him a few times, the Aunts would enjoy teasing Betty by winking or nudging each other in her presence and chuckling.

'Poor Betty. You can tell he's a goer. Are you *très, très fatiguée?*' And she would blush as they hoped she would and they would lapse into further French, as they always did when being filthy, saying things like, '*La bouche, c'est toujours efficace . . .*'

She had no points of comparison, the rich fiancé having been so very respectful, and had no friends with whom to discuss such things, but married life attuned her to the hints dropped in indiscreet conversations she overheard in queues at the greengrocer or baker. These, she swiftly realised, were either about a lack of sex or an excess of it. Terry prided himself on needing it every night. He said it had been that way since he started shaving, which made her wonder how he had managed at school. He could be apologetic about it, especially when the children were younger and days of caring for them could leave her shattered, but he said he simply couldn't sleep without release. He didn't call it that. He didn't call it anything, but she had learned from her eavesdropping and the occasional trashy novel lent her by the charlady, that release was an accepted euphemism. She mentally filed it in ladylike inverted commas, alongside that other piece of romantic novelese she and Pip could giggle over together, now that Pip was married and a mother, *his urgent need*. As in *He waltzed her manfully around the crowded ballroom until she heard him sighing in her ear and felt his urgent need.*

The funny thing was that, even though there were often nights where she would rather have talked or been held by him, she had become as dependent on sex to relax into sleep as Terry had always been. If he was sent away on a conference, she would sleep fitfully, if at all, and if he worked late, as he did tonight, she sat up in bed, yawning over a novel, knowing it was pointless to put out her light as she would only end up lying awake in the dark, making lists in her head.

They still had the bed her Aunt May had insisted on giving them when they married. It was from Heal's, a piece typical of the time, being a modern bed frame bolted to a headboard that was actually a salvaged mahogany dining table, and with sturdy posts at the foot end made from the table's legs. It was immensely comfortable for one person but on the intimate side for two, especially as Terry was twice Betty's size and weight. She had long become practised at sleeping with one arm hooked over the mattress edge so that she wasn't forever rolling downhill into Terry, who had a way of lashing out or even kicking in his sleep if she bumped into him uninvited. From Hollywood films and hotels where they sometimes took holidays, she knew that twin beds had become quite the thing, perhaps as people were acquiring larger bedrooms. But even though they were a little better off, with Pip settled and Whistle now working, Terry wouldn't have countenanced the expense. And he might have been hurt at the suggestion.

Even Georgette Heyer couldn't stop Betty from nodding off now. She had a terrible guilt dream in which her mother and all the Aunts, dead and alive, looked on in disgust as she led Father amongst them, her own clothes turned to rags to match his. She woke to find the light off and Terry on top of her. There was no tenderness, although possibly that had happened while she was dreaming. He was hammering into her with such force that the headboard was smacking into the wall. It hurt, rather, and, in the darkness and his haste, he had not reached into his bedside drawer for the Vaseline she left there to ease his way now that the change of life had so dried her out. She knew the way to bring things to a close more swiftly was not to lie there like a marble statue but to slide her hands so they held his bottom through his pyjamas – a piece of sauciness she would never have permitted herself without cover of darkness. Her grip had its usual effect, and he spent himself with a great, juddering sigh, muttered an apology as though he'd spilled his drink on her, rolled aside and soon was fast asleep. She cleaned herself with a tissue, crawled back uphill to the mattress edge, anchored herself in place and soon joined him in slumber.

TERRY

THIRTEEN

Terry had witnessed bad things in Sarawak. In his time as a policeman there, he had seen murder scenes, suicides, a drunkard running gruesomely amok in a market with a machete and several cack-handed executions. He had signed up because all he really wanted to do as a young man was ride motorbikes and drive fast cars – neither of which was on offer as a career option – and because he couldn't bear feeling less of a man for having missed out on fighting in the Great War. He had met men younger than he was who had been waved through by recruiting officers looking the other way, and it shamed him to his core. He found sitting still for any length of time intolerable, which was why he had only thrived at school once set loose on a sports pitch and, although he knew a desk job of some kind was his doom eventually, he craved adventure, danger and women, and his time in the Sarawak police offered all three. While out there, he discovered he loved jazz, was an excellent shot, could maintain a clear-headed calm in situations that had his superiors shouting and sweating and that he had something married women itched for. He was disturbed by how the sticky heat of the place brought out the animal in him, so that the merest whiff of musk beneath a woman's perfume had him in rut, or the chattering of a criminal made him want to slap them into the wall.

When he came home and found that, against all the odds, a girl as luscious as Betty was prepared to ditch an advantageous engagement to be with him, he felt he had been pulled back from a brink, saved from the profound cynicism that settled over old hands who stayed in any colony too long. She was not entirely innocent, thank God, and endured his moods and appetites like a trooper, but something in her tamed him a little, and becoming a father of two girls completed the process. Now, when a Maugham story or Conrad novel summoned up his brutal Sarawak self, it was like meeting some lethal stranger. And yet circumstance and a lack of other opportunity at a time when the work market was in crisis and his funds were short, had landed him in a job where an ability to look calmly on brutality, even to participate in it, and to look monsters in the eye and smile, was a prerequisite.

After Durham's jail, Liverpool's was extremely tough and needed toughness to stay on top of its challenges. It had a women's wing, which he always felt was asking for trouble, as it could bring out the worst in staff and men alike. He was also regularly obliged to take in busloads of juveniles, who had no chance of rehabilitation while locked up alongside so many hardened lags, in conditions that constantly had the henlike head of the local inspectorate on his back for cruelty. It also made giving them anything like education, or even teaching them a trade before they left to offend again, well-nigh impossible.

The other reason he was glad Liverpool was likely to be his last post before retirement was that it was the execution site for the north-west. It possessed the most modern facilities for efficient indoor hanging, so men condemned as far away as Shrewsbury would be sent there. There was an executioner, of course, usually Pierrepoint, but the governor had to witness the execution too, just as a doctor had to confirm that it had succeeded. Furthermore, given the understandable distaste many of the condemned had for the words of God come their last night on earth, it was often the governor with whom they chose to hold their last conversation.

Terry had daily meetings with prisoners. The men, as he preferred to call them, were brought to his office when they had grievances that could not be dealt with by officers on their wing and they were also brought before him when they broke the rules in ways he could punish by withdrawing privileges or company. If they broke the law of the land, of course, by assaulting an officer or one another, then they had to stand before a court and invariably their sentence would be extended. It was impossible on these occasions not to remember coming before the housemaster or headmaster at his sturdily minor public school, usually for what was deemed manly boisterousness of one kind or another, never for congratulations, until he started winning rowing cups and breaking opponents' collarbones in rugby, once a spectacular growth spurt made him newly dangerous. Terry had no sons, and his own father had been as distant as a mountain, but he tried to act as he imagined a kind father would towards a wayward son. He cracked jokes, offered them a cigarette and a chair if he had bad news from outside, kept them standing but still cracked jokes if they'd been bad.

Unless he was called to sign off on some building work or to inspect a site in need of a builder's attention, the only time he entered a man's cell was when it was his last night among the living. In the morning's case, there were two cells, two condemned men; they were boys, really, aged just twenty and twenty-two. They had been found guilty of murdering an old woman in the course of burgling her house.

It was a routine of Terry's to follow accounts of trials in his newspaper, a low-brow habit, he knew, picked up in late adolescence when an aunt gave him a copy of *Dramatic Days at the Old Bailey*. The guilt, or lack of it, in the man in his care was officially none of his concern, and he had long grown deaf to the well-rehearsed protestations of innocence among hardened lifers, most of whom would tell you, if prompted, how they had been variously stitched up by a bent lawyer or betrayed by far worse rogues or framed by lazy or corrupt police. If he was not utterly hated by them, it was because they knew he maintained the bars, but had played no part in putting them behind them.

When these two boys were on trial, however, it was hardly credible that they would be found guilty, since not one witness had testified against them who was not a criminal. It seemed blindingly obvious that the young men were petty housebreakers, not the sadistic murderers of every elderly householder's nightmares. The case against them relied on hearsay, circumstantial evidence and whatever it had been convenient for overworked detectives to believe. Terry shared the Liverpudlian outrage at the sentences handed down to them and believed the appeal against their death sentences had more chance than most. Evidently, letters from bishops and petitions from churchgoers were not enough, though. Perhaps the boys were simply too poor, too Catholic, too unappetising or even too male. The telephone call from the Home Office came through shortly before Terry would usually have left his desk to return home for the evening.

So, on the night that his long-lost father-in-law finally showed up, he had to leave the dinner table in order to visit each of the youths in person to tell them the appeal had failed, and they would indeed be hanged in the morning. The older and tougher of the two, who had stoutly refused visits from the Catholic chaplain, seemed utterly unsurprised.

'Of course we are,' was all he said. 'No judge wants to be made to look stupid.'

Terry let himself chuckle dryly at that. 'You're probably right,' he told the boy, then gently explained that he would now be moved to a different, more comfortable cell.

'So I don't have far to walk in the morning?'

'That's right. The officer who accompanies you there will be nearby through the night, so you'll have someone to talk to if you want, someone to be with until morning. Do you have any questions?'

'Is it quick?'

'It takes seconds,' Terry told him truthfully. He had witnessed the hideous process often enough.

'And you'll be there?'

'Yes. And the chaplain.'

'I said I don't want the fucking chaplain.'

'And the medical officer.'

At that the boy sneered silently and Terry knew himself dismissed.

The other boy, younger, softer, bewildered by all that had befallen him, clearly had put faith in the appeal because he broke down at the news. He stumbled forward and wept into Terry's jacket and Terry had to shake his head at the officer making to drag the boy off. He knew in that instant he had stood in for a comforting father figure he had probably never known. The lad's background was depressingly chaotic. He pulled himself together soon and sat back on his squeaky bed with a juddering sigh and an apology.

'That's quite all right,' Terry told him, touched that the boy had leaned on him, though Murphy, the hatchet-faced officer standing by, was not exactly comfort on legs. 'What nobody ever quite gets is that an appeal isn't actually an appeal for mercy. It's much colder than that. Cold as justice. It's an appeal against a jury's finding, and for an appeal to succeed the law has to admit that it made a mistake, and I'm afraid that is horribly rare.'

At that moment, a hideous ruckus was set up. The other prisoners knew what was afoot, of course, and somehow, though penned in their cells during the first boy's solemn progress to the cell of no return, they knew to make their harsh salute, banging tin cups on bedsteads, howling like wolves or just swearing loudly to high heaven, in ways they knew the officers were powerless to stop. The younger boy looked terrified.

'Don't worry,' Terry told him. 'It's a tribute, not a riot. They'll do the same for you in a moment.' He told him the same things about the last-night cell, how grim-faced Murphy and his radio and newspapers and cigarettes and endless cups of tea would help the boy through to morning.

'Do I get breakfast?'

'Of course,' Terry assured him. 'Though you may not feel like it first thing. I'm so sorry, old man.'

'That's all right,' the boy said. 'Was worth a try.' He stood and, for a second time, Terry felt himself dismissed.

Prisons were run by the Prison Service, which was part of the Home Office, so their every detail, from lightbulbs to slop buckets, was governed somewhere by a memo written in the coolly impersonal language of the Civil Service that Terry had never mastered. He knew he would never rise beyond the level of governor and suspected that his infinitely cooler-headed son-in-law, Mike, would.

Executions were no exception. As ever, just over a week before one was due, the icy mechanism had whirred into motion. Pierrepoint had been given the boys' heights and latest weights, with neither being fooled that either measurement was part of a routine health check, and accommodation booked nearby for him and his team. A letter on Prison Service paper had given Terry a chilly reminder of the series of procedures he needed to follow.

Armed with the weights of the boys – the *culprits*, in Civil Service language – he had then supervised the preparations as the officer of works tested the mechanism, first with no weight, to ensure the dark-painted trapdoors opened in response to the lever, then with two carefully measured bags of sand and much fussing over the official *Table of Drops*. Almost as a professional challenge to himself, Pierrepoint was insisting on a simultaneous double execution; he argued it was more merciful than to keep one *culprit* waiting. This meant that a second rope had been sourced and fixed beside the other to the beam above the trapdoors. These were not simply ropes with nooses tied at one end, like the ones in Westerns or cartoons, but carefully constructed pieces of equipment, with a leather lining to the business end covered with gutta-percha – a sort of rubber derivative he had heard spoken of by growers and agents out in Sarawak.

As with the trapdoor mechanism with its handle a little like something from a signal box, and the pin that restrained it to prevent hideous accidents during testing, Terry could not look on them without imagining the workshop somewhere where skilled craftsmen produced them to precise Civil Service specifications alongside other, less sinister items. Perhaps the handle-maker did indeed supply levers to the railways, and the cordwainer made hawsers for the navy. The word *gutta-percha* was now synonymous with trouble for him, as one of its inconvenient properties was that it stiffened with cold. There were, therefore, paragraphs in the two-page memorandum of instructions devoted to the need to warm it to flexibility both before testing and before fatal use.

Terry enjoyed gardening, more for the soothing excuse to spend time outdoors with his hands occupied than for any hopes of great results, though he did quite well with bergamots and dahlias. Lacking confidence in his own ability, he had a gardening manual – *your Bible*, Betty called it – and he would follow it to the letter when planting broad beans or whatever, using an old wooden ruler to measure the recommended depths and distances. There was a section in the execution memorandum which always reminded him of that in its mind-numbing detail concerning how to calculate the length of drop required to break a *culprit*'s neck using twine, to mark a point eighteen inches along the rope – deemed to be the average depth of the head and circumference of the neck after constriction *allowing for the lengthening of the neck and body of the culprit*. Copper wire and chalk were then used to mark off the required length of drop from that, and then the condemned man's height removed with a six-foot-six graduated rule and the rope adjusted by its chain and cotter so that the tip of the copper wire reached the man's height. A chalk mark was then to be made using a plumbline to indicate where the doomed man must stand.

Happily, these paragraphs were entirely the executioner's to follow – as even reading them out of duty made Terry's head spin as it used to with maths problems at school. There was even a paragraph saying that *these calculations will be attended to as soon as possible after six a.m. on the day of the execution so as to allow the rope time to regain a portion of its elasticity and, if possible, the gutta-percha on the rope should again be warmed.*

Terry assumed the double-barrelled execution meant that Pierrepoint had been at work since considerably before six a.m. When he called in, fortified by only a cup of tea and a couple of office digestive biscuits, to check all was going to schedule, he found Pierrepoint had recruited two assistants in addition to his usual one. Quietly deferential as a tailor or undertaker – and, of course, he shared some of their skills – he did not introduce his team as he shook Terry's hand. He murmured that the extra two pairs of hands would let him proceed with merciful speed.

Terry saw they had their straps and hoods laid out on a little card table and wondered how on earth one went about recruiting assistant executioners. He knew, from conversations he'd endured with some of the more unhinged lifers, that there were men, and quite possibly some women, who were aroused by taking life, or by being close at hand when it was taken. Why else had public executions attracted such huge and overexcited crowds? He saw how the second rope was brand new and looked, in its crisp brightness, more frightening than its seasoned neighbour. He saw two chalk marks on the trapdoors below the ropes and took in the room's unusual warmth being generated by a little paraffin stove exactly like the one Betty lit to take the chill off the bathroom on winter mornings.

'Ah. So you've warmed the wretched gutta-percha,' he said, sympathising with how the monarch must feel when meeting yet more industrious strangers and being obliged to think of something, anything, to say to them.

'We have, Governor.' Pierrepoint was not one for small talk.

The doctor arrived, clutching his bag, and apologised for his car having taken a while to start. He was new. Terry saw him glance at the two ropes with surprise.

'Where do you want your witnesses, Pierrepoint, so we're not in your way?' Terry asked.

'Against the wall over there will be fine,' Pierrepoint said, and glanced at his watch. 'Gentlemen,' he murmured to his assistants. 'Are you all clear as to your tasks?'

The assistants nodded. One said, 'Yessir,' like a soldier.

'Speed is of the essence. Speed is merciful.'

He handed two of the men leg straps and two of them wrist restraints and white linen hoods. The straps and restraints, like the ropes, were reused, but the hoods were new each time. *Somebody,* thought Terry, *maybe even Mrs Pierrepoint, sits at her sewing machine and makes them.*

At one minute to eight, two officers appeared in the doorway, glanced at Terry and the doctor then turned expectantly to Pierrepoint, who was looking at his watch.

At five seconds to eight, he said simply, 'Yes.'

While the assistants with the straps positioned themselves beside each noose, the two with the hoods and restraints walked swiftly out with the officers, who Terry could hear unlocking the cell doors on the dot of eight o'clock. Moments later, the two boys were marched in, their arms fastened behind their backs, collars tugged open to bare their necks. The slighter of the two was crying audibly. The bigger seemed stiffly resistant and gazed about him as though bewildered. They were steered firmly to each of the chalk crosses marked on the trapdoors. One pair of assistants swiftly strapped their legs together, at which point the larger of the boys, the one who had so vigorously barred the priest, began to pray, but he fell silent as though awestruck as the other pair of men swiftly brought the hoods over their heads and placed the meticulously measured nooses round their necks, pulling them tightly into position. They worked with such military precision that Terry knew Pierrepoint had made them rehearse each movement repeatedly while the gutta-percha was warming. The assistants stepped neatly back from the trapdoors, looked to Pierrepoint and nodded that all was ready. Pierrepoint removed the safety peg that stopped anyone opening the trapdoors by accident and smartly pulled on the lever. The two boys fell from view, leaving only two taut ropes that swayed and twisted.

The hinges were kept well-oiled by the officer of works, but Terry told himself the sound he heard was of the doors flapping hard back against the ceiling below and not that of two necks being broken. He nodded to Pierrepoint and glanced at his watch, as he was required to note the time in his report. It was just twelve seconds past eight o'clock. Terry paused at the doorway to shake Pierrepoint's hand and thank him, which seemed only proper. Then he took out his fountain pen to sign the two notices of execution an officer held out to him on a wooden clipboard.

'Once you've made your report to the coroner just before nine,' he told the doctor, 'one of the officers will bring you over to make your report to me. Paperwork, you know? You've a bit of a wait. There'll be tea and biscuits in the cell next door while you sit it out. The way into the pit to make your inspection is down that flight of stairs there.'

The poor doctor looked even paler.

The original memorandum of instructions had one ghastly amendment to paragraph twelve, the final paragraph. Where it had said, *The body will be carefully raised from the pit as soon as the medical officer declares life to be extinct,* an ink correction had changed it to say, *The body will hang for a minimum of forty-five minutes and will then be carefully raised.* Clearly there had been some incident where, despite all the careful calculations with heights and weights and bags of sand, someone's neck had failed to break. The sentence *hanged by the neck until you be dead* made cold-blooded allowance for strangulation and so, presumably, did the additional forty-five minutes.

The doctor had to enter the pit to confirm both men were dead and record the time. The bodies were then brought up, released from their ropes and straps, laid on stretchers (kept tactfully out of view until needed), then laid out in another room where the coroner would read the medical officer's report before making his own inspection.

The final sentence of the memorandum of instructions was as obsessively detailed as the rest. *In laying out the body for the inquest, the head will be raised three inches by placing a small piece of wood under it.*

Terry unlocked his bottom drawer to pour himself a splash of Scotch and had barely drained it and relocked the drawer than his deputy called by to report that a crowd of some thousand had held a vigil at the gates, but now had been peacefully moved on by the police, with no arrests or other trouble. Terry thanked him and rang Betty to check she was all right.

She was Caesar's wife, never showed a ruffled surface, whatever she felt inside, but he knew it was just the sort of thing that would give Whistle hysterics. There was no reply from Betty, so he set to writing a rough draft of his report, scratching through any hints of emotion such as one man's tears or the other's frantic last-minute plea to Jesus and Mary. His handwriting was so small and crabbed that even Betty had admitted she sometimes made out only one word in three. Once the doctor had come up to report, he would make the typist a fair copy using childlike block capitals.

BETTY

FOURTEEN

Terry was up before dawn to go about his grim business. Betty tended to oversleep if he got up much before her as, left alone, she would roll into the warm dip he had left in the bed's middle and often enjoy her best sleep of the night. Happily, she was woken by the rather unladylike clatter of Whistle's heels on the staircase as she remembered, thank God, to leave for work early.

Betty glanced at her little alarm clock and hurried through bathing and dressing as she wanted to be downstairs before Father, but clearly he kept farming hours and had been up long before Whistle, who he had sent off with a handful of toast and marmalade.

'She was in quite a state,' he said. 'Nearly didn't leave the house. Who are all those people? What's going on out there?'

'Oh dear.'

He had pulled wide open one pair of the dining-room curtains. Her practice on these, happily rare, mornings was to keep the curtains drawn in the rooms to the front of the house, partly as she felt it gave the house a respectful, mourning aspect, but also to stop any angry strangers from the desperate families from looking in. But Father had tugged the curtains back and, as the room had only a small patch of garden between it and the street, the hubbub of the crowd was as present as though people were in the hall or kitchen. Normally, there were twenty people at most, including the inevitable reporters, but today the crowd was huge – a demonstration almost – including hundreds of men, women and even some children. There was a priest, she saw, leading a group of people in prayer, all in black, several of the women with shawls over their heads as though at Mass. She knew, somehow, that two of these women were the boys' mothers, knew it for sure as one of them looked up from her praying and seemed to glare directly in at her.

'It's an execution, Father. Do come away. I wanted us to be in the kitchen, away in the back,' and she pulled gently on his arm, but he was fixed there, staring out.

'An execution in the prison?'

'Yes. Poor Terry has to oversee it. It's so ghastly that we don't discuss it. This one's particularly bad as they're both young men and he's fairly sure they didn't do it. Do come away. It feels wrong to stare.'

At that moment, the grandfather clock in the hall started to strike eight and Betty froze, her hand still on Father's suit sleeve, unable now to look away as the huge crowd fell silent. Several more people joined the women on their knees and the only voice that could be heard was the priest's. She could tell it was a prayer from his tone of voice, though presumably he was praying in Latin. Instinctively, she recited the grace in her mind, watching the shattered women.

She had barely reached *be with us ever more, Amen* than the priest led his followers in crossing themselves.

Then a kind of groan went through the crowd, half despairing, half angry. The people kneeling were helped to their feet as there was a surge towards the prison gates.

'Please,' she told Father, and pulled on his sleeve again. This time, he stepped back into the room so she could draw the curtains again and hide the crowd.

'Are they . . . trying to get in?' he asked her.

'No. The notices must have gone up on the gate. Notices have to be posted to certify that the execution has been carried out. It always strikes me as a bit ghoulish of people wanting to be there. I suppose in the old days it happened in public, and the posting of the notices has taken the place of that. And today was extra grim as there were two of them, and people will have come to support the boys' mothers.'

'Or to watch them suffer. People get excited by suffering. I've seen that before. There was a woman in Winter, a good, Christian type, who was always among the first to offer sympathy to the afflicted, but you could see from a light in her eye that proximity to pain stirred her up in a way that wasn't wholesome.'

'And there was I thinking Winter must be like *Anne of Green Gables*.'

She led him across the hall to the breakfast room. It was a luxury typical of the huge governor's houses that they could barely furnish, let alone heat, that this one included a pretty room, sunny in the morning, where they ate breakfast and where she wrote letters, often as not amidst the breakfast's toast crumbs.

She made them a pot of coffee and cooked him bacon,

eggs and a grilled tomato, then sat across from him eating buttered toast and marmalade. He seemed to have been shocked into silence.

'Let's do something jolly later,' she suggested. 'Something . . . wholesome. I think I need it after that. I promised Whistle I'd save the overhead railway for her to take you on as she loves it for some reason, but I thought we could visit the Walker Gallery. Do you like paintings?'

'Unless you count the table of watercolours at the annual North Battleford Show, I haven't been in an art gallery since, well, it must have been when I walked around the National Gallery with your mother.'

'Not that long ago, then,' she joked.

His laugh was dry. 'I should love that,' he said. 'But I know you'll have things to do. I wouldn't want to—'

'It's fine,' she assured him. 'Terry's quite used to me leaving him a cold plate for lunch. I just need to answer a couple of letters and pop round the corner to the shops. Stew for supper, I thought, and baked potatoes, so I can leave those to cook in the slow oven while we're out.'

⚓ ⚓ ⚓ ⚓ ⚓ ⚓

He came with her round the corner to Walton's short row of shops, as everything interested him, from the price of goods to the tough realities of rationing. He looked at everyone as though he was visiting some foreign tribe. Betty was always aware when shopping in Walton or going to church there, that many of the women were married to prison officers and that some might well know men on the inside. She hadn't a haughty bone in her body, but knew the need to avoid anything like favouritism. Her natural self-consciousness, combined with the way she wore a headscarf, which emphasised her rather determined chin, made her seem aloof. It wasn't helped by having a toothless and frankly rather shabby old man at her elbow. She knew not to introduce visiting relatives to shopkeepers or other women in the queue at the butcher's, but she sensed they were all wondering who he was.

Her discomfort was furthered by the palpable excitement the executions had caused. She knew herself associated with them at one remove. Her husband had been there, they were thinking, and would be telling her all the details. Terry wouldn't, of course. He was always professional, the soul of discretion, but others didn't know that.

Back home, Father volunteered to take Mollie for a walk while Betty hastily set a lamb stew in the slow oven, washed four baking potatoes then threw together a rhubarb crumble to cook later. Making up Terry an extra-nice cold plate, she resolved that she would ask him to take Father to his tailor on Saturday and have a frank son-to-father-in-law talk about money. She assumed there was a bank account Father could access, or a post office savings account. The fear that neither was the case, that all he possessed were the worn-out clothes he stood up in, made it impossible for her to broach the topic herself. With an extra mouth to feed, could they apply for more coupons, or was Father not planning to stay long? Driving him into town might help; driving was always a useful situation for tricky chats as it involved minimal eye contact.

'I love the Walker,' she told him as she drove him into the city later.

He had inexplicably dressed up for the outing, once again wearing his bizarre bootlace tie, like something from a cowboy wedding, and it fluttered distractingly in the breeze through the Morris's open windows.

'I try to go at least once a month,' she went on. 'It's not overwhelmingly large and it lifts the spirits on days like today, when Liverpool feels a bit much. When we go on holiday – for the last two years, we've gone to a sweet little place in Port Appin, in the Highlands – Terry always wants to go off shooting or fishing, but I find I simply want to rest my eyes on green, quite as though I'm thirsty for it. And it's the same at the Walker. Sometimes I catch a lecture, though I'm such a clot most of it goes over my head and nothing seems to stick for long, but more often I'll find an empty bench opposite one of my favourite pictures and just gaze at it.'

It was not a huge collection like the Tate's or the National Gallery's, and she already knew its succession of rooms as well as she knew her own and could lead him around with ease. She loved the Laura Knight view of springtime breaking over gardens in St John's Wood.

'I like the way its high viewpoint immediately makes you think it was seen from a bedroom,' she said. 'It makes me think of Granny's house in Strawberry Hill, as I had a room facing the street. The best bedrooms all faced over the garden to the river.'

He stared a while then mischievously pointed out it might be the view from a block of flats, or from a maid's cramped, shared attic.

She liked the Lowrys as well, like his grim little canvas, *The Fever Van*, but, praising them to Father, she realised they didn't trigger the same emotional response in her that her other favourites did – Clausen's *The Shepherdess*, for instance, or Spencer's *Saturday Afternoon*, with its smartly uniformed housemaids; like the Laura Knight view of tidy streets and treetops, they evoked her girlhood.

'It's funny,' she said, 'I know nothing about art, really, so does that mean the paintings I like are simply the ones in which I see something I know, or something I recognise? Which speak to you? Let me guess: the two horse ones!'

Father admitted she was right. He could almost smell the beautifully groomed horse in the Stubbs, and the Frank Bevan of a horse auction took him back to his childhood as the view of London gardens had Betty. He had circled a bronze sculpture of a half-naked farm labourer with a scythe, peering at its details so closely she had been afraid he was about to forget himself and touch it, but then he led her to sit in front of a painting she had not noticed before. It was predominantly grey and black, which was probably why she had passed it by on previous visits. Her eye was childish and untutored, she supposed, craving colours as an infant did sugar. He gestured to her to sit beside him, which she did, though it made her freshly conscious of his caved-in face and terrible tie.

'See the shooting star?' he asked. 'Now this is an artist

who has gone outside on a summer night and lain on his back to look up and really see.'

She saw, now, that it portrayed a night sky pinpricked by stars that were little more than paint flicks. Once she gazed and her eyes tuned in to the muted palette, darkened houses, and a barn perhaps, became visible as black shadows, or were they blue? And, at the canvas's dark centre, flashed a shooting star.

Most paintings were of stillness, of people sitting or lying, or flowers or fruit immobile on a tabletop, but this one dared to freeze a moment of swift motion. People reacted to it, she saw now, just as they reacted to shooting stars in real life, seeing nothing until the moment of brief triumph.

'Is this your favourite, then?' she asked, and Father simply said, 'The starlight in the prairies can be so bright you'd think you could read by it. The air here is so thick I don't know how you can breathe.'

'Believe me,' she said. 'There are days on end in the winter when you can't, and I wouldn't let the children go out, when it's foggy already, but every chimney is belching out smoke into it as well. Is it very beautiful where you were living?'

'Well . . .' he began thoughtfully. 'It's kinda flat, but then so is East Anglia. Sometimes the scale of it, the far horizons and the way you can feel so small in the middle of it all, can be overwhelming, but then the light and the wildflowers and the canopy of stars when a night is clear mean you wouldn't want to be anywhere else.'

'Do you miss it?'

He smiled at her kindly. 'Betty? I feel like some poor carrier pigeon that's been blown right off course. But meeting you all grown-up and married and—'

'And a grandmother.'

'Yes. That too. Makes it all worthwhile. Come on. You've been on your feet all morning. Let me buy you a cup of tea.'

He insisted on buying her a Chelsea bun and a cup of tea in a nearby tearoom before she drove him home. He nodded off in the car, his head vibrating against the window and his near-toothless mouth emitting soft, puttering sounds, gentler than a snore. Betty kept two faded old cushions on the back seat for picnics and, when they had to stop for some lights, she slipped one between his frail head and the window. There was something of the child in the way he accepted the cushion and nestled into it without stirring that made her feel a pang of something familial towards him, even as she registered the enormity of what she had done in encouraging him to stay.

She woke him gently once they reached home and she had killed the engine in the garage. He took up her suggestion of an afternoon nap with the same readiness he had shown towards the offer of the cushion.

'Father?' She caught his arm gently as he was about to head into his room. 'I know I mentioned a dentist last night, but let me book you in with our GP as well. You've been all alone in the middle of nowhere for so long and it would reassure me to simply let him check you over. Would you let me do that for you?'

By way of answer, he simply patted her hand and nodded, then closed the door quietly behind him.

She made both appointments for him as soon as she returned downstairs. The doctor would see him the following morning and nice Mr Eade had just heard of a cancellation so could fit him in at the end of that very afternoon.

'Just as a matter of interest,' he asked her, 'how bad is it?'

'Oh, I think he needs a full set,' she told him.

She checked on the lamb stew, which was cooking nicely, added more seasoning and gave it a stir then returned it to the oven and risked putting in the potatoes to bake as well, as the oven was so slow. And in a moment of frugality, she made use of the spare shelf in there by sliding in a rice pudding, which was unsummery but always comforting and might be eaten cold the next day with the clovey stewed apple Terry always praised. She always served the apples in a pretty blue-and-white antique bowl of Aunt May's. He would never talk about it, but she knew that the executions would have left him in need of extra comfort.

Then she took off her smart town shoes as she liked the feel of carpets through her stockinged feet, and sat in the breakfast room, which was deliciously cool now the sun had left it, to write her letters. While they were out, a second bulletin had arrived from Pip, a sure sign she was under some stress. It was in her usual breathless style, full of dashes rather than regular punctuation, so that it reproduced precisely the tone of her daughter's bubbling conversation. The grinding reality of new motherhood was truly hitting home. Pip complained that her days now seemed ruled by the ceaseless preparation, serving and clearing away of meals with almost all adult conversation replaced by performances of nursery rhymes at the piano, with baby on her lap, or recitations from *Cecily Parsley*, ditto. *The young lady is evidently both highly intelligent <u>and</u> musical, but how I wish she would eat more! A little stewed apple or mashed potato if I'm lucky, and then she turns on me an expression of the deepest disdain.* She had been rereading the *Forsyte Saga*, although, *really, it's terribly housemaidy.* She had paid the char to mind the baby for an afternoon so as to slip into a matinee of a new Lesley Howard film and confessed she had long fantasised about taking Mr Howard for a lover, *not for long, just for a trip to Italy where he would show me art while I wore a very fetching striped skirt with a wide, red leather belt like this* – drawing attached – *and make passionate, though very English love to me afternoon and night, before a particularly beautiful Botticelli virgin awoke my conscience and his, and he sent me home, first-class, naturally, to dear Mike and Miss Baby, who would forgive me everything after weeks of Mrs Coley's nameless stews* . . .

Betty had always been faintly shocked at the ease with which Pip joked about such things, worried that she had inherited the moral lightness of her great-aunts, even the sweeter of whom were vain to a fault and one of whom was said to have cynically encouraged her lover to marry her daughter, so as to enable the affair to continue on a more domestic footing. Mike was the perfect son-in-law, serious and attentive – a counterbalance to Pip's giddiness.

In the year of his engagement to Pip, he had become like the son they'd never had, churchgoing, shadowed, like all his generation, by whatever he had seen in the war, but also scholarly, which they respected, and dryly witty in ways that won over even censorious Whistle. Orphaned early in the war, and at the mercy of landladies, with one older sister married and the other keeping house for a great-aunt, he clearly loved coming to stay, bringing with him Susie, the huge dog that sent Whistle into ecstasies.

Pip adored the dog too, but mainly spoke of her now as a huge consumer of meat or fish they could little afford. An added worry was that Mike's best man was soon coming to stay with his new wife, who was Norwegian, in her forties, and what Pip called *a scary grown-up*.

Betty read the letter through a second time then took out her leather writing case, with its pad of Basildon Bond and the good fountain pen one of the Wicked Uncles had given her as a wedding present. She answered Pip methodically, as a long-ago governess had taught her, addressing her daughter's letter paragraph by paragraph – although Pip's paragraphs tended to flow into one another – before giving any news of her own.

She stressed the advice of her earlier letter that Pip try the baby on brains. She assured her that all children went through phases of picky eating, but that hunger always won in the end, and said the child seemed absolutely the perfect weight last time she came to stay, despite her traumatic and early birth having started her so underweight.

For Susie the dog, she suggested horsemeat, which could often be bought from a pet shop or, failing that, the local hunt. She sent her best love from Mollie and hoped she was not going to become territorial and defensive now the baby was crawling. *She's a sheepdog, after all, and might think other children or dogs who visit are threatening her precious lamb!*

As to the Scandinavian wife, she said to be her charming self and, if in doubt, to hand her the baby to dandle. *Nobody could resist her! Never be threatened by older women, darling. Remember they will be depressed by your very youth!* She also recommended serving cocktails and making them strong ones: *martinis or Gin and It will soon have her on your side!*

She then told her more about Father's arrival and the various shocks of his evident age, lack of teeth, down-at-heel appearance and distinct lack of luggage. She added guiltily that he was *an adorable old cove* who had passed the Whistle Test and was thoroughly approved of by the dog. *I have no idea how long he'll be with us or what his long-term plans are, yet. Tricky to ask outright.*

She ended by asking a favour. *As you know, your Pa and I are off on our little holiday to Port Appin soon and I know he badly needs rest as work has been Hellish recently. They're getting along fine but I know he'd relax properly if he didn't feel he also had to play host. And I don't like to leave your dear sis with the charge of him as she's working now (hurrah!) and a bit young, bless her, and also, she has her regimental ball coming up while we're away. You know what's coming, my pet. Could you bear to have Father for a bit? He'd love to meet you and Mike, I know, and to dandle his great-granddaughter and you could show him a bit of Yorkshire. Let me know what you think, and we can draw up a battle plan. We're off on the 12th for a fortnight.*

She enclosed some pretty knitting wool she had found – just enough for a little jersey for the baby – and slipped in some food coupons and a bar of chocolate for Pip and Mike to enjoy after supper.

For her second letter, she had to reach for her address book. She had never been close to Aunt George and wrote to her rarely. She had married Father's younger brother, Jack, when Betty was still a baby, and moved to be closer to his veterinary practice near Chester. Mother had been painfully tactful, but had always implied there was something too calculating about George, brutal, even. George had been the only aunt not to have attended Mother's funeral. She had sent a note claiming she had a bad cold she didn't want to pass on, so Betty had repaid the slight when Jack died, only she pleaded morning sickness, which had been perfectly true, though it was nothing that a couple of gingernuts in her handbag wouldn't have quelled. He was the handsome uncle she only really knew from photographs, after all. Well provided-for in widowhood, George had become a slightly pathetic figure, whose racy daughters were, by all accounts, given to chasing airmen as well as husbands not their own. George had developed a maddening way of thinking that, by virtue of being a prison governor, Terry was somehow an official authority figure she could recruit whenever she had a complaint with her local council, or MP, or neighbours. She made it worse by writing directly to him, bypassing her niece. Terry would sigh heavily then dictate what Betty was to write back when saying he couldn't help. But, in this instance, family ties were all that mattered.

Dear George, she wrote. (George forbade the use of Aunt, as she thought it ageing, though now well into her late seventies.) *I do hope you and the girls are thriving. Cheshire must be so beautiful at this time of year, and your lovely garden, too. Our little patch at the prison here bears no comparison, but it gives us much pleasure, if only so much of it weren't overlooked from the road.*

George, the funniest thing. After years of saying he was going to do it, Father has finally sold his farm in Saskatchewan and come home to his 'little girl', as he rashly calls this fifty-six-year-old grandmother! It's a delight to see him, but also a bit baffling, as I'm sure you can imagine, since he left when I was so very small. The worry is where he's to go now. As you know, this is Terry's last posting before retirement, so we hardly like to suggest Father put down roots in Lancashire as we've every hope of returning to the Island to settle, after being so happy all those years ago at Parkhurst. It's a delicate matter but I'm not at all sure how much money the sale of his farm will have raised – very little, to judge from his luggage and clothes! After me, with your dear Jack gathered, you are his closest surviving relation, albeit by marriage. I feel sure Jack would have loved to see him one last time and Father will certainly want to visit Jack's grave one day, as Chester isn't so very far from here on the train. Perhaps you might even have him to stay, since you'd have so much lovely catching up to do? Terry and I are off on our precious annual holiday soon and I'm hoping Father will be going to visit Pip, Mike and his great-granddaughter while we're away, but perhaps after that?

I'd also greatly appreciate any suggestions you have as to where Father might settle. You're so very wise in these matters. I had pictured him finding a little cottage with a smallholding or even a market garden, given what an outdoorsman he is, but now that I've watched the slowness with which he climbs our stairs, I realise that was naïve of me.

Terry is going to take him to his tailors at the weekend, so that he's a little more 'sortable', as dear Pattie used to put it once she was a Parisienne, and I'm getting him seen by doctor and dentist. Oh, and Terry will be looking into the pension Father is surely owed after such long years in the Empire's breadbasket. But any help you could give him will be gratefully received. Please don't say I asked, of course, as he'll have the Cane pride, but perhaps slip me a note?

With much love, and it has been too long, your affectionate niece, Betty.

She read it through with some distaste. It was what Whistle would call a chocolate letter, but it would have to do. There was no sound of stirring from upstairs. She would walk the dog to the post office in Walton and post both letters at once before self-disgust gave her second thoughts about sending the one to George. Then she would take Father up tea and a biscuit to rouse him for the trip to the dentist.

FIFTEEN

That evening, Whistle had one of her bad spells. In her less motherly moments, Betty had sometimes wondered if her daughter was manipulative. Ever since infancy, in her babyhood, even, she had a way of suffering medical problems from toothache and headaches to a racing heart or leg aches, which coincided precisely with her parents snatching some precious adult time together or merely being concerned with something other than their younger daughter. The onset of womanhood, to Betty's lasting shame, had happened while her school was evacuated, and it had fallen to Pip to help her through the pain – extreme, Whistle claimed – which came over her once a month. She was not a manipulator – Betty knew that really. Betty had grown up among manipulative women and fancied she knew trumped-up symptoms from the real thing. Rather, she decided, Whistle was at once physically vulnerable and a kind of human barometer, powerlessly sensitive to the shifting moods and needs of those about her. Some people acted upon life, able to impose their wills directly, others only reacted to it. Whistle was a reactor; her body responded with pains and panics just as some people's blushed or broke out in rashes.

The late afternoon had gone well. After his nap, she had taken Father to the dentist and Mr Eade had been extremely kind and interested as he first examined and polished Father's surviving teeth, then took impressions of his mouth. Then Terry had come home, obviously shattered from his long, grim day, but had been very sweet to Father and loving to her while she fetched them both drinks.

Whistle was late home from work, which was unusual, and rather stomped upstairs, muttering about how dirty trips on the crowded train left her feeling, and keeping them all waiting while she insisted on taking a bath and changing. When she joined them downstairs, she had put on a wilfully frumpy skirt and blouse and done something strange to her hair with kirby grips, as though she had let herself be tended to by some keen but clueless child. She was subdued at first, giving only short answers to anyone's questions, and there was the flush to her cheeks that Betty knew often warned her temper was about to be lost. She helped Betty bring the lamb stew, vegetables and hot plates to the dining-room sideboard and lit the candles, without having to be asked, so perhaps all would be well.

The men had barely joined them, and everyone served, however, when Whistle prodded at her stew – which, for once, was really delicious and not too greasy, thanks to some dumplings – and said, 'I don't know how you can bear to eat meat. It's so brown and stringy and, well, eating other animals is savage, really, isn't it?'

'Oh, not this again,' Terry muttered, and stretched across to top up Father's wine glass. 'Every few weeks, she announces we're as good as murderers for liking pork chops more than turnips, and claims she's giving up meat like bloody Bernard Shaw.'

'Well, you are murderers, aren't you?' Whistle muttered.

'Darling, do eat it,' Betty coaxed her. 'It's very good and you need the iron. You're looking so pale.'

'Don't indulge her, Bets, for God's sake.' Terry raised his eyebrows at Father. 'Next thing you know, she'll be making her cheese on toast.'

'It's not a joke,' Whistle shouted, and tossed her cutlery back onto her untouched plate. 'I hate eating meat. I always have, but you never take me seriously, because I'm just a girl.'

'Well, you're certainly not behaving like a boy,' Terry told her, at which Whistle tossed down her napkin and left the room.

Betty made to follow her, but Terry shot her a glare.

'Don't you dare,' he said. 'She's an adult and she needs to learn to act like one. She can't pull stunts like this when she goes to stay with your grand cousins.'

'But she—' Betty started.

'No!' Terry told her. 'Now do eat this truly delicious stew of yours and tell me all about your day, because mine, as I think you both know, has been bloody awful.'

So she fought all her instincts to slip up to see Whistle, even when she went out to the kitchen to take the main course away and bring in pudding. Whistle was an adult now, as Terry had said, and was just being childish at not being able to impose her will. Betty didn't believe the vegetarianism fad for one moment; so often, with Whistle, one thing stood in for something else, like parables in the Bible. Announcing that meat-eating was murder would be code for something less easily said at table, which Betty would have to tease out of her later.

Soon Terry was apologising between uncontrollable yawns and Father tactfully offered to take Mollie out for a longer evening walk than usual as she had been rather shortchanged earlier. So, while he took Mollie out and Terry went upstairs to run his bath, Betty cleared away and washed up supper then made a cheese-and-tomato sandwich to take up to Whistle.

Of course, Whistle pretended not to be hungry at first, and Betty pretended to be taking her conversion to vegetarianism seriously, asking if butter, eggs and cheese would be allowed. Poor dairy cows suffered dreadfully, she reminded her, with calf after calf taken from them before they were weaned. And as for hens . . .

'No, no,' Whistle said, starting to cry quietly. 'Though I really don't like meat much and I expect, once I leave home and it's no inconvenience to anyone, I'll give it up completely. No, it's—' She broke off, flinching minutely at the sound of Terry pompomming to himself in the bath. 'Daddy's a murderer,' she murmured.

'Of course he isn't. He was obliged to witness an execution, that's all.'

'You make it sound so ordinary, like him inspecting the Home Guard on parade.'

'Well, no, darling, but because it's an inescapable bit of his job, however horrid, it is ordinary. It has to be, or he'd go mad.'

'But that's obscene.'

'Whistle!'

'He killed two of them. They were so young: my age!'

'Mr Pierrepoint did the actual killing. Daddy only—'

'It's just as bad. That's like blaming the bullet, not the gun.'

'Who's been talking to you?' Betty felt a flare of loyal anger; the phrase Whistle had used wasn't one of her own but like something from a pamphlet handed out by agitators.

'Nobody,' Whistle insisted, and absentmindedly helped herself to a quarter of the sandwich. Betty sat on the bed by her feet and said nothing as her daughter quietly ate another two quarters. 'Thank you, Mummy,' Whistle said, not meeting her eye. 'I was hungry.'

'I know you were.'

'People got to me about it at work,' Whistle went on. 'I don't know how they found out who I am or where I live, but it was probably the ghastly moo who runs the payroll, who looks over her hornrims at me.'

'That's awful, darling.'

'They kept on and on with questions, though I said I didn't know anything, and they asked how I could sleep at night.'

Well, you don't, half the time, Betty thought, but she said, 'Well, it's Saturday tomorrow. By Monday they'll have something else to talk about.'

'But it was all over the evening papers, so people were talking about it in the lift at work, then on the station platform and then all around me on the train. The first train was so packed and smelly that I jumped off again. That's why I was late; I missed two more trains on purpose as they were both so full and I couldn't face having people pressed all around me talking about the dead boys.'

'Oh. I did wonder.'

Betty nudged the plate towards her and Whistle took the last quarter, but then a fresh wave of horror hit her, and she merely held the sandwich to her chest.

'To die that young!' she said. 'I don't want to die yet.'

'You won't die for years, pet.'

'You don't know that. I could die in my sleep. I could choke on this right now.'

She tossed the sandwich back onto its plate. 'I keep thinking about the ropes around their necks, and the napes of necks when boys have just been to the barbers, and Daddy helping.'

'He doesn't help. He just watches.'

'That's almost worse. To watch without intervening! If I knew I was dying so suddenly at eight in the morning, what would I do? There'd be no time to do anything or write anything or make any kind of mark to show I'd been alive. I can't bear thinking about it.'

'So stop.'

'I *can't* stop!'

Betty took a breath to ensure her voice was uninfected by her daughter's tension. 'Why don't I brush your hair?' she suggested.

'It won't help.'

'It usually does, darling.'

And so, when Betty was so ready to sleep herself, and worrying about Terry and his needs, she had to kick off her shoes and lie on the bed beside Whistle to hold her while she softly shook and cried, seemingly unable to say anything that would help. At last Whistle subsided sufficiently to consent to have her hair brushed, just a little. Betty was slowly brushing the spun gold length of it, her mind wandering to worry how any man could be found to continue this sort of attention, assuming Whistle's vulnerability did not evaporate on leaving home, when she heard the front door open and close and the familiar sound of Mollie's toenails trit-tritting over the hall tiles on her way to her water bowl and bed. Soon afterwards, she heard the creak of the stairs as Father came up. He surprised her by knocking softly on the door.

'Hello?' Betty said, and Father came in, his hair slightly awry as though he'd been walking under trailing branches. Perhaps it was windy out.

'An instinct told me you might be in here,' he murmured. 'Hello, dear girl,' he added to Whistle, crouching beside the bed with enviable agility. 'You were missed at supper; we quite ran out of things to say without you.'

'Sorry,' she said, and smiled.

'I think some of us are country mice,' he said, 'however smartly we try to dress, and will never be happy in the crowds and bustle.'

'I hate cities,' Whistle told him.

'I could tell,' he said. 'I wish I could invite you to come and live on the farm in Canada, but it's too late for that. You'll just have to find your way to a life in the country here somewhere. I can see you somewhere lovely, in Hampshire or Wiltshire, with a chalk stream nearby, maybe at the bottom of the garden, with a horse, of course, and dogs, but maybe doves in a dovecote and a very wilful goat you could learn to milk.'

'I'd like that,' she said seriously, at which Betty suppressed a smile.

'But you know there's a trick you can play on yourself. I learned it long ago when I still had to live in London while I saw Jack through veterinary college. You just live in the city as though it was the countryside. You walk whenever you can, rather than taking buses or trains. Those are full of people, and people you haven't chosen drain the soul so. And you focus instead on the little bits of countryside managing to survive between all the pavements and bricks – the trees, the birds, the patches of park and occasional bee. You might have to leave for work extra early and be a bit later coming back, but you'll see: it'll put colour in those pretty cheeks and do wonders for your appetite. Are you not eating that?'

He indicated the last quarter sandwich and Whistle, gazing at him sleepily, shook her head. He ate the sandwich in two quick mouthfuls.

'So good!' he said.

'I think I'm ready to sleep now,' Whistle said.

'Of course you are.'

'Good girl,' Betty said, and slipped off the bed to lead Father from the room.

'Did you have a nice walk?' she whispered to him, once the bedroom door was safely closed.

He nodded and smiled, remembering. 'The locals are friendly,' he said.

'You've got something on your lapel, Father. It looks like white sauce.'

Father brushed absently at the mark. 'Probably a

roosting bird,' he said. 'I turned off all the lights. Was that right?'

'Yes,' she said. 'And thank you for that just now.'

'She'll be fine,' he said. 'She's just very sensitive and maybe facing in the wrong direction.'

She felt an odd little flash of resentment at that. He had barely met Whistle, so that, frankly, it had been a bit off him coming into her bedroom. What could he possibly understand of her needs? And yet he seemed to have something in him Whistle responded to, something gentler than the stick-in-the-mud she so often now made of Terry.

'Sleep tight,' she told him, and crossed the landing to where she knew Terry would not sleep until she had joined him.

TERRY

SIXTEEN

Having a father-in-law suddenly was very odd. Of course, Terry had had one ever since Betty and he tied the knot as two giddily horny, penniless young things, but Harry Cane had been like Father Christmas, the stuff of legend, and less real to either of them than Betty's *galère* of formidable, big-bosomed aunts. Quietly addicted to adventure stories, frontier tales and Westerns, Terry had always rather enjoyed letting slip that his father-in-law was a pioneering homesteader in the Canadian wilds; it was as romantic and far removed from daily reality as saying he was a rubber planter in Malaya or farming ostrich in the Klein Karoo. Like most such boasts, it had become meaningless with repetition. Very occasionally, someone would ask admiringly if he and Betty had plans to visit Harry and, rather than enter into the ambiguous history between father and daughter, he usually shrugged and said, 'Maybe when I retire. Must cost a packet to get there.'

In fact, he had no idea how much it would cost to cross the Atlantic by ship and then most of a vast continent by train, and then two men in quick succession, the sort of men to inspire trust, told him Saskatchewan was as flat and dull as Lincolnshire, so dull even the horses got bored, and added that it held no building older than its railway hotels. That left him hoping Betty would not suddenly suggest they make the journey. His annual leave was far too short for such gallivanting and his income – albeit cushioned by a house that went with the job – far too modest.

Having Harry in the house suddenly – a charming, crinkle-eyed wreck of an old man, a Father William where he had anticipated a Davy Crockett or Hawkeye, was disconcerting as Terry was a man who liked certainties and there were so many imponderables in this case. At first, he could not quite believe that Betty, a careful planner, a woman who read even a familiar recipe through twice and lined up her ingredients before beginning so as to be sure she had them all in the larder, should have invited her father with no idea how long he was coming for or what his plans were.

On Saturday morning, when it was the last thing he felt like doing, Betty had wanted him to get the old man measured for a suit and some shirts, but that plan had been scuppered by two wretched journalists wanting Terry's thoughts on the double execution, neither of whom would accept his line that, as a prison governor, he had no view but was a viewless servant of the state. By the time he was free, and now in a furious temper, he wanted simply to work in the garden. Nevertheless, he agreed to take Whistle and Harry for a ride on the elevated railway that ran back and forth along the Liverpool bank of the Mersey.

Built for the practical purpose of bringing workers in and out of the city's teeming docks, it had inexplicably become one of Whistle's favourite excursions and Terry had to admit that he also enjoyed the drama of it, the height, the views, their raucous fellow passengers and the chance to gaze on his daughter's blonde beauty as she pointed things out to her grandfather, who responded with kind indulgence, as though her girlish excitement were wisdom. Terry's mood had so improved after their ride and a pork pie and pint of stout at one end of it, that he then cheerfully agreed to drive them out to Port Sunlight for a walk with Mollie, who wasn't exercised nearly enough now that Whistle was working.

On Sunday, the old man had surprised them by pulling a face at the prospect of church, though, admittedly, the parish church in Walton was hardly Durham Cathedral. Instead, he had chosen to go riding with Whistle, which gave Terry and Betty the best part of a day's respite. Grandfather and granddaughter had returned full of loud respect for each other's courage and horsemanship – although the old man claimed he was too used to the high pommel of a Western saddle to have felt very secure. He had matched Whistle's every jump, apparently, and taught her some Cree phrases to murmur in a strange horse's ear to win over its trust.

Harry had rather upset Betty by saying, with an outsider's tactless candour, that Whistle's anxiety vanished as soon as she was out of the city and on a horse and that what she needed was to stop working in a great, grimy metropolis and live in open countryside among the animals that everyone apparently teased her for being so mad about. And Whistle, with the tactlessness of the enthusiastic young, said in front of him that she hoped Cowboy Grandpa would live with them always now, as she felt finally there was someone in the family who understood her.

So now, on a weekday, because there were things that simply had to be sorted before he and Betty went off on their annual holiday and the old man was sent to visit saintly Pip and Mike in Wakefield, Terry had boldly left his deputy to hold the fort for the morning so he could take Harry to visit his tailor.

Taught by her late mother, who had been quite the couturier, Betty made a lot of her clothes from paper patterns and, having raised only daughters, was touchingly ignorant of what a tailored suit and a couple of good shirts would cost. Having suggested the mission, she took Terry aside to murmur, 'I'm not sure he has any money at all, really,' to which Terry responded that she was not to worry, and he could take care of it. Between them, they had enough fabric coupons saved up and, anyway, the tailor he was going to see would not be a stickler for legality.

When they first met, when Terry was still young enough to be still wearing shirts and suits made for him to mark his leaving Framlingham, he had used his father's tailor in Jermyn Street, where his father let Terry charge things to his account. But once he returned from Sarawak and married Betty, his stepbrothers had grown and were making their own demands on the paternal wallet, so Terry had been obliged to find tailors of his own. He still had a once-good tweed suit – now his weekend gardening suit – bought from a tailor in Norwich, and in Durham had been obliged to admit that his waistline and chest had expanded for good and had a new work suit and dinner suit made, telling Betty they would see him out.

He had liked the Durham tailor, a wry type, much given to weekend birdwatching. He had been recommended to him by one of the university dons they met regularly for bridge, a handsome man whose appearance Betty pronounced *devastating*, her highest praise. The Durham tailor had been well trained in how to flatter a man's figure without making him self-conscious by discussing or even acknowledging the process. As he measured Terry's depressingly descending chest and expanding girth, he spoke only of countryside matters, of trout fishing, good walks, the kestrels on the cathedral towers. The jackets he then fitted were cunningly padded here or boxed there so that, though larger, Terry's girth was kept in proportion.

When they were moved to Liverpool, he had assumed he would keep faith with the Durham tailor, if he needed more shirts or any gloom-inducing alterations in the suits the man had made for him. But then, just when he'd have thought the National Health and free milk in schools would have kept Labour in power for at least a decade of good will, the nation voted Churchill back in and, with him, the policy of imprisoning as many active queers as the police and sharp-eyed landladies could catch. There had always been that sort of thing in prisons, just as there had in boarding schools, the navy and, for all Terry knew, monasteries. Men had needs and would improvise to see them met. But, apart from the occasional burglar who just happened to be a chutney-ferret, these incidences were, he gathered, between men with needs and men prepared to debase themselves for a measure of protection – just as in boarding school, in fact. Now, however, an already overburdened prison system was filling up with men who were there for what they were, not for what they had done. He couldn't say that, naturally – they were in prison for having broken the law – but whereas a short, hard spell locked up could be shock enough to see that a young housebreaker signed up for a mechanic's apprenticeship never burgled again, it was highly unlikely that the same would make a homosexual cease to be one. Terry had caused a bit of a fuss at the last governors' conference by suggesting chemical or actual castration would prove cheaper and more effective in fulfilling the government's aims and he had recently fallen foul of the hen-like inspector for blocking all visits for queer prisoners who had reoffended.

The bottom line, a pun he found irresistible, was that the surge in queer prisoners was an administrative headache. Some were quiet and discreet enough to survive, but the flamers, as the officers called them, needed special protection if they weren't to be being constantly beaten up or buggered so savagely they had to be taken to hospital.

Vance, Terry's Liverpool tailor, had been one of the quiet ones, had been shopped by his landlord when the cousin he shared a flat with turned out to be nothing of the kind. He had served in the navy – which was, presumably, where he had learned to mask his nature – and had even won a couple of medals for valour, so that Terry had felt for him in the sudden, savage exposure of his sordid home life. On admission, he had asked not to have protective measures and, when Terry asked why on earth not, had pulled a pained expression and said that the company would be unbearable. He was put in a cell with a vast stevedore serving a term for grievous bodily harm, who proved unexpectedly hospitable, and Vance served out his short sentence with exemplary service in the prison laundry, receiving nothing worse than a black eye. At his release interview, Terry said, 'I suppose there's no point my telling you not to do it again?' to which Vance said, 'I shan't get *caught* again, sir,' which Terry laughed at and repeated to Betty in bed.

'What will you do now?' Terry asked him.

'I'll go back to tailoring,' Vance said. 'A friend from the navy has offered me a partnership and I've enough set by to go in with him. It's only a small concern, but the work is steady.'

A few days later, he wrote to Terry, thanking him for being *civilised*, and enclosing his business card. *I know it's probably not allowed*, he wrote, *and I dare say you already have a tailor elsewhere, but we'd give you a good price.*

Terry had initially thought this a little cheeky and just the sort of mild corruption that could land a governor in hot water – he had been offered cheap cars in his time, insider deals on shares and once, to Whistle's lingering outrage, had returned the puppy of a racing greyhound said to be a sure thing. Vance was not like the others, perhaps it was the service medals and dry humour, so Terry tucked the card in the back of his wallet in the little pouch where he put dry-cleaning chits and train tickets.

After a few months, once it was clear Vance had mended

his ways or found a sympathetic landlord, Betty announced that she had already turned the collars on all Terry's weekend shirts, and it was time to cut them into rags for cleaning the brass and silver. Terry had fished out the man's card and looked him up one Saturday. He decided enough time had passed since Vance's release for it to lie just in the realms of possibility that he had come upon the business by chance.

It was a modest operation, with a tiny, tidy shopfront the size of a tobacconist's, tucked between two of the smaller Georgian townhouses on Rodney Street. Two half-mannequins, very sharply dressed as far as their non-existent legs, faced the street as though waiting for a bus. *Uniforms a speciality*, an elegant, hand-written card promised from a small picture frame beside them. The interior was revealed as one of those precious survivors of the Blitz, with walls of oak shelving and drawers, a little fireplace now filled with pinecones, and wide floorboards, which must have been lovingly waxed since being sawn and laid down in the eighteenth century. The door had set a bell jangling on a spring. Terry had time to admire the dexterity with which about a hundred ties had been fanned out on a large round dining table, like the petals of an exotic flower.

Vance emerged from the rear, quietly dressed in a navy-blue suit and, if surprised to see Terry, hid it well. He hung Terry's jacket up and took his measurements, holding all the numbers in his head and writing them down in a small notebook at the end. He helped him choose some Tattersall check, letting slip it was named for a London horse market once famous for its checked horse blankets and, because the shirting felt softer and finer than that of the old shirts Betty had loyally repaired so often, Terry let himself be talked into a couple of linen ones for warm weather, a thrush-egg blue Vance assured him wasn't too bright and a dazzling white he knew was probably impractical but which would go with both his summer jackets.

Vance quoted him a price far lower than Terry had been expecting and said he'd have the shirts delivered. That was the one moment of anything like awkwardness in their exchange, when Vance was filling out a form and Terry began,

'Governor's House,' and Vance interrupted him, softly saying,

'That's quite all right, sir. I have your address by heart.'

The four shirts arrived the following week, neatly folded between layers of tissue paper in a box so smart Betty whisked it away as she said it would be useful for next time she sent Pip a parcel of baby knitting. He was not a vain man; even in his randy prime he knew it was his size and physique that reeled women in, not his face. He knew he had an odd upper lip, much improved by the thick moustache he had finally grown because Betty said moustaches brought out the twinkle in a man's eyes. His approach to clothes had always been the one inculcated in him by his father – that they should be of the best quality he could afford but that, if anyone noticed them, they were wrong. He was always happiest in uniform or on those occasions – like weddings, funerals or anything requiring evening dress – when there was a very clear set of rules for what a man should wear: another uniform, in effect. Whenever they went to an event calling for evening dress, Betty suffered torments over how she looked, asking was she mutton dressed as lamb and so on, but invariably said how handsome black tie or white tie made men look.

The shirts Vance made for him, folded and wrapped as they were like treasures, their fabric somehow even softer than it had felt when Vance threw bolts of it across his cutting table, excited him in a way he knew was not quite the thing. He made a point of wearing one of the Tattersall check ones at once, while doing muddy digging in his vegetable patch, as though to show himself it was simply a replacement shirt and nothing special. Betty noticed it at once, though, when she brought him out a mug of coffee in the garden.

'That's nice,' she said, fingering the collar teasingly, knowing he'd swat her hand away and tell her not to fuss, woman. But he was glad she approved.

'He gave me a good price,' he said, in case she thought him profligate, like the time he had splashed an inheritance on trading in the workhorse Ford of their early marriage for a Lagonda, when it should have gone into their savings account.

Perhaps because he had rested and had a haircut and several baths, his father-in-law presented less of a spectacle than he had on arrival in England, and he was wearing the better of his two suits, the tweed one. Betty had sensed he had developed rather flashy tastes after years of living in dungarees, and suggested he be steered towards a good grey flannel and away from anything with stripes or checks.

'It's our birthday present to you,' she insisted as Harry and Terry left the house. 'Think of all the birthdays we've missed over the years.' Terry heard the tinkle of desperation in her voice. She was worried about Harry's lack of plans and, tormented by her guilt since, on the occasion when Whistle had taken Harry to the cinema, she had actually said that she didn't think, with rationing and Terry's niggardly pay, they could afford the extra mouth to feed for very long.

The GP had given Harry a thorough check-up and said his heart was in fine fettle for his age, and the arthritis in his joints only to be expected after a long life of manual labour. He had, however, the first signs of prostate cancer. Just as doctors ridiculously persisted in treating wives as though they were too frail to cope with bad news that might instead be delivered to their husbands, so, it seemed, they felt they should shield elderly parents.

'Does he have long?' Terry asked.

'Hard to say without X-rays or investigative surgery, which a man his age really doesn't need, and, from the swelling, I'd say it was too far advanced to be worth the trauma of removal.'

Talking on his office telephone, Terry noticed he had instinctively crossed his legs in manly sympathy.

'Does he have any idea?'

'None,' the doctor said. 'And I'd keep it that way. More men his vintage die with it than of it, to be honest. No point worrying him needlessly. I thought one of you should know in case it, well, affects any plans you might be making for him.'

Terry had already made a plan: that if he told Betty about the cancer, it would be once they were happily on holiday in Port Appin, and forgetting their troubles, not now, when the dear girl so badly needed a complete break.

'I've asked my old pal, Bob, to look into your pension for you,' he told Harry as he drove him into town, amused at how the old man's eyes were on stalks, taking in lorries, buses, buildings, passers-by. 'See if it can't be paid to you over here, instead of in Canada. I'm guessing you don't have a great deal set by if it can't. Sorry to be blunt, but—'

'No, no. You're quite right and that's kind of you. And him,' Harry said. 'I fear prairie farms are not prized, exactly, for all the premium they made on grain during the war. And I was rather obliged to sell it to—' He broke off, cleared his throat and continued. 'Sell it to a neighbour's stepson who is empire building, rather than to another homesteader who might cherish it. The homesteaders have all gone. Seen sense, ha!'

In the confined space of the Morris, his short laugh was almost a cry of pain. He fell to staring out of the window again. Terry glanced across at him when they stopped at some roadworks and was reminded of the prison officers who had gone off to fight in the war as keen young men and returned, if they returned, aged by things they had seen and could not discuss. His son-in-law, Mike, was one such, only in his late twenties when he arrived at Durham to be Terry's deputy, yet carrying some darkness in him from the war that could make Terry feel much the younger man.

'If you could live anywhere,' he asked Harry, 'where

would you choose? I mean, when you used to lie in bed in your cabin and stare out at the marvellous stars there, where did you dream of being? London? The Riviera? Some pretty English village with a church and pub on the green?'

Harry smiled. 'On the good nights, especially in early summer, I wanted only to be there on the prairie, and for the starry night to last for longer.' Then something wiped his smile away and he looked back at the passing street scene. 'That's all over now. There's no going back.'

'Not even to some little cottage? Betty said you'd imagined a place with a little garden, somewhere more manageable, somewhere with neighbours.'

'Neighbours? A blessing and a curse. Living in prisons, I don't suppose neighbours are ever a problem for you.'

Terry laughed. 'Not when the neighbours are safely locked up. It's not so bad here, but in some places where the governor's garden is entirely overlooked by the cells or a prison workshop it's a bit unsettling for the women, especially when the dirty buggers whistle or call things out. When I retire, Betty wants us in a cottage with thick hedges and no neighbours, so I think prison life must have got to her a little.'

'So where's your fantasy spot to escape to?' Harry asked.

'The Island. The Isle of Wight. We fell in love with the place when I was deputy at Parkhurst early on in our marriage and promised ourselves that we'd go back, once we were free and no longer having our every move dictated by the ruddy commissioners. Land that time forgot. It's beautiful, even though there are three prisons there, which probably keeps the prices down a bit.' He cleared his throat, realising Harry had somehow got him talking about himself, which hadn't at all been his intention.

This time, he parked on the hill, so Harry could admire the view of Liverpool through the usual pillars of chimney smoke. Terry lit his pipe, and they strolled along Hope Street to one side to marvel at the huge Anglican cathedral, still not finished, though its nave was taking shape.

'Makes you wonder if the medieval ones went up any faster,' Terry said. 'With no unions demanding tea breaks or safety devices.'

'I doubt it,' Harry told him. 'There must have been masons who spent a whole life on the cathedrals in Salisbury or Winchester, with no idea of how the finished thing would look. People gaze up at them now and say, *Oh, what an exercise in faith they were*, but I suspect it was simply a matter of doing a job well and being grateful to be well paid. And hopeful they didn't fall off the scaffolding.'

Terry offered to take him inside. The transepts and east end were already functioning as a church, while teams of men slaved on, working towards the eventual west end. Harry gave a sort of shudder, however, and said he found the place sinister.

'So dark, and it looms over these poor houses and tenements like stone judgement.'

'How was your church back home?' Terry asked.

'Like all our buildings, it had to be made of things

that could come by a train then be carried by horse and cart, so it was a little, white clapboard barn with a small bell tower at one end and simple clear-glass windows with a blue surround. Nobody had the money for stained glass and the light through the clear panes was rather refreshing, as was the lack of Victorian pomp and gloom.'

Terry steered him away from any glimpse of the unholy mess of the emerging Catholic cathedral at the other end of the ridge. He was never very comfortable discussing religion as he was secretly an atheist, but he would rather die on an altar rail than admit it, least of all to Betty. They walked down the hill to Vance's establishment instead.

Vance's tall, red-haired business partner was in evidence at the shop this time, a big-pawed bear. He was easier to picture streaked with mud and blood on a rugby pitch than delicately wielding tailoring shears, let alone a needle and thread. Perhaps his bouncer's build fitted him more to a front-of-house role, Terry thought, while Vance did the actual stitching and machining. He couldn't bear to watch Betty or either of the girls use a sewing machine; the proximity of their fingertips to the jabbing needle was unbearable.

'Hello. I'm Terry Ennion,' Terry said. 'Mr Vance made some very good shirts for me recently, so I've brought along my father-in-law, all the way from Winter, Saskatchewan, for a suit and a pair of shirts.'

'Terry, really,' Harry began to protest, but Terry raised a finger to insist.

'Our treat. Is Mr Vance not in?'

'He just nipped to the bank, but I can take Mr . . .'

'Cane. Harry Cane.'

'I can take Mr Cane's measurements while we wait. Please sit, Mr Ennion, or did you have other business?'

Terry sat, picked up a copy of *Motor Sport* and pretended to read. The man was a local. After the nicely lugubrious tones in Durham, he still found the Scouse accent comically cheerful.

Just as Vance had done for him, the partner whisked off Harry's jacket to measure him more closely and Terry noticed that, unlike Vance, he had to write down each measurement as he made it. Harry's shirt had a very obvious patch sewn on one shoulder blade and was tearing at one elbow and, when asked to remove his shoes, he revealed socks beyond even Betty's ability to darn. The partner was as tactful as an undertaker, looming over the old man and handling him as though afraid he might break, murmuring instructions like,

'Just bend your elbow for me, sir,' then 'Legs slightly apart while I measure their inside, sir.'

'So you and Vance met in the navy?' Terry asked.

'We did, sir. But then we were assigned to different ships, and I ended up a POW after mine was sunk off Italy. One thing the navy expects is that each sailor can mend his own uniform and we both found we had a knack for it. This old place belonged to my grandfather, a tailor himself, and when the tenants gave it up in '48 it seemed like fate was calling. Ah. Here he is.'

Vance bustled in and immediately took in the scene and Terry's presence.

'Mr Ennion,' he said. 'How nice. Are you keeping well?' He fairly glowed when Terry said how pleased he'd been with the shirts.

'It was all I could do to keep Mrs Ennion from coming after you for blouses,' Terry added.

The partner handed over Harry's measurements, quietly explained he was Mr Ennion's father-in-law, Mr Cane, and was after a suit.

'Something serviceable and sober,' Terry put in. 'Like a grey flannel. And a couple of shirts, one blue, one white.'

Harry smiled like a boy in a toy shop as Vance rolled out fabrics and opened style books, noting down choices and checking that the finished garments would be sent to Governor's House. The suit would be ready for a fitting and last adjustments in twelve days.

As Terry drove them home, the old man was lost in thought for a while, then said he found it touching that a couple had found a way to shelter their relationship by running a business together the way the tailors did.

'You've misunderstood there, I think,' Terry said. 'Indiscreet of me to say, but Vance served time under me for gross indecency. He learned his lesson.'

'Really?' The old man raised an eyebrow almost flirtatiously.

'Besides, anyone can see that the ginger bruiser who took your measurements would knock the lights out of any fairy who came on to him. Unfortunately, in my line of work, you develop an instinct for these things.'

'Ah, well. I stand corrected,' Harry said. 'I just couldn't

help noticing they wore matching signet rings, both with bloodstones.'

'Really?' Terry was unsettled. The big partner had been so very like Frank Runciman, a totally dependable engineer who played prop forward in his Sarawak rugby fifteen, a man he had unthinkingly showered with times without number. 'Perhaps they both belong to one of those sinister little clubs, like the Masons or the Moose.'

SEVENTEEN

Among the usual little pile of prison-office memos and work-related post waiting in the in-tray on Terry's desk when he returned to the office after an early, rather irascible lunch with Betty and her father, was a personal one, pointedly marked *confidential* and addressed to him at the prison, not the governor's house. The handwriting was thick and jagged, making him think of ugly brooches and rheumy-eyed, wheezing lapdogs. He used his penknife to slash the envelope open neatly. The envelope was embossed with the name of a smart hotel, crossed out.

He tugged the letter out with a flash of impatience. It was surprising how often he received letters from the mothers, aunts or wives of prisoners, wheedling, cajoling or downright offensive, variously asking for favours, or complaining when those favours weren't forthcoming. The notepaper was heavy, the name of the hotel from where it had been lifted scored out with a thick line and a Welsh house name written below it with the date.

Heart sinking, he flicked the paper over and saw the short letter was signed *George* and realised it was from his least favourite of Betty's rackety aunts, Harry's widowed sister-in-law. She was a querulous, demanding type forever perceiving slights or injustices where none were intended, forever needing to be appeased. She was notorious among her sisters for meanness, hoarding soap, stationery, even lavatory paper from any hotel her fast daughters and their strings of men friends paid for. She had long struck him as the least intelligent of her family, not least because she was convinced that his position as a prison governor gave him the ability to challenge the granting of planning permissions, cancel speeding tickets and even change election results that displeased her.

Harry had not enquired after her. Terry made a mental note to ask what he made of his late brother's wife; to establish her as a shared irritant would dispel the slight discomfort of their conversation after leaving the tailors.

Dear Terence, she wrote. It had always amused her to use his full name although nobody else did. *This is rather awkward, but I must trust in your discretion and professional knowledge. Betty wrote to me with the news that Harry Cane has returned from his Canadian exile and is visiting you. I wonder if his plans have become any clearer? Betty wrote clearly hoping I would have him to stay with me, for my dear Jack's sake, or wave a wand to conjure up somewhere for him to stay.*

It is quite impossible. My health is not good. The girls, quite rightly, had the bulk of Jack's inheritance to set them up in life but I find it hard to make ends meet on my widow's pension and with everything so rationed and short, I can barely afford to heat this barn of a house. In fact, I have been seriously considering selling up and living off the proceeds by moving into a small hotel by the sea, somewhere not too louche. Eastbourne appeals. The house is mine, after all, and not the girls'.

So, no. I cannot have HC to stay but neither, I consider, should you. Dear Betty was always sheltered from the truth, as were my girls by Jack, but it's important you know he had to leave her mother and the country because he was, and presumably still is, a sexual deviant of the Oscar Wilde sort. Not at all someone I'd consider safe around grandchildren.

Perhaps if we all make our feelings plain, he will know he is not welcome and will return to Canada? Though I imagine these days even Canada has the same laws we do.

I hope you can understand why I wrote to you rather than responding to dear Betty. I think it best I leave her letter unanswered, at least for a while. Her requests in it were a little wild, and, as her husband, you are best placed to judge the situation.

She ended with her jagged signature and, bizarrely, a large kiss, which was surely unintentional and had slipped out like a belch. Perhaps the ghastly woman needed a nursing home, not a genteel hotel?

Terry tore her letter in two and tossed it into the bin. After answering a couple of work letters, he retrieved it to tear it into smaller pieces, which he then stuffed angrily beneath other rubbish.

PIP

EIGHTEEN

For as long as she could remember, Pip had experienced days when her feelings could not be contained. Sometimes sorrow, though more often joy, would well up in her so strongly that the sensation was physical, like a fizzing in her head she half expected to see reflected in shop windows or her powder compact. Since the baby, and her twin brother who lived only an hour and was scooped away by the midwife like a bed pan, this had become more the case.

After one swift perusal of a leaflet left by the health visitor, Mike had said it was clearly an excess of hormones flooding her body, and she had almost thrown stew at him.

'My feelings are real,' she wanted to tell him. 'There's not just some chemical making me feel them.'

Her love for the baby was intense. She could hardly bear not to be touching, kissing and sniffing her all the time, despite the strict timetable set by the health visitor and the bossy book by Mr Truby-King for when Baby, always with her capital B, was to have her set times for rest and Mother, capital M, was to go upstairs, remove her skirt and lie down.

Pip had watched courting couples in cinemas since she was a girl and knew that the desire to be always touching and fondling and kissing a baby was simply a version of what normal men and women did with one another, a natural spilling-over of that bonding love. She and Mike had never been one of those couples – *those mauling couples*, he called them – so perhaps it meant she had more to spare.

This morning, doing the day's shop with Henrietta gurgling in her pram whenever Pip stooped to tuck a bag of this or a tin of that below the baby's happily fidgeting feet, she felt that unique fizz that made her want to stroke the cheeks of the exhausted girl-women in the queues and made her love the smile lines on this shopkeeper's face and the way the butcher's boy turned beetroot when she gave him her order. In moods like this, she had to sing or whistle almost constantly to let the joy out like the steam from a kettle.

The teachers at their little school had tried in vain to impress on her that whistling was crude and unladylike; both she and her little sister were demon whistlers. It was how Whistle got her nickname, after all. If pressed, Whistle could render the Badinerie from the Bach suites almost as fast as she could play it on her flute, but a darkness had stolen over her with adulthood, so she whistled more rarely. It amused Mike, who said it was like living with a song thrush and meant he could always find her about the house and knew when she was in the lavatory.

Today's tune, going round in her head, was the maddeningly circular 'Early One Morning'. Back home, baby sleeping, she turned last night's leftovers into oxtail soup for their lunch then set to the task that always stopped her whistling or singing: updating her account book.

Ever since their engagement, when Mike paid money

into a joint account so that she could amuse herself buying antiques for their future home, he had expected her to itemise each day's expenditure into a neat little notebook. Maths had never been her strong point, but it amused her that, finally, she saw that this was what all those maths lessons had been for. It amused her, too, that he expected her to keep at it even on their honeymoon spent driving to Provence and back, itemising how they eked out their precious francs and traveller's cheques on lunches of thrillingly foreign baguettes, cheese, fruit and chocolate. It amused her far less now that, as his wife and the mother of his child, *his drudge*, she called herself on her darkest days, he still expected her to itemise pillow ticking, lamb's liver and the huge quantities of meat or fish (depending on rations) that she bought to feed Susie the dog. When his bank statement arrived each month, he would ask for the notebook and, sighing heavily, go through both, ticking and underlining to, as he put it, *balance the books*. For they never balanced, naturally, as Pip left little treats out of it, or boring things. As far as she was aware, her mother had never been expected to do this for her father, and it seemed an injustice that Mike expected it of her.

As always, Susie sensed any mood change in her and padded in, panting, to lean heavily against her legs. Pip looked away from her little clutch of receipts and slipped an arm through the thick white fur to hug her and plant a kiss on her noble head.

If Mike could be maddeningly serious and buttoned up, even when they were courting, if he could seem too far a cry from Leslie Howard or Cary Grant, Susie had always been his wonderfully impractical, openly emotional redeeming feature. Presented to his regiment as a puppy by the mayor of a little town they had liberated from the Germans, the dog had claimed him as hers and had been spoiled by a succession of landladies as she grew ever larger, with paws the size of side plates and a deep bark that registered in one's chest like thunder. Whenever Wakefield felt a bit too desperate, Susie made Pip feel safe and whenever she felt low the animal sensed it and came to lean on her or place a huge paw on her thigh to reassure. Mike insisted they feed her fresh meat or fish, although the succession of dogs Pip had enjoyed, growing up, had all been fed smelly dog food from cans and been fine with it. And yet her husband queried her maths over the cost of two balls of baby wool (shell pink).

She picked up her pen again and, beneath the day's groceries, and in her tidiest hand, added *triple rope of <u>very</u> good, heavy pearls à la Queen Mary: £150.00*. And, under that, *Eloping to Italy with James Stewart: no charge*, then closed the little book with a feeling of triumph.

Mrs Coley, the charlady, was coming that afternoon to clean the house and mind the baby while Pip kept a dreaded medical appointment. Pip felt the prospect entitled her to some sunshine and freedom. She gave the soup a stir, added pepper and salt for luck, although, as a pipe smoker, Mike seemed only to enjoy extremes of flavour, like whisky, Gentlemen's Relish and mint sauce. Then she woke the baby for her feed, following the wretched timetable, rocked her against her shoulder for a burp, whose ripeness seemed to surprise Henrietta as much as her mother, then loaded her into the pram with toys and a picnic rug. She clipped Susie onto her lead and set out for a short walk before it would be time to serve Mike his lunch.

The house, 5 Love Lane, belonged to the prison, as did the smaller houses in the street. The house was nice enough, restored for them by the prison commissioners so as to be ready for their return from honeymoon, but the best part of the address was its name. The outlook was drab in both directions. The prison, almost directly in front, was a baleful presence and its visiting hours drew a stream of the wretched to queue for entry just across from her kitchen window. Mike had been her father's deputy in Durham, but, during their engagement, had been moved to Wakefield. There he had been recruited to set up a course covering everything from history and literature to sociology and criminology at the nearby Imperial Training School, which was linked to the prison, and in which he had lived, like a sort of housemaster for the trainees, until he had been rescued by marriage.

She suspected that institutional life suited him, as he had been sent to a boarding school from just five until he was eighteen, then to Oxford, then into the army for the duration of the war. The company of other men would always reassure him, as would the words 'suet' and 'custard'. But she was conditioned by institutions as well, in her way, and, having grown up in a succession of prisons, which, of their nature, were never in the more uplifting parts of town, had an instinct for the most cheering walks on offer in a short radius of her home.

In Wakefield, this lay uphill from the prison and from

Love Lane to St John's Square, where elegant Georgian houses looked over broad, pram-friendly pavements onto a pleasant, tree-fringed green around St John's, the church she and Mike favoured.

Lonely, not a thing she felt she could confide in letters to her mother without seeming disloyal, she dreamed of making friends with a woman who lived in one of these houses, another mother, ideally, artistic and funny, worldly wise yet kind enough to lift Pip from gaucheness, a friend whose nice husband worked far enough away not to come home for lunch.

She wheeled the baby, who was Henrietta in honour of Mike's grandmother, a direct descendant of Nelson's sister, slowly round the square in both directions, to give Susie ample opportunity to attend to the trees. Then she crossed to the grass so as to lie on the rug with Henrietta and some toys while Susie walked around pretending an interest in whatever she found on the ground, but actually guarding them both. If anyone emerged from the church or one of the houses, Pip gave them a smile she hoped looked welcoming and not demented, in case they should prove to be the new friend, but soon she was far too absorbed in the pleasures of warm May sunshine, sounds from the nearby grammar schools and the beauty and evident intelligence of the baby, who, in turn, seemed to have discovered the charm of slow-rolling clouds and the thrushes that swooped and hopped across the lawn around them.

It saddened her that Whistle had no sooner been made an aunt than she had declared all babies and talk of babies boring. Pip missed her company keenly and wished she could coax her into visiting Love Lane, baby notwithstanding. Whistle had thrown one of her panic attacks on the morning of the wedding and had been prickly and ambiguous towards Pip ever since. It was a kind of sulk, Pip supposed, and only the stealthy processes of time or the finding of a fiancé of her own, preferably better looking or more grandly familied than Mike, would lift her out of it.

Apart from two older sisters, one unmarried and terrifically good, one married and given to salty marital advice, and an ancient great-aunt, Mike's family were all dead before she met him. He came from a wonderfully rooted clan of landowners that had tastefully improved a farmhouse acquired on the dissolution of the monasteries then stayed put for five centuries. They had done nothing remarkable other than marrying money at intervals to turn the farmhouse into a Manor House of honeyed beauty and, latterly, marrying a descendant of Nelson's sister. Sadly, Mike's grandfather had let the house, and his father sold it. Pip had been working in Durham University library when she learned of its existence, so had been able to track down a couple of tantalisingly illustrated articles about it in ancient copies of *Country Life* and a colleague had gleefully discovered that Mike was listed in *Burke's Landed Gentry*.

'Of course,' Whistle had pointed out thoughtfully. 'If he'd been living there still, he wouldn't have come to work for Daddy in Durham and you'd never have met. He'd have been snapped up by some Wiltshire landowner's daughter with a horse and a frightening chin. Poor White Fang!'

An incendiary bomb had destroyed five centuries of family furniture and paintings, but Mike brought a large trunk of Georgian silver to the marriage and a handful of pen-and-ink ancestral portraits, one of whom, dark and handsomely brooding, with the requisite cruel yet sensuous mouth, looked exactly as she had always imagined Mr Darcy. Whenever she brought home something from the kindly antique dealer in Durham, who had taught her so much about chairs and old china, she found herself mentally asking this ancestor, not Mike, whether he approved.

Because of the long engagement insisted on by her parents and, perhaps unflatteringly, readily agreed to by Mike, they had written to each other regularly, initially by hand, with him dropping off notes for her at the library and she dropping them in at his landlady's on her way home. Then, less frequently, by post, when he moved away to Wakefield. She undoubtedly revealed far too much of herself on paper – not least her fantasy about briefly leaving him for a hedonistic spell on the Continent with James Stewart. He had expressed himself far more passionately and touchingly on paper than he ever seemed able to do in person.

She was utterly inexperienced; he was her first and only admirer. Convinced she was too tall to be feminine, and odd-looking rather than beautiful, she felt she must say yes when he asked her. Cruelly, it was only once she was engaged that she had any chance of adventure. A school friend she had never liked much invited her to stay in Dartmouth, where her father was an officer at the naval college.

There, she had a couple of what-have-I-done crises and described handsome naval escorts in some detail in letters to Mike, thinking to stir a reaction in him. He barely acknowledged the stories she told, however, and certainly gave no hint of jealousy, merely writing, like a slightly superior older brother, that she seemed to be having a high old time, and he suspected Durham's university library would seem very quiet on her return.

Their honeymoon in Provence, with its balmy evenings, sun-warmed peaches, copious quantities of icy rosé and Châteauneuf-du-Pape, was idyllic, but their few attempts at lovemaking were clumsy, painful disasters and she was still a mortified virgin when they drove back to Yorkshire and he asked, with trepidation, if she wanted to be carried over the threshold of 5 Love Lane. They finally managed it after she followed advice she read in the charlady's magazine about taking a hot bath and using plenty of talc afterwards and she had no sooner become pregnant than he returned to treating her with attentive caution, like an invalid.

Mike loved her. She knew he did. His letters had not lied, but it was as though something in him had been choked off at the source. He adored Henrietta. His eyes lit up whenever he saw her, and he loved helping at bathtimes and folding her in a towel on his lap afterwards.

A thoroughly nice-looking woman emerged from one of the houses with a wicker basket over her arm and wearing a wonderfully full-skirted frock with a pattern of poppies splashed across it. Her basket had library books in it. Always a good sign.

'What an adorable baby,' she said. 'Is she your first?'

English very much spoken, as Whistle always put it when someone sounded like a Home Service announcer.

And Pip said yes and tried to coax a smile out of Henrietta, but then Susie decided she needed to guard mother and baby against the intruder and the nice woman retreated, laughing at least, as Pip called out pathetic apologies and used all her strength to tug Susie back to lie down and stop barking. Henrietta, startled, wailed.

NINETEEN

Pip's pregnancy had not been easy. Carrying twins had put a strain on her heart and then she had gone into labour so early she did not even have a bag packed. As it turned out, hospital might have saved both babies, but everything happened in a horrible rush, with the terrified char standing in until the midwife arrived on her bicycle.

Henrietta was born as tiny as a perfect, roaring doll, but her equally tiny brother never recovered from arriving with his sister's cord wrapped tightly round his neck. The midwife, who otherwise was kindness itself, spirited him away in a towel and Pip had never stopped worrying about what had become of him, unchristened, although she named him and stammered through the Christening service for him from her prayer book, hoping that counted. She had nightmares still in which she saw his body bundled into the midwife's black leather bag, like a blood-smeared slab of black-market meat. She could not look at his sister without remembering him, but hoped Henrietta would thrive and grow away from the shadow of her arrival.

Today's was a routine check-up to make sure that the twins' birth had not damaged her in some way, but, as she served Mike his soup and bread and cheese, settled Henrietta to sleep and welcomed Mrs Coley and introduced her accompanying two grandchildren to Susie and the toy box, she was dreading everything about it.

Pip had been raised to dislike her body or, at least, not actively to like it. Her mother had left the grim business of Dr White's towels and belts to the school matron and, even once Pip was engaged, her only advice or instruction was that she must endeavour to keep herself *clean and appealing* at all times.

She had acquired shame mysteriously, from other girls at school perhaps, where she was already made to feel awkward as a teenager by being told she had outgrown her strength, whatever that meant, and was to walk the school donkey rather than join in team sports. School had also seen to it that she was utterly innocent of proper medical terms. In her head, at least, because these were things of which she never spoke, periods were *Henry coming to stay* and her undifferentiated private parts and their shield of black hair were collectively her *Mary*. A thing that would always make it challenging to address, let alone befriend Henrys and Marys in adult life.

When she bathed, she soaped and dried herself briskly, without paying much attention, and if she wanted to linger in a bath for the warmth, she used bubble bath for the way it hid her body from her view. She avoided letting Mike see her naked, wearing ankle-length nightdresses and aiming to get into bed while he was brushing his teeth in the bathroom and tending to dress after he left for work.

So a visit to a gynaecologist, where she must not only call things by their adult names and let a complete stranger crouch on a little stool between her raised and spread legs, was a nightmarish prospect to be got through with gritted teeth, tinkling conversation – because to whistle would have been odd – and a resolute silence on the matter afterwards. Her mother was quiet on the subject, thank God, though always ready with revolting ideas about what to feed the baby or bits of weird medical advice cut from the letters page in her *Telegraph* or old copies of *The Lady*.

Her first visit to the clinic was made nearly two years ago, when she had begun to suspect she was expecting Henrietta and her brother. She had approached it as she might a trip to the dentist: as something a little grim but necessary and good for her. Once Mr Cannon had enjoyed a *little chat* with her, a nurse led her into his examination room, had her remove everything except her bra, then brightly saw her *popped* onto the hideous, stirrupped chair, eased her feet into position then, with grotesque coyness given the indignity just visited, pulled over a little device on wheels so that a ticklish floral curtain hung across her midriff, concealing everything from her view, presumably to save her and Mr Cannon's blushes. The nurse then laid a hot towel over an array of steel torture instruments, *to take off the chill, dear*. After she withdrew, Mr Cannon came in by the same door and sat behind the curtain to get busy with his ghastly toolkit. Pip thought she knew what to expect, having eavesdropped on an older woman in the university library, so was ready to be unpleasantly opened up and probed. She knew it would be embarrassing and was resigned to the idea that it might hurt.

A grim-faced mother of three in the waiting room had asked her who she was seeing then said,

'Oh, aye. Mr Cannon? He likes a tickle, does that one.'

This was alarming because Pip had always been extremely ticklish, and it was one of those things in life she had hated even as a child and now feared in case it made her widdle.

What Mr Cannon proceeded to do, however, all the while reaching for this device or that, was to stroke her Mary, or some part of it, in a way that sent uncontrollable shudders through her body and made it impossible to respond to his unbearably smooth small talk with anything more coherent than squeaks. It didn't hurt, it didn't tickle, but it made her feel entirely in his control, almost as though he had thrust his whole hand inside her to make her his pornographic glove puppet. It seemed to go on and on and, conscious of the genteel nurse on the other side of the door, she had to chew on the side of her index finger to stop herself crying out. She felt quite sure she had wet herself at least slightly, so it was surprising when he finally stopped what he was doing and stood up, taking off his rubber gloves with a practised *snappety-snap* that made her think of the Long Red-legged Scissorman.

He returned to his room without a word and the nurse returned to *pop* her out from behind the ridiculous curtain, off the stirrups and back into her clothes. When she returned to his consulting room, it was as though he were playing a curious game, all doctorly urbanity and patronage again, disassociating himself entirely from the man who had just made her so lose control.

His good news that she was expecting had made her so entirely happy, and he seemed so genuinely pleased to be telling her, that she left his office lightheaded and feeling a little drunk, and was promptly swept up on one of the tides of powerful joy she could never describe to Mike without alarming him.

She bought herself flowers for the dining table to celebrate; *narcissi: 1 shilling.* She easily lost the brief unpleasantness within the joy, and it only resurfaced when she had to be driven to the maternity hospital after the birth to be stitched. All the way there she worried it would be Mr Cannon who wielded the needle, but it was a marvellous female obstetrician, a sort of utterly fearless aunt, sternly kind, who said that her surviving baby was perfect and that there was nothing that could have been done about her brother.

'People will tell you to forget him,' she said. 'You can't do that. Ridiculous idea. But I'm afraid it will make people uncomfortable if you talk about him. You've given him a name, though, and that's good. It means he was here and will always be in your heart.'

And Pip *was* good and didn't talk about him, spoke only of Henrietta and the joy of her, but privately decided she would tell Henrietta about him when she was old enough to understand. She knew twins formed powerful bonds in the womb and worried it might be damaging to her if she was not told, like feeling a phantom limb. Naming him would give her an invisible friend, if not quite an imaginary one.

Nearly two years on, Pip had missed her period, and Henry's visits were usually so regular she could leave little red crayon dots in her diary, so she knew when to avoid anything too energetic. Also her breasts felt fuller, almost pendulous when she bent to pull on her shoes, which she knew was a sign, and when she forced herself to take a long hard look at them in the bathroom mirror she had to admit that her nipples and the circles around them, were darker than usual, and more pronounced, as though someone had outlined them with a make-up pencil.

The timing could not have been worse, as it had just been confirmed that Mike was to get his first prison governorship, of HMP The Verne at Portland, many hours' drive away, but surely a much healthier place to raise children than smoky Wakefield, with its mills and mines. There would be the upheaval of moving from a house she felt they had only just made a home, and the task of decorating and finding enough furniture for the governor's house, which would be thrice the size. Prisons had work parties of trusties, she knew, who could help with this task and that, but she knew from watching her mother's repeated battles as they were moving from prison to prison growing up that it was a matter of constant negotiation with the prison commissioners to have any improvements made or budgets approved.

People who said how wise it was to get one's childbearing done in a tidy cluster with two-year gaps – Mike wanted just two children, while she secretly dreamed of at least four – did not have jobs involving a change of house, schools and everything that went with it, every five years. With the plans for the move requiring attention, and the added kerfuffle of having Cowboy Grandpa to stay for two whole weeks as well as having Mike's best man and his new wife to visit, Pip was childishly tempted to ignore the symptoms. But she knew, could feel it bubbling through her, and understood it was all part of the rapture she had felt at the sunshine and the still ungrimed leaves fluttering on the trees as she pushed the pram along.

She had said nothing to Mike yet, as he would roll his eyes and say something like,

'Dear God, do you think I'm made of money?'

She simply rang the hospital to make an appointment.

'I really don't mind who I see,' she told them, throwing out the name of the fearless aunt obstetrician like a protective spell, but the receptionist fiddled with her index cards and said,

'I've got you down under Mr Cannon.'

'Yes,' Pip heard herself twittering in her cowardice. 'But I truly, honestly, don't mind seeing someone else.'

The receptionist was relentless.

'Best stick with Mr Cannon,' she said, 'as he knows your history.'

So there she was, back in the same waiting room, with different but similar exhausted women with dirty hair and whining children, and the very same genteel nurse, talking to her as though she were mentally deficient, leading her next door to strip off again and get into the ghastly chair with the stirrups. Usually, she found dreading things sufficiently meant that they were never so bad as feared. In this case it was worse.

When she admitted that, yes, she had, as he put it, been visiting the Little Girl's Room more often than usual, he asked her again how many days it was since her missed period, and she admitted it was nearly four weeks.

'Would you say there was any change in your breasts?' he asked, and when she stammered that, yes, they felt fuller and she thought their middles looked darker, he broke off from whatever he had been doing to her with his considerately warmed tools and rose so that he was standing between her parted legs with the stupid curtain thing across his middle like a skirt. 'Show me,' he asked.

She couldn't bear to meet his eye, so she turned her head and obediently tugged down her bra. It was a clean one, she had made sure of that, and she made herself examine the radiator, the sickly-green paint on the wall and the faded reproduction of an extremely beautiful Lippi annunciation hanging above the radiator while he handled both her breasts at once in his gloved hands and asked her quite sharply,

'Is this tender?' as he pressed his thumb and fingers around both her nipples, to which she could only nod meekly in reply, because actually it was quite painful but also rather good, in just the same way having a baby suckle them had felt.

He hummed to himself and disappeared back behind the curtain and, hot in the face, she was mid-way through fumbling her breasts back into her bra, which was difficult when lying down, when he started doing to her the thing he had done before, sending the unwanted, uncontrolled tremors through her body, waves almost.

'Please,' she began, then had to break off and, once again, bite her hand to keep the noise in. She actually heard the nurse discreetly clearing her throat from next door, quite as though sending him a signal. She looked back at the angel in the reproduction, looked at its exquisitely delicate robes, like something spun from rainbow, gossamer and the thinnest gold wire. She may even have prayed a little, though she had been sternly told by Mike once that angels could not receive prayers as they were merely manifestations of divine intelligence, God's thoughts, in fact.

Then Mr Cannon stopped at last, taking off his gloves, *snappety-snap*, and leaving her bathed in sweat like a labouring mare.

'Poor love,' the nurse said once she had unstirruped her. 'It is warm in here. It's not just you,' and handed her first a blessedly cold, wet flannel then a soft, dry towel.

'The signs are all good,' he told her, when she was back in his consulting room, both of them restored to respectability. 'Your scars from the last birth are barely visible and all looks healthy and welcoming.'

'Oh,' she said uncertainly, unable to meet his eye. 'Good.'

'But, to be certain, I would wait a couple of weeks, a month even, until you have definitely missed a second period before telling anyone. I hate to encourage deceit between husband and wife, but I also dislike fostering false hope.'

Again, she caught the bus home, feeling almost sick from her conflicting emotions: joy at the more or less confirmation of another baby, however inconvenient, shame and confusion at the things the doctor had done to her, which she could tell nobody. She wanted to buy flowers again, to celebrate – *lilac and hyacinths: 1s 6d* – but that would mean telling Mike the happy news, which she had been instructed not to do and which, anyway, might not make him happy. Instead, she impulsively stopped at the sweet shop to buy four ounces of dark chocolate ginger, which they both liked immensely.

She was not a naturally good cook – she lacked the patience, and her hands were too warm for handling pastry – but, luckily, Mike was not a *bon viveur* so she had been working her way through the less alarming recipes in the *Good Housekeeping Cookery Book* one of the women at the library had given her along with tried and tested favourites of her mother's – brains aside – which she carefully copied into the blank pages at the back.

Tonight, she made him a shepherd's pie, which she seemed to have mastered and which he liked, with cheap lamb cuts she had put through the green metal mincer she clamped to the table and then enriched with a stock cube and a bottle of Guinness. Mummy had taught her that mince – beef or lamb – always tasted better for being cooked in advance and left overnight to thicken up in the fridge, so all she had to do once she got home was make some mashed potato and spread it over the cold mince before creating pretty ridges over it with a fork.

TWENTY

She returned home to noisy chaos. She could hear Henrietta wailing even before she had her key in the lock and, as she opened the door, realised children were screaming and Mrs Coley shouting and swearing while Susie was producing her most thunderous growls. Expecting the worst, that the visiting children might have tormented the dog in some way, as ignorant children could, making her lash out, she hurried towards the noise.

It was coming from the bright, small room they called the nursery, where the baby had a downstairs cot and all the gifted and hand-me-down toys she had yet to grow into. There was a pretty old button-back armchair in there, where Pip sat to nurse her, and it was where, for lack of space elsewhere downstairs, she kept her old upright piano and a bookcase full of sheet music. Keen to pass on her love of music and old songs, she often sat the baby on her lap at the piano now and played and sang to her from a pretty book of folk songs illustrated by Kate Greenaway.

There was a lady loved a swine.
Honey, said she.
There was a lady loved a swine.
Honk, said he.

Mrs Coley was standing in the nursery doorway sweating profusely and waving the broom like a blunt lance.

'Horrible dog,' she shouted. 'Horrible. Nasty German thing! You let them go. Go on!'

Susie was between her and the shrieking, cowering children, who were either side of the cot where the baby, perhaps sensing her mother was suddenly near, had begun to bawl. Susie was baring her teeth and really snarling, her aggression entirely for Mrs Coley.

'Mrs Coley, stop. Please, stop! You're making it worse,' Pip cried, and knelt beside her. 'Susie, come.'

The dog immediately stopped growling and bounded over to paw and lick her, tail wagging, proud of a job well done. The children raced to their grandmother, noisily hysterical. Pip tried to explain.

'She was defending you, sillies. She thought you were sheep and Granny a fierce wolf come to eat you.'

The children were not to be so easily teased out of their drama and continued to screech and whinge as though she had taken a strap to them. Mrs Coley was having none of it and stalked off, wrapping herself in high dudgeon along with her summer coat and headscarf. Pip couldn't ring her to apologise as Mrs Coley wasn't on the phone and she couldn't walk round to apologise in person, as she had come to them through a recommendation in church and Pip had only a vague idea of where she lived.

Henrietta was swiftly appeased, at least, by another outing in her pram with the disgraceful dog. As she walked them, Pip's irritation increased. Susie, she felt sure, was quite blameless and had been provoked in some way even before the stupid woman started waving a broom at her and shouting. Mrs Coley was taking shameless advantage bringing her grandchildren to work, both of whom should surely have been in school by now, and had probably eaten as many biscuits as their grandmother invariably did. (Pip had overheard her once actually telling them to *stock up* when opening the tin for them.)

'She's not a very good cleaner,' she told Mike over supper, which didn't feel nearly as festive as she had hoped, because the lamb was too fatty or she had made too much gravy, and the potato on the shepherd's pie had turned unappetisingly gloopy rather than crisping up to the gold it always turned when her mother made it. 'She wipes rather than dusting properly and I'm always having to go over the bits she can't reach, like the top of the tallboy, because she's so short. Anyway, I fear she's mortally offended or frightened by poor Susie, and that's that, as I don't know where she lives so I can't write her a chocolate please-come-back letter.'

'I can,' Mike said unexpectedly.

'How?'

'Her husband's an officer at the prison. I can get her a letter care of him. But we can't keep a dog who's going to attack children.'

'She didn't! She was defending them from Mrs Bloody Coley.'

'And she's eating us out of house and home.'

'I've told you. We should feed her dog food.'

'It's filthy stuff. It would give her diarrhoea.'

'Or tripe. That's cheap.'

'Do you really want to stink the place out boiling tripe for her? Boiling nappies are bad enough.'

Pip felt the situation and conversation slip out of her control. She wasn't at all sure losing Mrs Coley wasn't a disguised blessing. She was a poor cleaner, had a sour disposition and was never going to become a dependable rock the way some of her mother's charladies had.

Pip cleared away the shepherd's pie, feeling more than ever like some caricature domestic failure in a magazine advertisement when Mike politely declined the offer of a second helping. She brought in Stilton and some ripe pears, which she knew he liked. If she had already felt far from tempted to go against Mr Cannon's advice and tell Mike about the new baby, she felt even less so when it emerged he had completely forgotten that she was going to her parents for the weekend then bringing her mysterious grandfather to stay for two whole weeks while they took their holiday in Scotland.

'But what about Titus and Dagmar?'

'They're only coming for supper, I thought.'

'I think they're expecting to stay the night. They're making a sort of royal progress to mark their wedding.'

'Well, Cowboy Grandpa is only a little old man,' she said. 'We can make up the single bed in Henrietta's room and bring her cot in with us for that night. Don't look so worried, darling!'

She laughed. He had a way of wrinkling his brow as though the slightest domestic challenge was a crisis. It made her see at once how he must have looked at five, in a sailor suit, and being sent away to board by his unnatural mother, and it made her love him all over again. She reached out a playful hand to smooth the worry from his brow, but he misunderstood and thought he had somehow got shepherd's pie up in his hairline.

'What?' he asked. 'Have I . . .?' He fussed with his napkin and the tender moment was lost. 'My bank statement comes tomorrow,' he told her. 'Could you leave the accounts book on my desk for me to check against it?'

'Oh, Mike, do we have to?'

'Don't be silly,' he said. 'Of course we do, darling. Money doesn't look after itself.'

TWENTY-ONE

As they took their leave after the weekend in Liverpool, Pip's mother had slipped her a little pamphlet she had picked up there of the story of Bolton Priory, saying the site lay roughly halfway to Wakefield so would make the ideal spot to stretch their legs, feed Henrietta and eat a picnic beside the ruins.

'It's so pretty,' she said. 'Breathtaking, really, especially if this weather holds.' She had kissed the baby one more time, hugged Pip with a 'Bye, darling,' freighted with far more meaning than the words suggested and, after a hesitation, added, 'Bye-bye, Father,' and hugged the old man, who was hovering on the edge of their loving, exclaiming circle, as he seemed to have been all weekend.

Only knowing him from old photographs, Pip had been irrationally shocked by his age at first and struggled to find any family likeness until he laughed aloud on meeting his great-granddaughter, who obliged him with one of her coyest smiles, and then she realised her mother had inherited his infectious laugh.

And then there was his voice. She knew he was Canadian, not American, but to her untuned ears American was what he sounded, like the GIs they had sometimes met on school trips during the war or the men she had quietly adored in the cinema all her life. And she wished they had never got into the habit of nicknaming him Cowboy Grandpa, to differentiate him from their altogether more sedate and respectable grandfather in Newmarket, because he clearly wasn't a cowboy and was insulted by the term. He was utterly exotic to her and also somehow sad. His lack of teeth didn't help – giving him a crestfallen, ancient look in repose.

Her one errand on the trip, other than taking him off her parents' hands and driving him back to Wakefield and a series of Yorkshire excursions, was to drive him into town to Mr Eade to be fitted with his new false teeth. She found Liverpool utterly bewildering in which to drive, but her mother had marked the dentist's address with a pencilled X on a roadmap of the city and Grandpa Harry, as she decided to call him in an effort to quell the urge to call him Cowboy, proved an expert map reader, if rather laconic and slow with each stage of instructions.

'I'm used to a horse and cart, dear,' he told her, which made them both laugh.

She wished her mother could see him with teeth. Quite suddenly the ghost of his youthful beauty was restored now his cheeks were no longer unsupported, even though the new brilliance of his smiles took a little getting used to. She felt in this one small measure his dignity had been returned, and resolved to take plenty of pictures of him during his visit.

Trained by her father, who had seen to it that both his girls were calmly capable drivers – although he could persuade neither of them to venture further beneath a bonnet than to check the dipstick for oil before any long drive – she had applied to the AA for their recommended route when her parents first moved to Liverpool, and she kept it between the relevant pages of her road atlas. Grandpa Harry pored over this, and the small diversion off it they would require to reach Bolton Abbey, then declared himself ready and they set off. Pip apologised for the car not being as smart as her parents'. It was a pre-war Morris 8 with which they had frugally replaced the contrary bull-nosed Morris in which Mike and she had valiantly toured to the Pyrenees and back on their honeymoon. Harry declared it charming, although it was so small and low it would be a relief to get out of the city and away from looming lorries.

Pip loved driving – far more so than Mike, whose eyesight was poor and who had only learned very approximately by driving a tank in the war. Mike regarded anything mechanical as out to get him, whereas with a steering wheel in her hands Pip invariably felt herself freer and more capable. She loved the moment when she slipped into the soft driving shoes she kept in a bag under the seat and pulled on the driving gloves she kept in the glove compartment along with the road atlas and a tin of humbugs. She could feel Grandpa Harry appraising her as she drove.

'You're making me self-conscious,' she told him.

'Sorry,' he said. 'You go straight over this roundabout. It's just there's always something compelling about watching a person do something confidently, whether they're splitting logs or playing the piano.'

'Oh, I play the piano, but I suspect I drive better than I play since this one arrived. I don't seem to have the time to practise and learn new pieces, so you're more likely to hear selections from Ivor Novello from me than Chopin, apart from the easiest waltzes and preludes.'

'I think you'd have made a fine pioneer.'

'Do women not drive in Saskatchewan?'

'Oh, they do now, I dare say. The few that are left. I never saw the point. The horse was fast enough for me.'

'How peaceful!'

She suggested he dig out the humbugs because she felt like one and her mother's bacon and eggs had been an age ago. They reached the AA's approved route and continued in happy, sucking silence, broken only by the baby's occasional cooing – she liked driving too – or by Harry's occasional murmured instructions.

It had been a lovely weekend – time out of time, in which she felt cosseted and spoilt with every compliment paid to Henrietta and temporarily suspended in parental love from all the things that had been worrying her still when she set off. For she had left Wakefield in rather a temper with poor Mike for his having forgotten about Grandpa and with poor Susie for being so hard to control when she had one hand on a pram and there were squirrels or other dogs at which to lunge.

Whistle had been on good form, too, excited at the prospect of going to stay with grand cousins and attend a regimental dance with them. She forgot to be bored by babies, conceding that Henrietta was a dear little thing now she was sitting up and gurgling and fixing any who came close with her keenly intelligent gaze. They enjoyed sisterly time in each other's rooms while their parents and grandfather enjoyed the baby, and then, after lunch on Sunday, there was the great dressing-up session for which Whistle let Pip brush out her lovely blonde hair and put it up in a chignon before dressing her in a breathtaking pistachio silk ball gown of Great-Aunt Pattie's their mother swore blind was Worth, or perhaps Vionnet, but was certainly exquisitely handmade in Paris for Pattie.

Whistle had worried it would reek of mothballs or be stained or simply look antique, but it fitted her perfectly except in the bosom, where it needed a few handkerchiefs to round her out convincingly. Pip completed the look with their great grandmother's double rope of pearls, filched from their mother's jewellery box, and ivory ballet pumps – a characteristically impractical choice insisted on by Whistle. On an impulse, Pip then cut and dethorned a pure white rose for her to hold, so that she looked like one of the Edwardian studio portraits to which their great-aunts had been so addicted.

The adults broke out in spontaneous applause when Whistle appeared downstairs, and she glowed in their admiration, walking back and forth on the sunny terrace outside the sitting-room windows while Pip took photographs of her. For once, Whistle seemed to forget her usual fear that prisoners were ogling her from their windows and, when she stopped taking pictures simply to gaze, Pip felt suddenly matronly, freshly aware of a waistline and chest she was sure were already visibly expanding and freshly reminded that she had not married a handsome hussar who could whirl her round a ballroom like well-dressed gossamer, but a shy, clever man who could barely waltz and swore, rather than apologising, when he trod on her feet as they circled a room and turned at corners.

She welled up. Whistle saw and laughed and hugged her in a sort of sweet triumph, recognising the power of her youth and beauty. Their grandfather grew misty-eyed, too, because, although he had never seen the dress, having left for the prairies long before Pattie attained French respectability, he recognised the pearls he had given their grandmother on their honeymoon in Venice. Everyone was agreed, though, that Whistle's looks came not from the Wells clan but from their father's late mother, a creamy-skinned English rose who had died in his childhood, so was known only from photographs his mercifully kind stepmother must have looked over in awe.

Father had been drinking heavily all weekend, even by his standards, noisily funny and comically obstreperous by turns, wilfully derailing any attempts to be serious for long about anything. Pip remembered Mike telling her there had been an execution of two young men recently, so she was extra sweet to him, feeding him the cues for funny stories she knew he told well and humouring his usually maddening way of insisting on reading things out from his paper or book. At the height of his jollity, on the Saturday night, he not only played his adored Louis Armstrong records but, against their mother's protests, dug out a terrible, suggestive 78 from the 1930s called 'My Girl's Pussy', whose words Pip had learned by heart and passed on to the girls at school, causing uproar.

There had been much talk about the Coronation, and how insufferable friends and acquaintances with televisions were being already, quite as though they had invitations to the Abbey and not some intrusive device demanding attention in their sitting rooms. Pip started to say she and Mike could be installed at the Verne by then, where he was threatening to rent them a television especially for the big week, although she liked the radio, she said, liked the way the announcers and the music helped you paint a vivid, moving picture in your head while leaving you free to knit or read a book or make a cake, or just gaze out of the window.

'The cinema's different, I think, because the screen is so big, but it must be dreadful for your eyes to stare at such a tiny picture, and don't those tubes inside give out rays that can hurt you if you sit too close?'

She had then become aware of an awkward atmosphere. Later, washing up with her mother, she heard that it had been decided to send Grandpa Harry *home* again before the Coronation.

'He hasn't a bean, really, poor love,' Mummy said, pretending she needed to wipe steam off her glasses with a tea towel, but clearly terribly upset. 'Daddy has sorted out his pension for him, which is a huge relief, but apparently it isn't transferable, so he had to be living in Canada again to claim it.' They had paid for his liner ticket, on the *Ascania*, but couldn't afford to send him in much style.

'Well, he shared a cabin with a stranger on the way over and didn't seem to mind much.'

'Yes, but I think this ticket is for a class below even that, whatever that involves. No porthole, maybe?'

'Oh dear.'

Then Mother had a little weep, which was so unlike her that Pip stopped washing up to hug her with hot, soapy arms and rock her a little from side to side, and when Whistle joined them, Pip sang, 'See me dance the polka,' and pretended they had been dancing and being silly, because Whistle was so very sensitive and everyone needed her to be strong and brave and happy about going to stay with the well-heeled and rather terrifying cousins in the south.

So, bundled into the car with a picnic lunch Mother had got up early to make, Pip found she was driving her grandfather to Wakefield in the spirit she imagined one might jolly along a child soon to be left at boarding school, and talking about anything but Canada or, indeed, the Coronation, which seemed to be standing in for everything that might be cowardly or underhand in the family not taking this elderly relative in.

They made the short detour to reach Bolton Abbey, where Harry, who had been managing to read the pamphlet without it making him carsick, pointed out that it was important to realise that, while the place name was Bolton Abbey, the magnificent half-ruin in its heart was properly Bolton Priory, 'because it was an Augustinian foundation'.

'Mike would be proud of you.'

'Is he interested in church history?'

'His father and grandfather were priests, and he reads pamphlets like that in bed,' she said, at which her grandfather giggled. 'You can guide us,' she added. 'I love being guided and told what everything is; it's soothing.'

When they stopped the car, Henrietta was briefly

furious at being woken up, but soon calmed down at being bundled into her mother's arms and cooed at for how pretty she looked in the new, very Kate Greenaway sun bonnet her Aunt Whistle had given her. Pip carried one bag of picnic on her spare arm and Harry brought the other and slung the picnic rug over one shoulder in a vaguely Scottish fashion.

'The author, Mr Raistrick, recommends we approach through the famous Hole in the Wall,' he said, and led them through a ragged breach in a massive, buttressed wall, which ran alongside the road down the hill. On the other side, they paused to take in the spectacular view of the priory ruins on a bend of the river, with the rectory just in front of them. 'Those are the monks' old fishponds,' Harry said as they passed some deep hollows in the meadow. 'And this rather lovely building is the rectory from 1700 but including an older portion that was part of the priory infirmary. Apparently, there's a fine fireplace and chimney by the gate, left over from a guesthouse. Oh. That's it, I guess. Do you want to hear everything?'

'Maybe just the highlights,' she said. 'Isn't it lovely?'

'It is, rather.'

Perhaps because it was a weekday, they had the priory all to themselves, though she expected coach parties would arrive later.

'That looks lived in,' she said, indicating a large house constructed from the picturesque ruins of a towered archway across the lawns.

'Mr Raistrick says . . .' He consulted the little pamphlet

again. 'It's a residence and shooting lodge of the Duke of Devonshire.'

They approached the church, admiring the large, square outline of the ruined cloister, then passing through an elegant arch and incongruous garden gate into what would have been the south transept, where she was briefly transfixed by the hypnotically interlaced arches of the choir arcading before catching up with her grandfather, who had set down the rug and picnic the better to gaze up at the emptied tracery of the windows.

'Mr Raistrick says that one is *flamboyant*,' he told her, gesturing to a stunning example on the south side of the choir. 'Is that an architectural style, or is he turning Yorkshire scorn on its design?'

'You'll have to ask Mike. Just be warned: he *will* tell you.'

The sun was deliciously warm on her bare legs and the baby, who had fallen asleep again, felt suddenly much heavier in that irrational way babies seemed to when they relaxed and gave you their dead weight. 'Shall we picnic here?' she asked. 'Is that allowed? Are you hungry?'

'I don't see anyone here to disapprove,' he said, and spread the rug on the ground for her.

She lowered herself, lying Henrietta on her tummy on the rug before tugging off her suede driving shoes, which she had forgotten to change out of when they left the car. Henrietta began to explore the rug and nearby daisies and grass with her fingers, dribbling happily.

While Pip sunned herself, Harry set about opening the various little packages her mother had wrapped very neatly in the greaseproof paper and paper bags she smoothed out and saved in a drawer after every shopping trip. There were ham sandwiches with slices of her father's delicious tomatoes, four boiled eggs with a tiny packet of celery salt to dip them in, a wrinkled apple each and a slice of fruit cake. And her mother had filled the Thermos with icy lemon barley water. Henrietta showed no interest in her bottle yet, so Pip joined Harry in eating, leaning back on a convenient piece of ancient, sun-warmed masonry.

'You don't really think he's boring, do you?' he asked.

'Who?'

'Mike?'

'Gosh no. How awful. Did I sound as though I did? No, he's just very clever and well-read compared to me and I suppose I tease him, even when he's not here, to feel less stupid. We're quite a teasy family.'

'You are, aren't you?' he said, and laughed. 'But I like it. It reminds me of your grandmother and her sisters, though en masse they could be intimidating. She was much the kindest and sweetest of the bunch. I'm hardly educated, either, you know.'

'Really?'

'I mean, I went to school, but I never learned much, and I left at eighteen and wasn't encouraged to carry on. Jack did, of course, to become a vet, but I was a bit useless, really.'

'I'm sure you weren't.'

'Oh, I was. It wasn't until I started homesteading that I knew the meaning of work and began to feel I could achieve anything. What's Mike like, then?'

She laughed nervously, taken aback at the directness of the question.

'Well . . .' she began. 'He can seem very serious – he is very serious – but he also has a very dry sense of humour. I like to think he's a bit like one of the kinder priests in Trollope, or Mr Knightly. He's very good. Not in a pious way, but I somehow knew the moment we first met that he was a man who would always put others first. He loves dogs and old widowed ladies, and he always shows an interest in people, even though he's terribly shy and has no small talk. Poor Mike. His idea of conversation is to interrogate people – fire off question after question at them – but afterwards the sad old lady or desperately dull vicar, or whoever it is, will always tell me, "Mike is such a good listener." I'm very glad you're coming to stay.'

'Well, so am I.'

'No, I mean because you can protect me.'

'Whoever from?'

'Mike's best man, Titus, who is coming to stay too. He's lovely. Very clever and handsome, just like Mike, but I'm always a bit shy and silly around him because they've known each other since they were boys and fought in the same regiment in the war, and I think all the people around Mike thought he would marry Titus's lovely sister, only I suspect she's far too clever for him and he preferred an ignorant clot like me. Titus – that's just a nickname – is bringing his much older new wife, who's Norwegian and a criminologist or something brainy, and bound to be very worldly as well as clever, but now I can hide behind you.'

'I'll protect you. I knew several Scandinavians in the

prairies. Some Danes are delightful, and some Norwegians too. And, yes, they can be very direct. But in your condition, I bet she'll be like a sister and wait on you hand and foot.'

'M-my . . .?' she stammered. She had told nobody.

'I'm sorry. I can be a bit spooky sometimes and can just tell. My friends in the Cree used to say I should have been a medicine man or a shaman.'

'It's not official yet,' she said. 'I haven't even told Mike. The doctor said not to. I mean the gynae—' Unshed tears choked her, and she broke up. 'I'm so sorry,' she managed. 'Bally hormones all over the place. Oh, poppet, don't worry!'

Henrietta had begun to cry, as though sensing an abrupt change in mood, and Pip scooped her up, needing the comfort of her warmth suddenly, and for a few minutes they cried messily together, until she offered the baby her bottle again and was gratified to find her hungry this time, her tiny hands resting on Pip's as she held it in place.

'He's an evil man,' she heard herself say, unexpectedly. 'Mr Cannon.'

'Is that your . . .?'

She nodded.

'How is he evil?' Harry was meticulously peeling one of the apples with his penknife, the tired peel snaking off in one long coil. It was like a magic trick.

'Oh, I'm probably just being silly.'

'I doubt that,' he said, and his eyes, she saw, were just the same china-doll blue as her mother's.

'He touches me in ways that . . .' she started, then

shuddered violently and pulled herself up just in the time. 'Well, none of them can be entirely right,' she suggested. 'Choosing to specialise in a thing like that. There's a very nice, wise woman at the clinic as well. Sometimes, though, I think having a woman down there would be even worse. I'm terrified of lesbians! Women prison officers. Traffic wardens. So silly. There was a games mistress at our school, Miss Vaughan, with hair like two iron buns and hands like a roadmender, and we used to joke about her, which was probably very cruel and silly of us. Little girls can be vile. But she was the stuff of nightmares. And ever since then . . . Oh!'

The baby brought up a little sick and looked faintly outraged as Pip mopped it up with one of the old napkins she kept for the purpose.

Harry passed her the peeled apple in chunks, one of which she gave the baby to suck, and began to peel the second one.

'What do you want to do in Yorkshire?' she asked him. 'Wakefield's pretty tough, but there are lovely places we can drive to nearby. York's not so very far and there are beautiful walks, and Mike will want to show you any number of ruins and distinguished churches.'

He smiled at her with a new look that she realised was kindness, or even pity, and something deep within her was riled, used as she was to being the strong one, the resilient daddy's girl.

TWENTY-TWO

The schoolfriend, Vivvy, who had Pip to stay with her parents in Dartmouth and who had taken her on all those glamorous and flirtatious outings with naval officers, the one she instinctively thought of as awful and who she had brutally scratched out of the address book when she and Mike were writing their first Christmas cards as a married couple, had been a proper friend once.

The awful label had been acquired by degrees. At their little school, which had been friendly but ineffectual, they had become firm friends when all girls must have one special friend. Then, with wartime evacuation, the friendship intensified with much sharing of secrets at just the point where Pip began to feel they had less and less in common.

On Armistice night, as the eldest, a group of them was allowed out with one of the younger, giddier teachers to join in the public celebration in the nearest small East Anglian town. Shy of the drunk crowds, especially all the men, Pip had rather clung to the teacher, probably cramping her style, but Vivvy had shocked her by fairly flinging herself at a pair of GIs and laughed in their room later at how she had let them both kiss her and how one had clasped her hand to rub it against his uniformed erection.

After they both secured their school certificates and left shortly after that, she had Vivvy home to Durham on a visit.

There were no GIs, of course, though she did ask a lot of questions about the prisoners and how much they could see of the garden and house from their cells. She behaved perfectly well, otherwise, and they explored Durham together and went to the cinema and a grown-up dinner party, but otherwise her mother let slip oddly pointed comments about the girl being *advanced for her age* and *a bit sharp* and Pip found herself agreeing, disloyally distancing herself at last with a kind of relief.

She had begun to put her quite out of her mind, consumed as she was first by the job she landed assisting at the university library, and then by the dizzying business of being wooed and then engaged to Mike, when Vivvy's invitation to pay a return visit to her came through. Fond though she was already becoming of Mike, her mother was concerned about Pip marrying a man ten years her senior when she had seen so little of the world. As soon as she knew that Vivvy's father was a commodore and that the visit would involve plentiful but respectable socialising, her mother abruptly withdrew her reservations about the girl's suitability as a friend and urged Pip to go. Perhaps she had been testing the strength of the engagement – guessing the socialising would involve young, unmarried officers. Perhaps she simply wanted Pip to be more informed about the choices she could make and avenues she could choose. Pip was to have an innocent enough adventure and return to Durham and the engagement as an act of adult choice and not in girlish innocence.

The Commodore and his wife – a well-upholstered, tanned, immensely comfortable woman called Diana – were a welcoming delight. They said they felt they already knew Pip from all Vivvy's letters home from school and had long regarded her as a steadying influence.

'Vivvy can be giddy,' Diana said.

Vivvy said her mother had done something hush-hush in the war and could kill a man with a biro. There was little common ground between them, little love lost and very little attempt to disguise the want of warm feeling. Diana regarded her daughter with distaste, the commodore regarded her with bafflement. They spoke only briefly of Vivvy's engagement, with undisguised relief.

Pip's long walks and conversations with Mike had raised her intellectual and cultural standards, as had her quiet months of working in the library, and she was surprised to find herself seeing Vivvy with new eyes. Her friend had always been bossy and controlling, but now she seemed actively coarse, and without any discernible inner life. There was a devilry to her that remained compelling and Pip soon noticed that, while Vivvy was by far the bolder in dancing and drinking and answering back any cheek from the men she drew around them, she set off Pip to advantage as, simply by juxtaposition, she made her seem quiet and thoughtful. This, in turn, meant that Pip drew the attention of quiet, thoughtful men, who were the sort she secretly preferred.

One such was her escort for the evening when they were invited to dine in the officers' mess on board a battleship. He was called Oliver Anstruther. He was tall and blond, with kind grey eyes, a dusting of gold hair around his watch strap and thick, humorous eyebrows she longed to stroke. Amidst all the noisy chatter, and despite Vivvy's raucousness, he was attentive to her. She had come to realise attention was important. Mike was attentive too, sometimes stolidly so, not always following when she was being fanciful or flighty for the fun of it. In the Jane Austen novels she had come to love through his recommendation, and regular gifts of them, the most romantic moment was always when the serious, older hero seemed not only truly to see the heroine at last, but to pay her close attention. Oliver had been reading Greats at Oxford when the war broke out and, as a former Pangbourne boy, had unthinkingly enlisted in the navy, and now found it meant more to him than returning to complete his studies.

'I still read Virgil for comfort,' he admitted, 'and Cicero, when I need something bracing.'

Pip was honest at once about being engaged to Mike, but it made him no less attentive. There was dancing after dinner, and he held her close, didn't step on her feet, and murmured witty observations close in her ear, which felt more intimate than kissing.

'You smell delicious,' he sighed, and instead of demurely saying *thank you* she stupidly told him,

'That's the Floris Rose Geranium in my bath and Yardley's Bond Street afterwards . . .' which made him chuckle and say,

'How thorough.'

He smelled of very clean laundry and Bay Rum, which her father also used. He drove the little launch that took them back to shore in the moonlight and she felt so woozily romantic she was filled with grateful, guilty affection for Vivvy and resolved to be less stiff and goody-goody around her.

She wrote an excited letter home, all about Oliver and enclosing a tin of American coffee for her mother and smart new pyjamas for her father from the Senior Service Stores. Oliver and another young officer picked them up in his Triumph sports car that afternoon to take them to a tennis club and, two nights after that, Oliver and yet another officer squired them to a dance. Pip was shameless, as she was hundreds of miles from home and no one but Vivvy knew her, and she danced with nobody else all evening, prompting Vivvy to leer at her when they briefly retreated to powder their noses, and shock her by saying,

'I won't breathe a word to Mike if you keep schtum with Kenneth.'

They both had a lot to drink, and this made her lean on Oliver rather heavily as they danced, which perhaps he misinterpreted, as suddenly he was kissing her, which felt thrilling and wrong at once. She lurched off the dance floor in need of fresh air and he followed her onto a terrace, which seemed to be a kind of lovers' lane as paired cigarette glows and sighs and laughter revealed couples in the darkness on every side. Oliver apologised, sighed heavily several times and mumbled,

'It's all such a godawful mess,' or some such repeatedly before driving her home in silence, Vivvy having made other arrangements. He apologised again on the doorstep, and she apologised as well for having been silly and he all but clicked his heels in respectful farewell and looked so devastating in his uniform and the moonlight as she closed the front door that she hurried to her room, weeping like a lovesick ninny.

Sitting on her bed, still dizzy from drink, she brushed her hair thirty times on either side and felt she had just made some kind of sacrifice and rededicated herself to Mike, rather than behaving badly. She found her writing case and wrote him one of her more rhapsodic letters, which she suspected would unnerve him and which she'd quite possibly shred come morning.

Vivvy came back very late and barged into her room on a cloud of Dubonnet and cigarettes and woke her up, asking with some urgency if she and Oliver had had a lovely evening. Sitting up in bed, fumbling for the bedside light switch, Pip pulled her dignity about her like a shawl and said they'd had a very nice time, thank you, but that he'd been a perfect gentleman and had driven her home once she had had enough.

'So you're n-not in love with him?' Vivvy stammered.

'Don't be daft, Vivvy. I'm engaged to Mike. Oliver's a lovely man, but . . . no!'

At this point, Vivvy broke down so noisily Pip worried she'd wake her parents, and confessed she was madly in love with him but was promised to Kenneth, who had much better prospects, and that she had hoped pushing him at Pip would cure her of her longing, but it hadn't.

'If anything, watching you dance together . . .' She broke off and started afresh. 'You're made for each other, you know. Everyone is saying so. An ideal couple, Mummy said, damn her. If anything, watching you dance only intensified my feelings.'

Flattered and rather thrilled by this, but also humiliated that her little adventure had actually been a piece of social manipulation, Pip felt suddenly sorry for silly, coarse Vivvy, who had made such a mess of things while she had stepped neatly back from the abyss and found herself still very much in love with Mike and longing to see him again.

'But surely you can break up with Kenneth? It's not too late. Your invitations haven't even gone out yet. Money isn't everything and your pa would be thrilled to see you marry a well-educated officer like Oliver.'

But then Vivvy shocked her by admitting she was carrying Oliver's child, though Kenneth thought it was his, and confessed further that her wedding to Kenneth was to be a private affair because he was under rather a cloud. He had killed a woman. Run her down with his car. It was an accident, and he hadn't been drinking much, though the poor woman had, apparently, and his parents had managed to keep it out of the papers or from going to court. Pip had never heard anything so appalling and found her heart racing at being made a party to such confidences. It confirmed the low opinion she had instinctively formed of Kenneth, who was so hard-boiled and charmless it was hard to believe a broken engagement would dent his self-belief nearly as much as being deceived over the paternity of a child.

'Poor Vivvy. Poor, poor girl,' she said, drawing the quilt over her not-really friend's shoulders and rocking her gently. By the time Vivvy finally stopped weeping and blew her nose and took herself off to bed, Pip felt much the older and wiser and happier of the two.

For what remained of the visit – and there were several days still to go – Vivvy was cold towards her, quite as though she were some friend of her mother's, not a confidante of her own, and Pip realised she bitterly regretted having confided things she could never unsay, and which would always lie between them. Her parents had clearly seen this sort of rude behaviour in her before and were kindness itself, arranging outings for Pip without Vivvy, trying to teach her bridge, taking her sightseeing. It became intolerable, and she told a fib and pretended Whistle was having one of her medical crises, so she was abruptly needed at home. Vivvy saw to it that she was not around to say an awkward goodbye.

Refusing to stoop to her level, Pip had made a point of inviting Vivvy and Kenneth to her wedding. They had given her an ugly hairbrush and hand mirror made from silver plate and Mike, who for all his goodness could be quietly catty when it was needed, gratified her by writing to her mother (who of course had copied it out for her in a letter of her own) that he found them *so sleek, patronising and prosperous that they were really rather intolerable.*

All these months later, sitting in the sun in a ruined priory, Pip worried that she had revealed too much to her grandfather just as Vivvy had to her. Not babies out of wedlock or a hit-and-run killing, but, in its way, just as destabilising. She watched Harry meticulously peeling the second apple. He had playfully wound the first peel round

Henrietta's edible dimpled arm and the child was fascinated by it, frowning at the way it flexed this way and that and curled about her skin.

Whatever were they going to talk about now? And how was she going to fill his days with distraction and entertainment for two whole weeks? Perhaps she could persuade Whistle to bring Mollie the dog to stay for the weekend – the two dogs adored one another and would provide the perfect excuse for lots of walks.

Harry smiled as he wound the second peel round the baby's other arm.

'Look!' he told her. 'Just look! You're an empress!' He started to eat a slice of the second apple then remembered he had new false teeth in. 'This new, dazzling smile will take some getting used to,' he said, and so precisely echoed the thought she'd entertained in the car that Pip laughed.

'They take years off you,' she said. 'Honestly.' And he looked at her with an understanding directness that disarmed her so that she feared she might cry again.

All weekend she had been trying to put her finger on what it was that made him different, and finally she realised it was that he didn't smoke. All the men she knew smoked, and the stink of it on their clothes and breath when they came close was indistinguishable in her mind from their maleness. Sometimes she thought the difference between the onscreen romances she so loved and reality was all in the smoking and teeth. Mike had superb cheekbones and good, black hair and could look film-star handsome in evening dress or in tweeds for a country walk and could deliver rectitude and heroic self-denial as well as

Jack Hawkins or Leslie Howard. But when Jack or Leslie smoked a pipe, the heroines never wrinkled their noses at the smell and ash, and when they were pictured at a bedside in decorous silk dressing gown and Jermyn Street pyjamas it was never without their teeth.

'People without secrets,' Harry said, 'are like people with very tidy houses: usually not worth knowing.'

And she remembered that he was being sent home, betrayed by them all, in only two weeks.

'There's so much I want to show you,' she said. 'And so little time.'

'In that case, we had better get our skates on,' he said, and rose with the agility of a far younger man and held out a hand to help her to her feet.

MIKE

TWENTY-THREE

Nothing had prepared Mike for how precious weekends would become: time away from the relentless demands of work, with wife and child and dog. As a boy, they had begun on Saturday afternoons and been merely the time when schooling didn't happen, but were never times for selfish pleasure as they were entirely given over to God, honouring him through charitable works on Saturday afternoons – visiting the less fortunate, visiting hospitals and alms-houses, usually with gifts of clothes or food – and attending Evensong, and honouring him in worship two or even three times on Sunday.

His sweet, otherworldly grandfather, who would otherwise have been an archaeologist, had been swept up as a history student and inspired by the Oxford Movement to break the family's centuries-old tradition of complacent land ownership to rent out house and lands, study theology instead and become a priest. He remained in Somerset and became a canon of Wells Cathedral, raising three children in Trollopian comfort and still finding time to become a distinguished amateur archaeologist. Mike's father had become a priest of a more severe cut and had distanced himself further still from the family's history by selling house and lands to take on a parish on far distant Romney Marsh.

Mike had been handed to a village wet nurse at birth and sent to a sternly Christian boarding school at just five, so his parents were figures he discovered by degrees and only in the school holidays. He was devoted to his older sisters and their mother was as round and merry as God allowed, but it was a household where every meal began with a solemn grace and every day ended with them and the servants kneeling around the dining table for family prayers. Lent was a reliably grim season, with sugar in all forms removed from their diet and each day closing with a slice of a forbidding confection called supper cake, whose lack of sugar and acrid, salty spiciness was designed to awaken a sense of the bitterness of sin.

It was small wonder, then, if Mike came to feel most unconstrainedly himself first at that little prep school, then at his public school and even more so at university, and especially in the company of dogs. He had always longed for a dog, been disarmed by the frank affection of them, the minor miracle of their singling one out with paw swat or invitingly dropped toy, but his parents preferred cats for their mousing and relative self-sufficiency and his sisters were quite uninterested, so he continued to long for a dog well after the age when his school friends had moved on to yearning for girls. Even as a student, reading Modern Greats at Oxford, his head stuffed with Corn Laws and the relative merits of the Reform Bills of 1867 and 1884, he would amuse his friends by breaking off mid-argument to cross a street to pet a dog tied up outside a shop or taking itself for a walk.

The declaration of war interrupted his studies, and he

enlisted along with most of his contemporaries and several of his lecturers, faintly baffled that the accidents of class and education made him an officer in command of men he always suspected were both braver and more battle-wise than he.

Mike was devoted to the men in his platoon, rather as his father and grandfather might have been to their parishioners, with the difference that he was prepared to die to save them. He was, he supposed, an instinctive Christian. Raised in an atmosphere and in institutions where not believing was as unthinkable as ceasing to take in air, he had packed a tiny lectionary and travel Bible in his kitbag and relied on the focus and silent observance of daily readings as a fragile thread of civilisation, first in the banality of officer training camp and then in the horrors and brutality in which he was called to participate and witness once they sailed to the theatres of war in North Africa and Europe. But, despite his lifelong Christian instruction and practice, he was surprised by the deep love he felt for his men and the unquestioning instinct to put himself in danger to keep them from it. He was mentioned in despatches and awarded an MC for an act of almost wild cunning and murderousness, in which he crawled ahead on his stomach through a wood in order to take out a three-man enemy-gun emplacement with a grenade, and two sentries with his sidearm. His passion for cricket made his grenade-throwing lethally calm and accurate. The men he so slaughtered were shockingly young. He saw their unlined faces and heard their laughing chatter before he struck, continued to see and hear them in his dreams for years to come. Killing them, though, was preferable to seeing the equally young men under his command mowed down by machine guns, as they surely would have been.

Dogs were a constant throughout Europe – robbed of their owners or homes by war, they would attach themselves to the nearest battalion in hope of food and treats and affection and many become temporary mascots, trotting alongside the men as they marched. He always reminded himself they had probably been temporarily adopted by the retreating enemy forces up ahead, and responded with the same heedless enthusiasm to German endearments as they did to English ones, bought from one loyalty to another with no more devious argument than a cold sausage or a hard-boiled egg.

The puppy was different. No canine refugee, she was formally presented to the platoon in the first, mildly hysterical and extremely drunken hours of the peace by the mayor of the little town from which they had routed the enemy just before the good news came down the line. The mayor sought out the most senior officer present, who happened to be Mike, shook his hand, all but kissed it, in fact, and solemnly handed him a snowy, black-pawed bundle he said was the pick of a litter born only days before.

'She will keep you safe as you have saved us,' he said in halting English.

Mike was so overcome by the relief of peace and the searing tin mug of local brandy he had just knocked back and then the sudden surprise of a tiny dog being thrust into his hands, that he didn't ask any of the questions of which he later thought, and soon lost sight of the mayor in the merry chaos breaking out on every side.

'Of course,' he felt he should say, 'she belongs to us all. She should go home with one of you who can give her a good life, someone with a farm and sheep, perhaps.' And the men said yes, yes, and made offers and suggestions, insisted she be called Susie for her one black eye. None followed through, however, and he soon found the puppy was his to feed, to lead on a rope and then to buy bowls, collar and proper leather lead for. Unhappy and homesick at first, she cried at night unless he took her into his bed and let her snuggle inside his pyjamas, and soon the whimpering ceased, and she bonded with him utterly. He found himself, now in his late twenties, and doubtless against any number of military regulations, unexpectedly the master of a small dog.

She did not stay small for long. She ate pounds of fish or meat each day and was soon identified for him by the vet he took her to after he was demobbed as a Pyrenean mountain dog.

Although a quiet, scholarly life suited his shy nature, he turned away from the place held open for him at Oxford, taking instead the honorary degree conferred without further examination on all veteran undergraduates. Following his father and grandfather into the church, which had once seemed likely, was impossible to him now, and only partly because of the innocent blood he felt the war had left on his hands. Inspired by the memory of a lecture by a prison governor given in his years as a teenager at Tonbridge, he entered the Prison Service. He was trained up, working with delinquent youths at the HMP Borstal, where he contracted double pneumonia from bitterly cold afternoons refereeing football matches, and no less bitter nights spent chasing young escapees along the railway tracks. Then he was promoted and came to Durham as deputy to Terry, which of course was how he met Pip.

All this while Susie grew in charm and boldness, indulged by a succession of landladies. Pip and Whistle adored her, spending happy hours brushing and teasing out her thick coat, producing buckets of loose hair each time, which nesting birds seized gratefully. He suspected it had been Susie's charms that had best argued his case with Pip and her family.

⚓ ⚓ ⚓ ⚓ ⚓ ⚓

He could no longer afford to feed his dog. Even with the cheapest meat or fish he could source on rations, the bills for her upkeep seemed to climb ever higher. He wanted wife and child well and secure and for Pip not to worry about money. His work saw him in daily contact with people driven to desperate measures often through no worse motive than wanting a piece of security. It was a daily reminder of how comfortable and lucky he was compared to them. Yet there was an instinctive frivolity in Pip when it came to money, a cheerful carelessness about bothering to fill out her cheque stubs properly that frightened him. Once, having yet again forgotten to fill out a stub, she wrote *silver lamé frock £80* with such confidence he believed her until she saw his expression, pointed and laughed at him.

He had confided his concerns to his one married sister, whose husband was a salaryman at a bank, earning far more than Mike, even with no higher education than he had picked up in the engineering corps, but that had only left Pip saying how bossy she found her.

Though larger and nicer than the boxy new-build they had first been assigned, their little house in Love Lane was still too small for a dog of Susie's bulk and energy, and her size and sounds dominated in a way he knew undoggy people found oppressive. While fine for a toddler, the garden was quite unsuitable as a playground for her, as she soon demonstrated by the ease with which she could vault its low wall if another dog passed by that interested or threatened her. Although Pip loved her dearly, and took her for two walks a day, the need to take a pram and baby along meant that they were never walks that tired Susie out the way a large dog needed, and weekends always seemed to start with a list of tedious chores to be done. This meant it was only once a week that Mike got to drive Susie out onto the moors, where he could walk her for two or three hours, and even then he usually tired before she did. She needed to be working on a farm, ideally, if it was not too late for a farmer to train her.

He wrote regularly, and confidentially, to Pip's mother. Even before their engagement, Betty had been like a second mother to him, feeding him up, concerned for his health, even mending his shirts sometimes. She was kind and amusing like all her family, but never teased him the way Terry and her daughters did. Even more than Pip, she was conscious of her scrappy education and hungry to learn, so, from the start, their friendship had involved him recommending or lending her books and she had seemed flattered by the way he engaged her seriously and wanted to hear her opinions. Beneath a flirtatious femininity, he recognised a reflex in her – a protective impulse almost certainly developed to protect herself from the influence of the aunts who had raised her, and later sustained to balance out Terry's faintly parodic masculinity. There was a grounded practicality to her that won Mike's immediate trust. They began exchanging letters early in the long engagement on which Betty had insisted, he knew, in the belief Pip would either lose interest or come to her senses or whatever. Pip would have been upset, he felt sure, at his disloyalty in writing to her mother without asking her, but increasingly the privacy of the correspondence was precious to him.

He had written to Betty weeks ago about his worry that he could no longer afford to keep a dog he loved but had not, in all honesty, chosen and she had very wisely suggested he place an advertisement in the *Yorkshire Post* and *Farmers' Weekly*. *And perhaps ask to put up a card in your local vet's. Families who are sad at having just lost a dog will jump at the chance of such a lovely one who is already housetrained. No need to tell Pip until you've a definite offer, Mike. You know how she gets. And Susie is your dog, after all.*

Even as he read that line, he could imagine Susie flopping a huge, possessive paw on his knee and gazing at him with her dark, tragic stare.

'I am your dog,' the stare said.

With a heavy heart, he wrote and rewrote the advertisement, laboriously counting the letters and spaces to keep the cost down. *Pyrenean Mountain Dog. Female. 8 Yrs. Sweet nature. New home regretfully sought. Free to right owner.*

He had written *glorious* as well but struck it out as it pushed the advertisement into a higher cost bracket. He called her glorious on the little cards he pinned up in the town's two vet surgeries. He gave his work number and alerted the college secretary that there might be extra messages for him.

There were no responses, even after he paid to advertise for a second week. Eight was quite old, of course, especially for a large dog. Even the prospects of a glorious dog free of charge would be shadowed by her just reaching the age when there would start to be vet bills to meet on top of the cost of feeding her.

Then, last night, he came home to relative uproar and the story of how something in Susie's usually docile nature had cracked and she had fiercely kept the wretched charwoman from coming near her own grandchildren. No blood had been shed, thank God, though he was prepared to bet the children, unsupervised and unused to dogs, perhaps, had tormented poor Susie by sticking crayons in her great felty ears or by shrieking in her sensitive face.

Pip had turned the whole thing into a glorious escapade, naturally, and was already working it up as a story to tell Whistle and her parents, complete with a rough approximation of Mrs Coley's outraged Yorkshire accent. She was all for laughing it off until the following week, but Mike was more aware than she of diplomatic sensitivities in a tight community in which they were no more respected than any out-of-touch colonial functionaries. In any case, he was fed up that she was bringing her long-lost Canadian grandfather to stay for two whole weeks, when they already had other guests coming. He was equally fed up with himself for having clean forgotten. So he took himself off after supper to track the Coleys down and apologise.

Reg Coley was an officer at the prison, so it was easy enough to drop in on the gatehouse, gently pull rank and obtain his address. Ordinarily, Mike would have taken a peace offering, some bottles of stout or a box of jellies or whatever, but the shops had long closed, and Wakefield was hardly a spot for the sort of after-hours flower stalls that served late or errant husbands in larger cities. He hadn't thought to bring a map so had to ask first a policeman, then a passer-by, for directions.

The Coleys lived, as he'd supposed, in one of the poorer parts of town, the kind of hugger-mugger terrace where wives scrubbed their doorsteps and knew their neighbours' business. It was a balmy evening, and he guessed the little houses must be hot from cooking, as there were gangs of children out playing well past their bedtimes, and women and a few elderly men leaning on walls or sitting on windowsills to chat. It being pay night, every pub he had passed was noisily full.

As Mike approached number fifteen, he wished he could forget how his pronouncement, on the char's appointment, that *Coley is a sad, grey fish* had passed into the litany of phrases that made Pip laugh. He felt hot and self-conscious in his work suit and Tonbridge cricket eleven tie, when the few men he saw were in shirtsleeves or simply vests.

Mr Coley answered the door and solemnly said,

'Well, you'd better come in,' when Mike said he was after his wife.

Mrs Coley hurried out from the kitchen, where their radio was audible, and ushered him into a spotless front room, mopping at her hot face with a tea towel and loudly apologising for not expecting him.

He said he had come as soon as he heard and had her repeat her assurance that the grandchildren had been frightened but quite unharmed.

'I can't come back, though,' she said. 'Not while that beast is there. I know you're fond of her, but, well, she scared the life out of me, and Albert said I'm not to.'

'If she is gone by Monday,' he asked, 'would you come back then? We'd be so grateful.'

She seemed flustered all over again and he wondered if she had been expecting a fight and felt deflated by his so readily acceding to her demands. Perhaps she was about to demand a pay rise? He already knew she insisted on being paid cash in hand rather than by standing order, and suspected it was so tax was only paid on her husband's wages. Albert Coley, near mute, saw him out, perhaps to keep the neighbouring gossips at bay, but Mike felt eyes on him as he walked away, and stopped, once he had turned a corner, to light his pipe in relief.

He told Pip that Mrs Coley had been talked round on

condition the dog was removed, and, to his surprise, she accepted the news sadly but without a fight.

'Dear, dear girl,' she said, sitting on the foot of the stairs to give Susie a two-armed hug. 'I shall miss you, but I suppose it's for the best. Will the vet be able to help?'

'I'm sure they can,' he said, adding meaninglessly, 'They're always having people asking.'

He took Susie for an extra-long bedtime walk. Usually, they only strolled up Love Lane and back, but that night he led her to the lane's furthest end and on into the rough ground, a park of sorts, bounded by Balne Lane, where there seemed to be a surprising number of other men off smoking under the trees and between the scrub, but without dogs.

In the morning, he gave her a big breakfast before loading Pip and Henrietta and all the inevitable baby paraphernalia into the little car and waving them off once Pip had given Susie a last, slightly teary farewell. Then, with as much brightness as he could summon, he called Susie for a final walk, visiting the trees she liked to sniff around St John's Square up the hill before calling in at his office, just in case any messages had come in after he had left his desk the afternoon before, and then, heavy of heart, crossing the town to the vet. He took down the optimistic little card he had pinned on the waiting-room noticeboard and made a mental note to call round to the rival vets later to take down the one there.

The vet, Mr Thwaites, had long admired Susie so she was always pleased to see him, and Mike half hoped he might offer to adopt or at least foster her, so much so that he voiced the thought aloud, encouraged by Mr Thwaites's sympathetic gaze as he told the sorry tale.

'Alas, we have three timid Burmese cats – my wife's particular passion,' he said. 'I have to get my fill of beauties like Susie at work. It's quite a painless procedure,' he went on. 'She'll be sound asleep before I give her the dose that actually stops her heart. Why not stay here to reassure her until she's asleep, and then . . .?'

So Mike crouched beside Susie, an arm round her, as Mr Thwaites expertly slipped a syringe of sedative into the great ruff of her neck. She panted in expectation, licked his face, gave one of her settling-down rumbles and slowly slid to the floor against him. She was, as promised, deeply asleep. Her belly rose and fell, her huge head nestled between her front paws.

Mr Thwaites had filled his second syringe.

'Would you mind awfully if I . . .?' Mike said, standing.

'Of course not,' Mr Thwaites said. 'Would you like us to take care of her disposal?'

Mike nodded, not trusting himself to speak, and stole away.

He made himself walk directly to the other surgery to take down the card there. By the time he had reached their door, he knew it would all be over. He hadn't thought to ask of how euthanised pets were disposed. Were they cremated or buried? And where on earth did it happen? Horses, he knew, often ended up butchered for dog meat. Part of his horror of commercial dog food stemmed from his having once strayed to the back of a pet shop in town in search of the owner, to find the remains of a partially flayed horse stretched out on a butchering table beyond a fly screen at the back. At Durham, he had once visited the town dump to enquire about the logistics of disposing of a ripe consignment of old prison mattresses, and seen a grim sign announcing that the dead-animal bin was temporarily unavailable.

He wondered if he should ring Mr Thwaites to ask him to wait until he had the car again to collect her, but the soil in the garden was not deep and it would have taken a team of men with pickaxes to break up enough of the rubble beneath it to make a deep enough grave. Besides, it would have felt wrong to leave Susie behind in a garden they were so soon to abandon.

He was unlocking the door back in Love Lane before he realised he was still holding Susie's lead. He bundled that, along with her carefully washed-up food and water bowls onto a shelf in the cupboard under the stairs. There would be other dogs, he knew it, just nothing quite so magnificently large. What unmanned him, in the end, was her bed, a much-chewed and mumbled mattress affair – she had rapidly destroyed the wickerwork basket that briefly housed it. It was richly redolent of her and released a little cloud of her hair as he picked it up and struggled to roll it into a parcel he could then tie with string to leave beside the dustbin.

He poured himself a large whisky and wept silently. He had the place to himself until he left for work on Monday morning; he could do as he liked.

He wrote a fond letter to Betty as he drank and wiped his tears, saying how Pip and the baby were safely en route, how much he looked forward to meeting her mysterious pioneer father at last and joking that, just like Terry, he was rereading *Our Empire Story* by way of homework to remind himself of the highlights of Canadian history. He told her in confidence about having Susie put down, knowing she would agree that both Pip and Whistle would be happier to think she had simply gone to a better home. He wished her and Terry a very happy holiday in Port Appin and signed off with much love.

The house felt unbearably quiet and empty. He tuned the radio to a ball-by-ball commentary of a test match and poured a second whisky.

TWENTY-FOUR

It was a peculiarity of most boys' boarding schools that Christian names were so little used that they were often only revealed, with some hilarity, at school confirmation services. The norm was to use surnames, small boys addressing one another with the formality of so many work colleagues and the awkwardness of attending siblings worked around by the addition of major, minor and, where three brothers attended a school simultaneously, minimus. Nicknames were common, a mark of affection or derision or, as was often the way, an ambiguous combination of the two.

He had known Titus for three years at their oppressive little prep school before discovering that he was really a Clough. Mike was not unpopular, too good at cricket to be one of the pariahs – as such unfortunates were even known to the staff – but he was shy, his manner could be stiff and formal, and it was a sign of something that his nickname had withered and been forgotten from disuse. He did not have the knack for friendship.

They were thrown together because Titus's family were in India so couldn't have him home at half-term and Mike's parents felt it would be disruptive, even upsetting, to take their boy from school for a few days only to send him back again, so paid a little extra for him to be held there. With no other boys but them in it and no masters present, the school was transformed, even idyllic. They walked in the grounds, read in the library, listened intently to the radio Titus had built from a kit and climbed trees they were usually forbidden to climb, yet still, with heartbreaking adherence to the regulations, separated after supper to sleep in their own deserted dormitories at opposite ends of the building. They didn't single each other out when all the other boys came back, as they belonged to quite different tribes, Mike to the sporty one and Titus to the smaller group that collected stamps and held Sunday-night play readings, though Mike saw Titus watching him sometimes now in matches and they nodded and smiled when they passed in corridors. When full holidays came round, it never occurred to Mike that Titus would be all alone in the place, partly because it never occurred to his parents to ask if he had a particular friend he'd like to invite home to stay.

But then they progressed to Tonbridge, the nearest public school, where they were in the same house and dorm and where Mike developed a passion for history, and Titus, whose nickname mysteriously travelled with him, discovered one for modern languages. They might have gone on just as in their prep school, but Titus's family moved back from India, and he invited Mike to stay for the Easter holidays.

They were quite unlike his own family, being artistic, funny and godless. Professor Oates was a philologist, attached to King's College, London, Mrs Oates was a rather good painter and a cheerfully terrible pianist, and

Titus had a sister, Mary, two years older but with none of the bossiness of Mike's own sisters. At Tonbridge, sisters were a kind of currency, safely invested with erotic allure because they were unlikely ever to be met. It had always amused Mike that having not just two sisters but two older ones, gave him a quite unearned cachet among older boys, who would have crumpled in the face of his sisters' withering scorn. It surprised him that Titus had never mentioned Mary's existence.

Both parents and sister were quite unremarkable in appearance and, as Mrs Oates liked to say, *built for comfort*, which had the odd effect of suddenly revealing Titus as a beauty. Mary acknowledged this, calling him their *Star Child*. They lived in a beautiful, chaotic old farmhouse inherited at some point by Mrs Oates, who came of bohemian stock.

Mike was put to sleep in Titus's room, as though it was the most usual thing, ostensibly because the spare room had a leak in the thatch directly over the bed, so was currently unusable. He continued to be put in Titus's room on subsequent visits after the house had been rethatched. They were hormonally charged fourteen-year-olds and one thing initially led to another because, though it was a double bed that had belonged to his grandmother, there was not much room in it, and it was a bitterly cold night, and they had only one hot water bottle between two. Subsequently it happened because they were powerless to resist.

Mike was utterly innocent of sexual experience and had believed all the stories he had been told about masturbation sapping one's strength and leading directly to other unhealthy depravities. Titus, however, turned out to have enjoyed all manner of experiences and quite a sexual education at the hands and mouths of older boys at their prep school, and wasted no time demonstrating all that he had learned.

Holidays with the Oates family were a sort of Arcadia, full of marvellously unstructured days walking the family's terrier, pottering about in the garden, catching buses to the seaside, visiting ruins and old churches on their bicycles, often with Mary leading the way, a delightful hybrid of jester and governess. Nothing was discussed, naturally, even between the boys, but it seemed accepted and even celebrated that Mike was Titus's particular friend and therefore a cherished part of their family.

'You do know you could always come to stay with us at the vicarage,' Mike felt he had to say. 'But it wouldn't be anything like as much fun.'

'Then I'd much rather not,' Titus said, at which they laughed, and it was agreed he wouldn't.

Mike painted a judiciously edited version of the Oates household in letters to his mother, emphasising their scholarship and aesthetic pursuits and saying nothing of their letting him learn to smoke a pipe and the equally dizzy sensation brought on by their complete lack of religion.

His faith was intrinsic, as impossible to deny as the warmth of sunshine on his face, but spending time with a family whose days were not dictated by the church calendar and discovering that he could miss church on Sunday and feel perfectly fine, made him realise that his faith was also a deeply private source of strength, independent of church or ritual, which was unexpectedly empowering.

Back at Tonbridge, they reverted to their own tribes, but the undiscussed thing between them emerged, undimmed, at every half-term break and holiday. They both applied to their fathers' old Oxford colleges and were accepted – Mike to read Modern Greats, Titus to read Modern Languages – and, to celebrate, their families sent them off on a train tour to Venice, Florence and Rome.

Travelling alone together somewhere so beautiful was a kind of dream and Italy was full of young men walking arm in arm – not that they would ever have gone so far. Still, they did not discuss what they were doing. Titus seemed not to need to, blithely accepting whatever happiness came his way, and Mike did not dare to. He knew that to talk about it was to make it what it was, an impossible, illegal thing that would have to be put aside with adulthood. He even fantasised that he could marry Mary, as a means of somehow enabling it to continue, only he liked her far too much to practise such a deception on her and very much doubted she would have let herself be deceived.

Curiously, for all the bragging and lusting after distant sisters there had been at school, there seemed to be remarkably little socialising with women at Oxford, despite the presence of women's colleges on the fringes of the city centre, and the presence of women studiously note-taking in the front row of many a lecture. All around them were intense friendships carried over from school, and the strict rules imposed by the college bulldogs on the entertaining of women in college rooms meant that all-male socialising was quite the norm.

Shamed by the beauty of the place where his father and grandfather had studied, prompted, too, by the monastic design of his college, with chapel and cloisters only a short walk from his bed, Mike began to attend church again regularly, enjoying the sparsely attended early morning communion services in the college chapel before his first lectures. This, in turn, somehow made it easier for him to make excuses when Titus visited his rooms and suggested they sport his oak to have guaranteed privacy.

Because they had never discussed the intense pleasure they took in one another in the holidays or on their trip to Italy, Titus was slyly inhibited from raising it to protest now. With the cruelty of virtue, Mike made a point of including him in chaste little lunches when one of his sisters visited, or a woman student and her friend with whom he had been talking seriously after history lectures.

What changed everything was the declaration of war. They both enlisted in the same Kentish regiment, but Titus was summoned to London midway through their six months of officer training in Colchester, so Mike assumed use was being made elsewhere of his advanced language skills, as he had not only fluent German but Russian and Norwegian. Obviously, they couldn't discuss what either was up to, but the extremity they were both in, especially once air raids began, released any inhibition Titus had felt about acknowledging what they had been doing or had become to each other. His letters were often short but always frank and passionate. Cunningly, he did not sign them, and never used Mike's name or any proper nouns that could specify the where and when in them. Mike froze after the first letter, overwhelmed by the strength of answering feelings it stirred up in him, but replied to the second and every letter he received thereafter. Grateful, Titus assured him he burned them after repeated re-readings, but Mike found he couldn't bring himself to do the same. He carried the ever more battered bundle with him in a Petticoat Tail shortbread tin stuffed to the unsavoury bottom of his kitbag.

And, like so many other illicit wartime couples disinhibited by the proximity of violent death, they found ways to meet when their home leaves coincided, rarely for more than one sleepless night in some hotel or over one pub or another.

With the peace, each officially recognised for some feat of bravery they could not begin to discuss, Titus took a job teaching languages at Tonbridge and had to become the model of probity, and Mike entered the Prison Service and was increasingly confronted with the harsh treatment meted out to men who had been acting just as he and Titus had, crudely trumpeted in the newspapers. Initially, they were not so far apart, both in Kent, working at institutions for teenage boys almost comically alike and opposed – Tonbridge and HMP Borstal – but then Mike was sent to assist Terry at Durham and met Pip and her mother at cathedral evensong within weeks of arriving.

Pip later joked that he didn't stand a chance because a magazine horoscope had said she would meet the love of her life that month. As their growing friendship stumbled towards a formal engagement, fed by often very funny letters from her and increasingly serious ones from him, his growing love for her blended with his faith to cause him to believe Pip had saved him.

Titus behaved impeccably, agreeing to be best man provided Mike would one day do the same for him, charming Pip, as did Mary, but of course his letters all but ceased, and when he did write now they were rinsed of anything indecorous, which felt like a rebuke of sorts.

The wedding was in London for the convenience of relatives largely based in the south-east, and the reception catered by Searcy's in a fine old house on Cheyne Walk. Mike and Titus spent the night before in adjoining rooms at the Sloane Square Hotel. Titus bought him as extravagant a supper as his schoolmaster's salary and rationing permitted and afterwards they drifted, with no discussion, into Titus's room where, in cautious, fumbling silence, they slept together one last time. And they did sleep at the upsetting, tearful end of it, Mike extricating himself from under Titus's arm and leg at some point towards dawn and dressing again only to undress again next door, and moments later to slip into his own tidy bed.

They had met only once since the wedding, when Titus travelled north to be godfather at Henrietta's christening. Mike had been deprived of the chance to be best man in turn. Titus supplemented his income in the holidays by working as a translator for the United Nations, which was how he had met his Norwegian wife, Dagmar, and married her so quietly in Geneva it felt like a sleight of hand.

Perhaps Mike imagined it, but Pip's reaction to the

happy news of Titus's marriage had seemed charged with relief, as though she had felt Titus's single state as a threat to her own contentment.

'He's such a honey – he deserves to be happy,' was all she said. 'I want everyone to be as happy as we are.'

She helped choose a set of exquisite old coffee cups: white porcelain with a dark blue band and a thinner rim of gold, admiring them one last time before she wrapped them in layers of tissue paper and parcelled them up with cushions of sawdust. 'You should always give people something you want yourself,' she said.

TWENTY-FIVE

Harry Cane, the mystery grandfather, was not what Mike had been expecting. With all the chat in the last two years of Cowboy Grandpa, he had been anticipating some swaggering figure in fringed shirt and gun belt who was, of course, American. In reality, Harry was no Robert Taylor, though one could see he might once have been startlingly handsome. He was wiry the way some roadmenders could be: strong, without bulk, his hair snowy white, his skin nut brown and as wrinkled as a fisherman's from long exposure.

The really incongruous trait was his voice. Because she was shy or nervous around him for some reason, Pip would keep producing a rather crass imitation of him to his face – her idea of an American accent – but to Mike's ear Harry's voice was almost a spectre from the past, its Edwardian vowels and delivery like something heard in old phonograph recordings yet overlaid with Canadianisms like a half-hearted fancy dress.

He seemed to be no trouble at all as a guest – years of living alone on the prairies had made him entirely self-sufficient; Pip said he made his bed as tidily as any nurse, washed and pegged out his own laundry and would even have helped in the kitchen had she let him. He read incessantly, happily treating their bookcases as his library; he said books had been in such scant supply where he had been living that people read the latest shopping catalogue as eagerly as the latest John Buchan and that even the village schoolmistress had been known to use the Eaton's catalogue as a reader for children when she had nothing else upon which to draw.

Titus and Dagmar were only coming to stay for the Saturday night, as her sister had also married an Englishman, and the couple were to call in on them in Lincoln for a night before heading home to the school for the end of half-term. Pip had been in a kind of frenzy of cleaning and cooking in advance, apparently so she could pretend, once the happy couple arrived, that her life was one of civilised leisure. At first Mike believed it was the thought of Titus that had her in such a state, but of course it was the prospect of Dagmar that unnerved her. In her head, she had built up an intimidating picture of a crisp, professional sophisticate who would look down on her for having a baby and no career.

'Knowing Titus, that hardly seems likely,' he said, but Pip had awoken an answering fear in him, and he polished his great-aunt's sherry glasses so vigorously he snapped the delicate stem of one and hid the fragments in a bundle of newspaper in the dustbin, like a guilty housemaid.

In the event, Dagmar gave the lie to their fears. She was short and round-faced, with a blonde pageboy haircut and not a trace of make-up. She wore a rather sexy scent – French, Pip said, definitely not Yardley – perhaps to mask the effects of the long cigarettes she smoked with elegant relish whenever she stepped into the little garden. She complimented Pip on how she looked even prettier than in her photographs and roared with laughter when Pip admitted why she hid their wedding photographs. When the florists had merely delivered a box of gardenias and not the expected Alice band with gardenias attached, a bossy bridesmaid had cut up Pip's bullet bra to fashion her an emergency hairband and stitched the flowers to that; so her hair looked pretty but her bosom misshapen.

Dagmar charmed Harry, saying she wanted to hear all about crime on the prairies. She exclaimed at the elegance of the spare room, admiring the Queen Anne tallboy Pip was especially proud of having nabbed for next to nothing in a sale room because the crucial minutes of the auction coincided with the Grand National. Finally, she begged to be allowed to hold Henrietta, who had diplomatically remained delicious after her bath and responded with delighted giggles to a Norwegian folk song. Over sherry and little decorative canapés Pip had never once served before, she said she wanted to hear all about Mike and Titus's friendship; only Dagmar insisted on calling him his real name, Clough. Twinkling at Harry, who was sharing the sofa with her, she declared,

'These Englishmen with their *amitiés particulières* that last well into adulthood, mere women cannot begin to compete, but I thought at least by insisting on his real name rather than a schoolboy nickname I could make it clear that adulthood has arrived!'

Titus smiled kindly at Mike in a way that made one see how the boys in his care must love him, and shrugged, 'Dagmar is insatiable; I've told her everything but still she wants to know more.'

'Mike's boyhood was so sad it makes me cry,' said Pip. 'I think Titus was the only thing that made it bearable. To send a child to boarding school at five!'

'Barbaric,' Dagmar agreed, then added with a grin at Mike, 'and probably quite damaging.'

'I've just realised,' Titus said. 'Where is Susie? They have the most magnificent beast of a sheepdog,' he told her.

'We had to let her go after she rounded up the wretched charlady's grandchildren and wouldn't let poor Mrs Coley near them,' Pip said. 'It's so very sad.'

'But she was a sheepdog,' Dagmar said reasonably. 'What did the silly woman expect?'

And Pip went on to re-enact the scene, growl by growl, shriek by Yorkshire shriek, as Mike could tell she had already done for the benefit of her parents and Whistle and her cowboy grandpa, until he thought, *Please stop or I might cry*, and poured everyone another sherry. Dagmar drank like a man, which was another point in her favour.

They had invited a distinguished widow from church to make up the numbers and because she was nearer Harry's age. At supper, Mike was between her and Dagmar, so could do no more than occasionally catch Titus's eye as he topped up wine glasses or took away plates. He heard everything about the nice widow's long life in the house in which she still lived and about Dagmar's genuinely interesting research into the link between crime prevention and early-years education, but there was desolation in his heart because he wanted to be alone with Titus, even if only to talk quietly about Mary and his parents, but he knew that wasn't going to happen.

It was a lively, happy evening. Pip had made the house atmospheric and interesting; everyone was attractive by candlelight, even funny old Harry Cane, and Mike thought it would never end. At last, the nice widow said she had to be up early for churchwarden duties and, in one of the Americanisms to which her excellent English seemed prone, Dagmar yawned like a little cat and declared herself *bushed*.

Pip led Dagmar upstairs and the two of them could be heard laughing as Pip explained the house's eccentric plumbing. Harry appeared to have nodded off.

'I thought I'd take a moonlit walk,' Mike said. 'I can't seem to lose the habit even now Susie has gone. Want to join me?'

Titus gazed at him a moment, let his eyes flick to Harry, who was just waking up. Mike could almost feel him calculating. The women's laughter reached them again.

'I should probably join Dagmar,' Titus said. 'An excellent dinner after a long day of driving is catching up with us both.' He made a fetching show of stifling a yawn just as Harry came to life.

'Fresh air and moonlight are a fine thing before turning in,' Harry said to no one in particular, and he stood, spry as ever.

So Titus said his goodnights with, Mike was sure, a just detectable touch of mischief, and Mike led Harry out of the front door. He lit his pipe – always a useful little ritual when faced with any awkwardness; men lit pipes in much the way cats fell to washing themselves. Then he took the route he might have taken with Susie, right out of the front door, left up the hill under the railway bridge, past the station, past the handsome Unitarian chapel and on to circle homeward along Balne Lane.

He drew Harry's attention to buildings of interest, but it was a little like dropping pebbles into mud, it drew so little response.

'Clough seems like a fine man,' Harry said at last.

'I can't get used to that name.'

'You knew him as Titus?'

'Since we were boys, yes.'

'It's not easy,' Harry said, then fell quiet.

Mike stopped walking to relight his pipe. 'What isn't?' he prompted at last.

'When you're so close to a man and you have to watch him grow away.'

'Well, we all grow up. Good thing too, probably.' He hated his falsely hearty tone, like the worst sort of schoolmaster.

'He's almost as lucky in Dagmar as you are in Pip.'

'Not an easy woman, I'm guessing.'

'Clever people never are. The thing is she's quite unshockable. Has he always drunk so heavily?'

'Is he drinking heavily? I hadn't noticed.' He had. Titus had been drinking with a kind of feverishness all night and it was quite unlike him.

At last, they turned onto Balne Lane. Mike was aware he was pressing ahead rather, being discourteous to an old man who perhaps needed to walk more slowly. He made an effort to check his pace, though he longed to be home and upstairs in bed with the reassurance of his young wife and the new

C. P. Snow. It was a warm evening and once again there seemed to be quite a few men loitering under the trees. There was hardly enough light to cross the rough patch safely, but every now and then one or another would light a cigarette, and the flare of his match would briefly reveal him.

Harry was now watching the men openly. 'Like fireflies,' he said. 'It is interesting, though,' he went on, 'that you chose to marry an innocent, and he went quite the other way.'

'We ought to be getting back,' Mike said.

Harry would not be deflected, however; he was as relentless as a horsefly biting through a thin summer shirt. 'She knows everything, you know, Dagmar. Not Pip.' He laughed shortly. 'Pip knows nothing, bless her.'

'I'll thank you not to talk about my wife like that. She knows we've been close since our schooldays.'

'But Dagmar knows you were lovers.'

The word sounded with dreadful clarity. Happily, the street was deserted. They were nearing the prison and, even though it was long past lights out, the occasional shout or jeer rang out from the nearest cell block.

'She made it quite clear when we were chatting in the garden before supper,' Harry went on. 'You have nothing to fear. She said Clough has no secrets from her, that she insists on complete candour as the bedrock of their marriage. But she said she was glad that, how did she put it, that a man who has lived fully was less likely to wander after novelty.'

'I'm afraid you have, both of you, badly misread the situation.'

'You think so?'

Mike's blood was racing. Was this strange old man with his bright, new teeth a blackmailer?

'Pip is keenly looking forward to the move to Dorset,' Harry went on. 'She thinks it a much better place to raise children.'

'What a lot of confidences you've been receiving.'

Harry shrugged, smiled a little sadly. 'Women talk to me. They always have. Perhaps it's because I don't smoke? You go home to her. She'll be dying to talk everything over and I'm sorry if I've made you uneasy.'

'Not at all. Was I walking too fast for you? Pip always says I have a bad habit of striding and forgetting when I'm not walking alone.'

'It's all right. Can I let myself in in a while? I don't sleep much in town, and I'd like to walk a little longer.' Harry glanced back the way they had just come, to the waste ground and the human fireflies.

Relieved he had misinterpreted the tenor of their conversation, Mike was briefly concerned. It was not exactly the Gorbals, but parts of the town could be rough after dark, especially this side of the railway.

The old man seemed to read his mind. 'I'll be fine,' he said. 'I'm a pioneer, remember.'

Mike smiled at that. 'I'll leave the door on the latch,' he said. 'Just click down the snib to lock up when you come in. Goodnight.'

Harry just lifted a hand to his shoulder in response, already turning away.

When he'd brushed his teeth and washed his face, Mike

found Pip sitting up in bed with the baby, who, far from grizzly, was all affability and smiled at him as he climbed in beside them.

'I know,' Pip said. 'It's against all Truby-King's rules and regulations, but she was so pleased to see me and says she hasn't seen her father for hours.'

'Your Cowboy Grandpa is still walking,' he told her, reaching for his library copy of *The Masters*.

'On his own?'

'He'll be fine,' he told her. 'He's a pioneer.'

HARRY

TWENTY-SIX

The homeward crossing was far more comfortable than his outward one had been. The weather was perfect, warm enough for sitting out on one of the steamer chairs lined up around the decks, the Atlantic surprisingly calm and one of the family – he suspected it was Mike – had very discreetly contacted the shipping line to upgrade Harry's ticket so that, while still in tourist class, he had a cabin to himself.

Flattering their tourist-class passengers that they were just as precious, and possibly as distinguished as their first-class ones, and making no allowances for the shy, Cunard handed out a little printed booklet with all the tourist passengers listed in it, which even contained a couple of blank pages for the gathering of autographs from new shipboard friends. Similarly, the tourist-class dining room, smoking room and reading room echoed the country-house comforts he could only imagine of the public areas on the higher decks, but with unadorned metal ceilings, which caused the din of any gathering to be magnified. His cabin, though, was quiet and inviting, with leaf-patterned carpet and floral bedspread and curtains. It had a comfortable armchair and a little dressing table he could use as a writing desk.

Coming out to Liverpool, he had felt he was sailing

home, but of course it wasn't home any more. The entire trip had been an exercise in misplaced nostalgia. Even if he had been returning to old haunts in London, to Piccadilly and Strawberry Hill, he suspected it would still have felt utterly alien to him; too much time had passed, and too many old certainties had been swept away.

Betty and her daughters could not have been kinder, and he loved his smart new suit and beautiful shirts and was slowly getting used to his bright new teeth, but the thoughtfulness and the care had unwittingly made him an old man, and the politeness and consideration reminded him that he was indeed a stranger to them. A Canadian stranger, who made them awkward and uneasy.

As Mike was away, busy with a tape measure and notebook, seeing what needed to be done to ready the governor's house at The Verne for a young family, Pip had been all set to drive Harry back to Liverpool, but he wouldn't hear of it. She had done enough, he insisted, and a train journey would be an adventure. So he had caught the train to Liverpool and found his way back to the tailors – Martin Vance and his bear of a friend, Cushty – who had made him try on the new suit, which was perfect and needed no further adjustments.

They were themselves, of course, without Terry looming at his elbow, and insisted he have a cup of tea with them. They were shocked that he was sailing home to Canada that evening with nobody from his family to see him off, so Cushty had driven him to the impressive Cunard liner terminal at the docks, quite like a dutiful son. Harry thought of the wordless men he had met under the trees in the dark in Wakefield, of the ones he had met in a back alley in Walton while taking the dog for a late-night walk.

'How do you cope, the two of you?' he asked Cushty as they sat in the car, because they were still a little early for embarkation to have begun.

'We're careful,' Cushty said with a wry smile. 'You know how it is.'

'Oh, I know,' Harry said.

That was all. There was no big discussion or confession, just a small flicker of recognition in a small car at the dockside, but it made him feel seen for himself as he had not felt in four weeks among his blood relatives.

For all their generosity with suit and shirts, the false teeth, the sorting of his pension and having him checked over by their doctor, nobody had asked him what his plans were, and it was only now that he was sailing home to Canada that he admitted he had none. Paul had been his reason for living, then it had been the duty to support Paul's widow. The treadmill of the farming calendar, if not a reason for living, at least gave a ready excuse for continuing and made it impossible to stop or look further ahead than the next season, the next crop. And with the sale of his farm Harry was rudderless.

Encouraged by all the letter-writing, he had thought some spark of family chemistry might change that, once he was reunited with Betty and meeting his English family, and that they might even take him in, but, from the moment he had seen her, dear, sweet woman, gazing hopefully up at the passengers on the first-class gangplank as he walked down the one from tourist class, he realised that had been the fond fantasy of a lost old man.

He took a while, on his strolls around the one open-air deck to which his ticket gave him access, to find a suitable spot. Suicide for a first-class passenger was simple, as they had private balconies off their staterooms, from which they could slip, unseen, into the night ocean, but Harry had only a porthole that could not be opened without a steward to unlock it and through which only a child would have fitted if it could. He would have to jump from a carefully chosen public area at a time when there was nobody around. Unfortunately, the only outdoor parts of the decks open to tourist-class passengers opened onto further decks further down. But then, during a bracing daytime stroll, he came across a smartly framed and labelled drawing of the ship and realised that by nipping down a crew staircase at the dead of night he could access a sort of service deck at the aft of the ship. Just above the proud, gold-painted words RMS ASCANIA, there was a railing giving out onto an uninterrupted void. To judge from the picture, it would land him a few yards safely behind the ship's giant propellers.

Having chosen the spot and identified the door onto the service staircase he would need to take, he sat down to order what was left of his affairs. He settled on Mike as, in effect, his executor, as he was sensitive and intelligent yet, Harry had ascertained, touchingly close to Betty, who was Harry's next of kin. There was no need for a will, since everything would go to her, but he wrote Mike a letter, giving details of the bank account in which the pitiful sum raised from the farm sale was saved, less what he had spent on the train ticket and boat ticket to get to Liverpool.

There was nothing else. He had no treasures, no family portraits or grandfather clocks. He had stripped himself of all such stuff when he left England to be a homesteader in the 1900s, and, for simplicity, had included all the house's simple furniture, his two horses, tractor and plough in the sale price offered by Davy O'Connor. All that remained were his silver half-hunter watch he hadn't used in years, the serviceable wristwatch he had bought himself in Moose Jaw when learning how to farm, and the initialled cufflinks he had worn for so long he could not remember where they had come from. They might well have been a confirmation present from his disgraceful father. They were not much, but they were something, small tokens that he had existed, by which Mike and Pip's children, or Whistle's, assuming she had any, might keep his memory alive. He wrapped the watches and the cufflinks in three clean handkerchiefs and tucked them into an envelope addressed to Mike at what would soon be his and Pip's address in Portland.

He then wrote a letter to Betty, thanking her for her hospitality and saying what a great delight it had been to spend time with her finally, but he tore it up, realising it would be read as a suicide note and he wanted to leave her the option of thinking his death had been accidental. Mike would know the truth, but Mike, he could tell, was an expert keeper of secrets and sparer of feelings.

He spent a peaceful afternoon on deck, under a rug on a steamer chair, finishing *The Longest Journey*. He had only just discovered E. M. Forster and Pip had insisted he take it away with him. He dined as usual then waited until the early hours, when even the seasoned merrymakers had staggered to their cabins, and he could be sure nobody would be about. He then quietly made his way through the deserted corridors and down the humid staircase to his chosen spot at the ship's stern. Unlike most of his fellow passengers, he had remained utterly sober all evening and was completely clear in his thinking.

It was bitterly cold, of course, and he knew the water would be icy. In fact, he had every hope that the shock of his plunging into it would stop his heart before he drowned. There was a significant five-bar railing to climb over, with a thick mahogany banister on its top. He had often thought how odd it was that older people were so much more cautious of physical risk than the young, when it should, by rights, be the old who hurled themselves into danger and were more devil-may-care. Climbing the railing, he found he was clinging tightly, watching his grip, afraid of a fall. He had planned to stand on the mahogany rail and jump from that, but there was quite a swell compared to when he had been reading on deck earlier in the day and, instead, he found himself cautiously sitting on it, watching the moonlit sea rush up and fall away, rush up and fall away.

'There is nothing now,' he told himself. 'Nothing at all.'

He thought of Paul in his sturdy prime, riding a horse towards him, remembered how he had once taken Paul's musky flannel work shirt to bed and fallen asleep with it pressed to his face in longing. He unlocked his feet from the railings.

Then, all at once, there were arms around him and he was being dragged back to safety.

He recognised a young member of staff from his corridor, a green-eyed Irishman with a cheeky smile.

'I'm sorry,' he started. 'I was just—'

'You're fine,' the young man said. 'You're safe now. I've got you now. Let's get you to the warm.'

He threw a tartan blanket around Harry's shoulders, which was suddenly the softest, warmest, most richly coloured thing, and led him along the deck, up the humid staircase and along the corridor back to his cabin. He heard his teeth chatter as the young man opened his cabin door.

The plumped-out envelope addressed to Mike and the note of thanks and tip to his steward were clearly displayed on the cabin's little table and said all that he could not deny. The young man, it turned out, was the very steward for whom the tip was destined.

'Fellows don't normally leave me that until the journey's end,' he said as he helped Harry into bed and brought him two biscuits and sweet tea with a hefty splash of brandy in it, which should have been revolting, but just then was quite delicious. 'Are you going to fall asleep or are you going to tell me all about it?'

EPILOGUE

Harry was alone on the boarding house's little terrace, watched from a distance by the landlady's gooseberry-eyed black cat, that was also sunning itself. The delicious smells of breakfast – pancakes, crisped bacon, maple syrup, coffee – lingered on the air from the open French windows to the dining room behind him. He loved this time of day now, when everyone else had bustled off to work and he was left alone with a full stomach and the day's possibilities and promises.

A family of raccoons lived under the shed at the far end of the small garden and, just occasionally, he had seen them at play, their clever, hand-like paws busy finding one another's fleas or picking at scraps they had found in the neighbourhood. Most people regarded them as vermin, no better than gophers or rats, but Mrs Tresidder, the landlady, said she always had room for waifs and outcasts, being one herself.

She had been orphaned back home in Cornwall, when her father died in a mining accident and her mother gassed herself. Little more than ten, she had been bussed out of Redruth, with a clutch of other unwanted children, without her consent, and put on a boat to Canada to be trained up as a servant. Her employer in Toronto, some kind of bigwig on the city council, had got her pregnant five years later and signed her over to an enforced abortion and indefinite stay in the city asylum to silence her. She declared proudly that her diagnosis had been *moral turpitude*. Happily, a hospital orderly, another Cornish exile, recognised her accent, fell in love with her and helped her escape. They had taken on his late mother's rooming house. He had died in the war, and now her boarders were her only family.

Harry heard all this from her the night after he moved in. Dermot, the kind young steward from the *Ascania*, had brought him here once they disembarked at Montreal, knowing she would take him in if she could. She had given Harry the use of a little maid's room in the house's attic, with a calming view into the trees which lined the neighbouring ravine at the lane's end. The room was promised to someone else in a month, but Mrs Tresidder said something else would come up, as it usually did.

Her boarders weren't itinerants precisely, but she favoured the bohemian and restless: actors and dancers, who came and went like migrant birds, and performers of another sort, obliged to maintain a false front to survive. One of these was Dermot's lover, Liam, who worked around the city's building sites. Then there was the nesting pair of schoolmistresses in the large garden room, whose frequent arguments meant that they rented a second room – nominally their boudoir – into which one of them would move until noisily forgiven.

Dermot came and went, of course, according to Cunard's demands and the schedules of the *Ascania* – a ship he always called the Ash Can. When he returned, he and

Liam would be shut in their room for a day-long reunion. They were quieter than the schoolmistresses, letting out only the occasional gasp or laugh from in there, but Harry enjoyed the sense that the entire household shared in their satisfaction, and that it responded to the shifting weather of either couple's love.

Since arriving, Harry had walked himself silly, since he had little money and walking was free entertainment. Mrs Tresidder gave him a little street map and he was slowly falling in love with Toronto's streets, villages, lake shore and the unexpected valleys and patches of wilderness that erupted here and there into its orderly grids. Inspired by his visit to the Walker with Betty, he spent hours feasting on the museums and galleries. Once or twice now he had also accompanied Mrs Tresidder – whose first name remained as secret as the undergarments she never pegged on her washing line – to the theatre, when theatrical boarders had slipped her free tickets to make up rent.

Dermot had been at sea for the Coronation, but the rest of the household had gathered to listen to a recorded relay on the radio and celebrated with a roast chicken and crackers and paper crowns, quite as though it was Christmas. Despite the tribulations of her early life, and with no desire to return to the country that had so traduced her childhood, Mrs Tresidder was a staunch royalist and the official photograph of the young queen, looking fresh and tiny in her robes and huge crown, now hung over the dining-room sideboard where her father had hung until recently. His portrait had moved to a table on the landing, where she honoured it with candles and a thriving Christmas cactus, and made of the table a sort of altar.

Harry had written on arrival to Dimpy, who had written back by return, wishing him well and saying she was guarding his precious pension book, which had arrived for him at Winter, asking where he wanted her to send it. He had written, too, to Pip and Betty, thanking them for their hospitality and giving them a judiciously edited version of his return crossing. He sent Betty a copy of *Chatelaine*, whose title he thought might amuse her, and posted Pip an outrageous present for Henrietta of a pair of bearskin gloves, complete with carefully preserved claws, which he had found in a thrift shop. He imagined that one day she would enjoy dressing up in them to play at being a wild beast.

'Morning, Sunshine.' Mrs Tresidder came out in the big-skirted floral housecoat she wore for her morning chores. She touched his shoulder. He was fairly sure Dermot would have told her about his desperation on the ship. He might even have asked her to keep an eye on him. She set down a saucer of sardines for the cat, which jumped down lightly to feast, then she turned and set a letter on the table for Harry as she headed back in. 'Mail for you,' she said, and patted his shoulder again.

The stamp was British, the postmark from Liverpool, though the handwriting was unfamiliar. It was a short letter, barely two sides, but the pages were crammed by the writer's enthusiasm. He flicked to the back page and saw Whistle's signature.

Dear Grandpa, she wrote. *Heaven only knows how*

long this will take to reach you. I'll post it in the beastly office (where private mail may not be sent through our system, etc., etc.) and hope it reaches you soon.

It was so sad that you had to leave. Stupidly I'd misunderstood and thought you were coming to <u>live</u> with us, so didn't pay nearly enough attention or ask any of the important questions. My mind is like a squirrel looking for lost nuts most of the time. It was so lovely to meet you. You look just like your old photographs, so I can see why we're all so bloody beautiful! And it was so kind of you to have spent that precious day riding with me on the beach at Crosby, especially when we didn't have the sort of saddles you're used to. I wish Mummy and Daddy had seen you ride. I think they just saw you as an old man, but seeing you on a horse, you suddenly weren't old at all, just a man very happy to be on a horse. I've remembered those secret Cree phrases you taught me, by the way. I shall use them always. Much more special than that silly English trick of blowing up a horse's nose, which I'm sure is bad horse manners, and better for them than sugar lumps.

Anyway, I think you must have murmured some secret Cree magic to me as well, because something changed in me after you left. I trotted off to the frankly terrifying cousins like a very calm show pony and wore the beautiful pistachio dress with my hair up, so I looked almost like Grace Kelly, though I felt more like Mrs Tiggywinkle inside and, Grandpa, I met the loveliest man! A calvary officer, devastatingly handsome. Dress uniforms are so flattering but even so. And we danced far too many dances, probably, but the terrifying cousins approve because his family are Wiltshire aristocracy, even though I suspect he hasn't a bean and Daddy will be appalled and, guess what, he loves animals as well. In between dances we talked and talked and agreed that we must live in the countryside, proper countryside, with grass in the middle of the lanes because there's so little traffic, and have not just two horses but dogs, at least two, as they're happier in a pack, and bantams for the eggs and because they're funny and maybe a donkey as company for the horses and a goat, as you suggested, so I can make cheese. And guess what even more? He is coming to Liverpool next weekend to meet Daddy!

I just wanted to thank you because I was in a silly state when you came and something you did straightened me out, or this wouldn't be happening. Dear Grandpa, my Cowboy Grandpa, this comes with mad hugs and probably more than a whiff of horse sweat, from your Whistle. Xxx

He read the letter again and realised he was smiling to himself like a madman. He would write back to her later, perhaps after he'd found something suitable to send her. A scarf, perhaps, to match the fabric of the old dress that had looked so good on her, not that he could afford much. And he would describe Mrs Tresidder's raccoons for her.

Instead, he wrote to Dimpy, asking her to hold on to his pension book as he would soon be catching the train, or succession of trains, back out as far as North Battleford.

He might not find anywhere as appealing to rent as the place he had seen before he made this trip, but he would find somewhere because he had to.

He had seen another world, several in fact, but he was too old and tired for more adventures. His fellow boarders and Mrs Tresidder were kind and funny and he couldn't help but fear North Battleford represented a kind of slow death by comparison to this lively boarding house: painless, genteel, possibly even skirted by a pretty, white picket fence, but a death, nonetheless.

ACKNOWLEDGEMENTS

The real-life Harry Cane, my maternal great-grandfather, did indeed end his days at North Battleford, Saskatchewan. He died in the care of the Salvation Army there and was buried in an unmarked grave, being penniless. His wristwatch came down to my sister, the baby he had met on his trip back to England and I am proud to wear his cufflinks. We know very little of his years as a farmer at Winter other than a few tantalising details I gleaned from the postmistress's sons: he chaired the wheat farmers' cooperative, he had lovely table manners and he kept the best horses in the district. The formidable bearskin gloves were indeed in the dressing-up case when I was a child, along with some Cree beadwork slippers, long since destroyed in play, which should properly have been in a museum.

Even more than its related novel, *A Place Called Winter*, *Love Lane* draws on the memories, stories and letters passed down to me by my family. It is a novel, not a memoir, but I am still hugely grateful to my brother, sister and cousins for their forbearance of this terrific piece of cheek, and hope that none of it will give offence. It would be nothing without my grandmother's unfinished memoir or the extraordinary trove of letters between her and my parents, with the occasional illegible PS from my grandfather, Terry.

I'm indebted to writer and friend, Neil Bartlett. His First World War anniversary project to get several of us writing

ACKNOWLEDGEMENTS

the letter we imagined in the hands of that beautiful statue of the reading soldier on Paddington Station's Platform 1 set me wondering about the scant two letters that pass between Harry and Paul and what their afterlife might have been.

Thank you, too, to Jo James, Cunard (Carnival Ltd) and the Cheltenham Festival at Sea, for bringing me across the Atlantic on *Queen Mary 2* and unwittingly nourishing several chapters in this novel. Thanks, too, to the University of Liverpool's Special Collections archivists, for letting me browse their amazing Cunard collection to feed my descriptions of Harry's rather less happy experiences on the Atlantic.

As ever, a teetering pile of novels, memoirs and histories fed the writing of this, and I'm hugely grateful to my wise friend Marina Endicott for her suggestions of books to further my understanding of the Canadian prairies during the Depression and the Second World War. Liverpool Central Library was also a great help in my research into the many executions carried out at HMP Liverpool both before and during my grandfather's time as its governor, not least in leading me to find the Prison Office memorandum on preparations to be carried out before an execution.

Good editors do so much more than simply correct, and Imogen Taylor is a great one, understanding what I'm stumbling towards and helping turn stumbles into strides. I am blessed in the support I get from her amazing team at Hachette, not least for Joe Thomas, Ellie Freedman, Alexia Thomaidis and my long-lost cousin, Patrick Insole. My career would be getting nowhere without Caradoc King and Jen Thomas of United Agents.

Cumberland Sound
Meta Incognita
Hall Pa.
Hudson Strait
Frobisher B.
Resolution I.
C. Chudleigh
Ungava Bay
Godthaab
New Hernhut
Lichtenfels
Fiskernæs
Frederikshaab
C. Desolation
Julianeshaab
Lichtenau
Nennortalik
Friedrichsthal
C. Farewell
York to
Clear Water L.
R. Koksoak
Whale R.
Labrador
Nain
Hopedale
Hamilton Inlet
C. Charles
Quebec
Gulf of St. Lawrence
Newfoundland
St. Johns
C. Race
Sydney
C. Breton
Great Bank of Newfoundland
Halifax
Sable I.
Boston
C. Cod
Rhode I.
Philadelphia
Delaware B.
Chesapeake B.
C. Hatteras
To New York from Gibraltar 3,206, Genoa
Colon to Liverpool 4,530
Jamaica to Liverpool 4,026, Bristol 3,996
699 miles
Bermuda Is.
New York to St. Thomas
Colon to N.Y. 1,972
Bermuda to St.
850 m
Mail Steamer St. Thomas to South
Liverpool to
Glas
Barbad
Gibral
O C E
A T L
N